Chan for *e*

OTHER BOOKS AND AUDIO BOOKS
BY TRACI HUNTER ABRAMSON

UNDERCURRENTS SERIES

Undercurrents

Ripple Effect

The Deep End

ROYAL SERIES

Royal Target

Royal Secrets

Royal Brides

SAINT SQUAD SERIES

Freefall

Lockdown

Crossfire

Backlash

Smoke Screen

Code Word

Lock and Key

Drop Zone

Spotlight

STAND-ALONES

Obsession

Deep Cover

Failsafe

Chances Are

Kept Secrets

Twisted Fate

Chance

for Home

a novel

TRACI HUNTER ABRAMSON

Covenant Communications, Inc.

Cover image: *Decorative Outdoor Party Lights and Lanterns in Garden* © timnewman; *Loving Couple* ©
GoodLifeStudio, courtesy istockphoto.com

Cover design copyright © 2017 by Covenant Communications, Inc.

Published by Covenant Communications, Inc.
American Fork, Utah

Printed in the United States of America
First Printing: April 2017

23 22 21 20 19 18 17   10 9 8 7 6 5 4 3 2 1

ISBN 978-1-52440-188-7

For Jon
Thanks for sharing my love of baseball

Acknowledgments

THANK YOU TO PAIGE EDWARDS, Ellie Whitney, and Jen Leigh for your continued support and advice in the early stages of each manuscript, and thanks to Paige and Mandy Abramson for your help during those initial edits. My continued thanks to my fabulous editor, Samantha Millburn. I so appreciate your guidance as I take each new story idea from concept to finished product.

My sincere appreciation to everyone in the Covenant family for allowing me to continue this career that I love. A special thanks Kathy Gordon and Robby Nichols for all your support and to Jessica Parker and Peyton Cram for your comments that helped this novel reach its potential.

Words cannot express my appreciation for the time and effort Tiffany Hunter and Tom Whalen expended in gathering the medical insight for this book as Dianne Hunter gave us a first-hand look at MRSA the hard way. Thank you to the doctors and nurses who helped bring about a modern-day miracle.

Finally, thank you to my family for your love and support.

Chapter 1

AUSTIN MUELLER DESERVED TO DIE a slow, painful, agonizing death. Kari had entertained a hundred variations of that thought over the past week after discovering her boyfriend of the past six months had neglected to tell her he was already engaged.

His fiancée had certainly managed to surprise him when she'd arrived home from a year studying abroad to find Kari and him hanging out at his apartment, watching a movie. At least Kari had the satisfaction of knowing that in less than three minutes, Austin had gone from having two girlfriends to none. Apparently the fiancée didn't appreciate cheating any more than Kari did.

Austin had tried to talk to Kari several times since that unfortunate day, but she wasn't about to grant him the privilege. She briefly considered letting him explain himself, but that had been before the internship she had been promised mysteriously got canceled. Knowing Austin's father sat on the selection board for that particular position, she hadn't needed to look far to place the blame squarely on Austin's shoulders.

At least the breakup had come at the end of the semester, and she would have the whole summer to decide what she wanted to do next. After all, without the internship to occupy her time, she didn't have a reason to stay in Nashville.

Though she wasn't normally one to run away from a challenge, Kari found herself wondering if she even wanted to continue her studies at Vanderbilt. Since her closest friend, Maya, had left school last fall, nothing had been the same. Admittedly, Austin had helped fill her time socially, but academically she wasn't sure this school was still the best fit.

After helping Maya through her early treatments for cancer, Kari had discovered an aptitude in something she had never before considered:

medicine. Unfortunately, Austin had expressed his desire to become a doctor, and Kari wasn't particularly fond of the idea of spending the next two years as his classmate. Even worse was knowing his father was the department chair of the biological sciences department.

The idea of transferring to another college where she could start fresh held an appeal, and she hoped living with her brother and Maya this summer would give her time to explore the possibilities. She thought of how her brother and best friend had come to be married and the way Ben had helped Maya battle and ultimately beat the cancer that had threatened her life.

At first, Kari had been hesitant to spend the summer living with the newlyweds, but knowing that Ben's career as a professional baseball player would keep him on the road much of the time, she had reconsidered. Besides, she missed her friend.

She loaded the last of her luggage into her car and slammed the trunk shut. With one last look around, she slid behind the wheel. By tonight, she would be in Washington, DC, and by tomorrow night, she would be sitting in the stands with Maya, watching her brother play ball.

* * *

He was swearing off women. Done. Finished.

Ryan thought of the woman he had almost married, of all the sacrifices they had both made when his baseball career had kept them apart. He had been so sure Brandi was the person he would build his future with, but when they had started planning for that future, he'd finally realized they wanted completely different things in life. Brandi shared her entire life on social media. He preferred his private life to stay private.

She expected them to travel during his off-season and experience the world together. He wanted to spend his downtime between seasons in one place, where they could build a home and start a family. Discovering her stand on children, or, rather, her preference not to have any, had ultimately been the last straw.

Since their breakup last winter, he had dated more than a dozen women, and not once had he found anyone he wanted to take out a second time. Maybe he wasn't ready, or maybe he simply wasn't attracting the right type of woman. Lately, everyone he dated seemed more interested in being part of a public couple than genuinely wanting to know the man he was when he didn't have a bat in his hand.

Regardless, after spending the past two weeks dodging phone calls from the last four women he had dated, he was in desperate need of a break from the opposite sex.

Ryan pulled into the players' parking lot and climbed out of his car. He noticed one of his teammates parking a few spaces away, and his spirits lifted.

Ben Evans had been called up to the majors only a week before he had. They both stood several inches over six feet and had dark hair, and their physical similarities had caused a few people to confuse them in those early days. Now in their second season, the two had become friends, even though the media often used their stats to compare them in a way that made them seem like they were in some kind of competition.

"Hey, Ben." Ryan altered his path and approached Ben as he climbed out of the car.

Ben nodded a greeting and circled the car to open the passenger door for his wife. Petite in stature, with black hair falling well past her shoulders, Maya took a moment to gain her balance, a reminder that months before she had nearly died from cancer.

"Hey, Maya," Ryan greeted her.

"Ryan. It's good to see you," Maya said, her voice carrying the cadence of India. She put a hand on the car as though to steady herself and waited patiently while Ben opened the rear door to collect his duffel bag. "How are you doing?"

"Glad to be home for a while. I needed a good night's sleep."

"What do you mean?" Maya asked.

"Some of our teammates ordered some wake-up calls for us at our hotels. We were getting calls at three, four, and five in the morning," Ben said.

"And everything in between," Ryan added.

"No wonder you were so tired when you got home."

"You know, I think it's time we dish some payback," Ben suggested.

"Any ideas?" Ryan asked.

"I'm sure we can come up with something." Ben slipped an arm around his wife's waist, and they all headed toward the clubhouse.

"Let me know if there's anything I can do to help," Maya offered. She glanced around the parking lot before adding, "Revenge is best served when your victims aren't sure where it came from."

"You're absolutely right," Ryan agreed.

Chapter 2

KARI SHIFTED THE BACKPACK ON her shoulder in an effort to redistribute its weight.

Ben had convinced her to come to practice early with him on her first full day in DC. After showing her to the dugout, he had promptly disappeared down the tunnel that led to the clubhouse.

She glanced over at the camera crews setting up for tonight's game, a little surprised they were here so early. The game wouldn't start for another six hours.

Her phone vibrated in her pocket, and she looked down at it to see a message from Ben. *Meeting is starting.*

Are you sure about this? She texted back.

Absolutely. Marty will let you onto the field.

Kari looked over at the broad-shouldered security guard standing a short distance away. She had met him both times she had come to Ben's games last year, but her brother had made a point of introducing them again today. After assuring Marty that no one would end up on the disabled list as a result of their planned fun, he had agreed to help. Shifting her backpack once more, she climbed the dugout steps.

"Hey, Marty," Kari said in greeting. "Is it okay if I go check out the field?"

"You're sure no one will get hurt, right?" Marty asked.

"Positive."

Marty's bright eyes twinkled in the folds of his dark skin. "In that case, you got it." He motioned her forward, but Kari took only one step before addressing him again.

"Could you shift a bit to your left while I'm on the field?"

She glanced at the television cameras.

"Absolutely." His grin widened.

Kari moved forward, her own lips curving into a smile when she heard Marty greet the cameramen.

Hoping the distraction would work, she made a beeline for second base. Skirting by the pitcher's mound, she reached back and unzipped a pocket. In a smooth motion, she reached inside and pulled out a can of shaving cream.

A quick glance over her shoulder revealed the camera crew deep in conversation with Marty. Without hesitation, she leaned down and sprayed the edge of second base. The thick foam painted the side of the base in the same bright white. Standing, Kari looked down at her work, satisfied that the added substance wasn't noticeable without a close inspection.

Pleased, she continued toward third base. A quick glance at the camera crew, a brief inspection of third base, another thick spray of shaving cream, and her job was done.

Kari shoved the can back into her pack and returned to the dugout. Marty's voice carried toward her as he debated with a member of the television crew about whether it was warm enough for them to see some home runs tonight.

Marty apparently sensed her approach. "What do you think, Kari? Is your brother going to hit a home run tonight?"

"Of course," she responded automatically. "It's the least he can do since I came so far to see him play."

"Who's your brother?" The tall, dark-haired man to Marty's left asked.

"Ben Evans," Kari answered.

"Kari Evans, this is Alex Donaldson. He's one of the broadcasters for the local station," Marty said.

Alex extended his hand. "Good to meet you, Kari."

"You too." They fell into simple small talk, Alex conducting his informal interview even though Kari was hardly newsworthy. No, she hadn't flown in from her hometown of Cincinnati. Yes, she was staying with her brother for a few weeks. Yes, her sister-in-law was doing well.

Kari was touched that the reporter would ask about Maya, but she also felt awkward talking about her best friend with someone who made his living sharing others' personal business.

Her cell phone buzzed, a message from Ben that the team meeting had ended.

She took a step back. "If you'll excuse me, I think I'll go find my seat before the team comes out for practice."

Marty moved to her side. "I'll show you the way." He escorted her to the gate that would allow her to enter the stands. As soon as they were out of the reporter's earshot, he asked, "Did everything go okay?"

"We'll see soon enough."

The words were barely out of her mouth when the first players walked onto the field.

"I suggest you get comfortable. It'll be awhile before they start working on the bases."

"Is everyone going to know Ben was behind this?"

"Ben or Ryan."

"Ryan Strobel?" Kari asked. She had heard the name often enough from Ben. The two had apparently become partners in crime since coming up as rookies together last season.

"Yeah. Third base."

"It always amuses me how everyone is identified by their position." She thought for a moment. "I don't remember meeting Ryan when I came to visit last summer."

"You might have missed him when he was out with an injury for a couple weeks."

Several players made their way to the edge of the field and began stretching. Stretching gave way to playing catch. Kari was starting to think the real practice would never start when finally the infield players walked onto the field.

Ben took his position at second base and glanced into the stands. Even from this distance, she could see him stifling a grin. She put her feet up on the seat in front of her and settled back to watch the show. This should be good.

* * *

Ben struggled to keep a straight face. He could see the thick white foam on the edge of the base. Kari had done a great job of layering it on, and he doubted his teammates would be able to spot it from a distance.

Lanski stepped on first base and then took a three-step lead as he prepared to steal second. The pitcher on the mound practiced his pick-off move twice before he threw home and Lanski sprinted toward second.

Ben took the throw from the catcher, but instead of sweeping his glove downward, he deliberately bobbled it and stepped back. He was glad he did. Lanski's foot impacted the edge of the base and shaving cream flew into the air, globs spraying his cleats, pants, shirt, and arms.

Ben stifled a laugh.

"What the . . . ?" Lanski popped up to stand on the base, staring down at the white splotchy mess all over him. "Ben!"

"What?" Ben pasted on his best innocent look. "What did you do to yourself?"

Lanski wiped at the shaving cream, throwing the excess onto the ground. His eyes lifted, and he glared at Ben. "You're going to pay for this, Evans."

"Hey, I didn't do anything. I was just standing here."

"And this stuff . . ." He lifted his hand and took a sniff of the goo on his fingers. "This shaving cream got here by itself?"

"Maybe the grounds crew was having some fun with us." Ben shrugged innocently. "After all, everyone knew we had a team meeting today."

"What's going on out there?" Jack Wheatley yelled from the sideline.

"Nothing," Ben shouted back to their manager. "Nothing at all."

Lanski shifted his attention back to Ben, a look of determination in his eyes. "I know you're behind this. I don't know how you did it—"

"Before you go making threats of getting even," Ben interrupted him before he could finish, "don't you think you should make sure you're getting even with the right guy?" He stuck his hands in his pockets and pulled them inside out to demonstrate the lack of evidence against him. Maintaining his claim of innocence, he added, "I'm just a bystander here."

For the first time since receiving his shaving cream shower, doubt crept into Lanski's eyes. He shifted his attention to third base, where Ryan was standing, his expression carefully neutral. "I know one of you is behind this."

"Or maybe Gavin's having fun again and making it look like it was one of us."

"Stop the chattering out there," Jack called from the sidelines. "Play ball!"

"You heard the man." Ben shifted away from the base and into position, all the while biting the inside of his cheek to control the laughter struggling to break free.

When Lanski repeated the exercise going from second to third, Ben couldn't contain it any longer. The shaving cream shower exploded once more, and this time, Ryan got the close-up view.

* * *

Kari couldn't contain her laughter. The first player who had run through the drill still had splotches on his uniform. The second player apparently hadn't been paying close attention to the action while he waited his turn and received a similar shower when he took his slide into second base.

The look on Shawn Nill's face was priceless. Shock and confusion followed by a reluctant laugh. Kari was glad she had thought to pull out her phone and record the joke. She wondered who would try to get even with her brother first. That thought amused her over the next several hours.

Now, with the stands filling up, Kari scanned through her program and familiarized herself with this year's team until she heard someone calling her name. She turned to see Maya heading her way. Kari stood and jogged up the half dozen steps to where Maya was holding on to the rail as she descended to their seats.

"Here, let me help." Kari took Maya by the arm and supported her as they walked down the last few steps.

"You know, I really can walk by myself now."

"Yeah, I know." Kari didn't release her arm until Maya was comfortably seated.

"And like your brother, you're ignoring that fact."

"Yep," Kari said good-naturedly, delighting in the friendly banter she and Maya had shared since her senior year in high school. She really had missed her.

Though Maya was ready to regain her independence, her strength still wasn't consistent enough for her to come early with Ben to his games every day. Several times a week, Ben arranged for a driver to pick Maya up from their apartment to bring her to the game so she wouldn't have to drive herself.

"I don't know what you and Ben are going to do when I go to the doctor next week and he takes me off all my meds."

"What do you mean?"

"Once I'm done with this last round of chemo drugs, the doctor said I should start feeling like my old self." Maya put her hand on Kari's. "I can't wait."

"Sounds like you and Ben may need to go car shopping," Kari said.

"Oh, he's been shopping for weeks, and not just for cars."

"What do you mean?"

"His lease came up last month, and he didn't renew. We're on a month-to-month now, but he wants to buy a house."

"Really?" Kari shifted to face Maya more fully. Even though Ben had spent last winter in Washington, DC, she had never considered that he would settle here year round. "I thought you guys would buy a house in Cincinnati near my folks."

"We talked about it, but my doctors are here. I also like the nursing program at the community college here."

"It's already May. Have you applied yet?"

"I applied for spring term," Maya said. "Ben and I decided I needed some time after I finish chemo to get my strength up before tackling school again."

"That makes sense." Kari let the new reality take hold and felt a sense of excitement for her friend. "Just let me know when you want to go house hunting."

"I was hoping you would want to tackle that adventure with me." Maya's eyes met hers. "Are you sure you're okay with hanging out with me this summer?"

"Of course I am, as long as you don't mind having me," Kari said.

"You know you're always welcome to stay with us as long as you want, but I feel bad that we're talking about me and Ben buying a new house when all of your summer plans changed so completely."

"It's water under the bridge," Kari said, trying to believe her words.

"Can't you do anything about the internship?" Maya asked.

"I put in a grievance, but that's all I could do. By the time they review my complaint, the summer will be over."

"I'm sorry, Kari. I know you were really looking forward to working at the imaging center."

"Yeah, I think that's the worst part," Kari admitted. "It was annoying to have the internship ripped away from me at the last minute. I love working with MRIs and sonograms. It's fascinating how technology can be so effective as a diagnostic tool."

Maya rolled her eyes. "I'm certainly well versed in all of those tools."

"Yeah, but now we go in expecting good news instead of bad," Kari reminded her.

"That's true." Maya's attention shifted to the section to their right. "Uh-oh."

"What?" Kari followed Maya's gaze to where several women were chatting as they made their way to their seats.

Maya shifted closer. "See the redhead over there with the Strobel jersey?"

"Yeah. What about her?"

"She's Ryan's ex-fiancée, Brandi."

"And?"

"I'm just wondering what she's doing in town."

Kari watched Brandi greet several women sitting in the rows in front of them before taking a seat. "Looks like she has a lot of friends here."

"They're the other players' wives and girlfriends." Maya shifted her attention back to Kari. "How did practice go today?"

"Better than expected." Kari's eyes lit up at the memory of Lanski sliding into second. "I was hoping for an encore at some point tonight, but someone sent the grounds crew out to check all the bases. They cleaned up what was left of the shaving cream."

"I wish I would have been here to see it."

"Oh, I figured you would say that." Kari pulled out her phone and showed Maya the video of Lanski sliding into third. In the background, the player going into second was also visible.

Maya giggled. "Now I really wish I had been here."

Kari noticed Ben and a few of his teammates wandering out onto the field to start their warmup. "I have to say, after sitting here all afternoon, I'm ready to see the actual game."

"I usually bring a book or something with me for that gap between stretching and start time."

"*Now* you tell me."

"Hey, sometimes you have to find things out the hard way yourself."

"I may resemble that remark," Kari admitted. "Did you want me to get us something to eat?"

"I think we can do better than concessions." Maya opened her oversized purse and pulled out two plastic containers, handing one to Kari.

"Is this what I think it is?"

"If you think it's curry chicken, then yes." She took out a plastic bag that contained three plastic forks, opened it, and handed one to Kari. "Ben helped me make some on his last day off. I promised to make some for my friend Henry."

"Did someone call my name?"

Kari looked up to see an older man with a huge grin. His skin was dark and weathered, his eyes bright with humor.

"You're just in time." Maya motioned to Kari. "Henry, this is Ben's sister, Kari. Kari, this is Henry. He's the angel who used to help me get home after my treatments before Ben and I got married."

Kari offered her hand. "It's so good to meet you. Maya and Ben have mentioned your name quite a few times over the past several months."

"I've heard plenty of stories about you too." Henry shook her hand and took the seat on the other side of Maya. "Now, where's that curry chicken you promised me?"

Maya retrieved a third container from her bag. "Here you go."

Kari took a bite and rolled her eyes in appreciation. "This is just as good as I remembered."

"Glad you like it."

"I keep telling her that if she's not careful, she could put the food court out of business." Henry scooped up a bite and wagged his fork in the direction of the concourse. "Seriously, this is a golden opportunity."

"I only cook for my special friends," Maya said with a laugh.

Kari leaned forward and grinned at Henry. "We both have excellent taste in friends."

"I agree."

Chapter 3

RYAN SAT ON THE GRASS between Ben and Gavin while all three men stretched. Ben nodded toward the stands. "Ryan, it looks like your friend is back."

"Which one?" Gavin asked with a friendly smirk.

Ryan winced as Gavin's question echoed through his own brain. He deliberately didn't look in the direction Ben indicated, instead waiting for an answer.

"Brandi."

At the mention of her name, Ryan had to fight the urge to look. "I wonder what she's doing here."

"I don't know," Ben said. "I stopped following her on Twitter after you two broke up."

"I didn't," Gavin admitted. "But she didn't mention anything about being in town. My guess is she's here to surprise you."

"I don't like surprises."

"Sure you do," Gavin countered, "or you wouldn't have helped Ben line the bases with shaving cream."

"What makes you think I had anything to do with it?"

"I saw you jump out of the way when Lanski slid into third, just like Ben did when he came into second." Gavin stretched his back and glanced over at some of their teammates playing catch. "What I want to know was how you managed to frame me."

"What do you mean?" Ryan asked.

"I came back from practice to find my helmet filled with shaving cream," Gavin told them. "Coincidence? I don't think so."

Ryan tried to smother his laughter but couldn't quite manage it. "Sorry, Gavin, but we didn't have anything to do with that."

"Yeah, man. We didn't know you'd be the only person called out during our team meeting."

"My mom called. She was having an emergency."

"She was asking about doing a soup commercial with you," Ben countered.

"For her, that's an emergency," Gavin insisted. "It had something to do with styling her hair."

"Makes me glad my mom isn't into that kind of stuff," Ryan said, thinking of how down-to-earth his mother was. She wouldn't even let him buy her a house or upgrade her tiny two-bedroom apartment.

"What are you going to do about Brandi?" Ben asked, bringing his attention back to his ex-fiancée sitting in the stands.

"Pretend she isn't here."

"Good luck with that."

"Thanks."

* * *

Kari waited with Maya outside the clubhouse door while Ben finished doing whatever it was he did after a game. She glanced down at her watch. The final out had occurred over an hour ago. "Does it always take him this long to change?" Kari asked.

"It depends on if he was responsible for the winning run," Maya said.

"Which tonight he was."

"The press conference should be over in a few minutes," Maya assured her.

"Do all of the players have to stay for those?"

"No. It's usually just a few of them. Tonight it was probably the winning pitcher, Ben, and Ryan who got roped into it."

"No wonder Ben's sleep schedule is so crazy."

"Don't I know it," Maya agreed.

Kari glanced around and noticed the redhead Maya had pointed out earlier. She stood talking to another woman a short distance away.

"Looks like we aren't the only ones waiting," Kari said softly.

"I wonder how Ryan is going to feel when he walks out here and finds her waiting."

"I wouldn't know. I've never met the man."

"I'll have to introduce you to him," Maya said. "He's a good guy."

Kari sensed movement and turned to see Ben and Ryan heading toward her. She didn't miss the way Ryan's gait faltered when his eyes swept over his ex-fiancée.

Ben must have noticed the change too because he put a hand on Ryan's shoulder and leaned over to say something to him.

They were too far away for Kari to make out the words, but she saw Ryan nod as they continued toward them.

"I'm glad you waited for us," Ben said, and to Kari's surprise, he hugged her instead of approaching Maya first. He lowered his voice and whispered, "Do me a favor. Pretend you and Ryan know each other."

Before she could respond, he released her. As Ben turned his attention to Maya, Ryan stepped forward. "Thanks for waiting for me, Kari."

"No problem," she said. Though confused, she continued to play along. "Are you guys ready to go?"

"We are." Ben draped his arm around Maya and started toward the exit.

Kari turned to follow them, surprised when Ryan stepped beside her and put his arm around her shoulders. When she saw the ex-fiancée heading toward them, she clued into the favor Ben had really asked of her. Now aware of her role as stand-in girlfriend, she pushed aside the bubble of awkwardness, looked up at Ryan, and smiled brightly. "Are you guys still up for going out to celebrate?"

"That's a great idea," Ryan said, a look of relief flashing in his expression. "We could go to that all-night diner you like so much."

"I could go for a milkshake," Kari said.

"Me too." Ben shifted and nearly succeeded in cutting off Brandi's progress but not quite. She skirted past him and stopped in front of Ryan.

Brandi's gaze skimmed over Kari, a touch of disdain appearing in her expression before she focused on Ryan. "Ryan. I hoped I could talk to you for a few minutes."

"Oh, hi, Brandi. I didn't realize you were in town." Ryan turned to Kari. "Kari Evans, this is Brandi Snyder."

Kari gave her a nod in greeting. She felt bad misleading this girl, but she figured Ben must have his reasons for asking her to help. Determined to play her part well, she said, "Nice to meet you. Are you a friend of Ryan's from back home?"

Apparently shocked that Kari didn't know who she was, Brandi stiffened. Her voice turned haughty. "Ryan and I used to be engaged." She waved a hand toward Kari as though dismissing her. Her words went shrill when she added,

"Unlike his current dating behavior, where no one ever lasts longer than a date or two."

Whatever sympathies Kari had felt for Brandi dissolved in an instant. Ryan dropped his arm around her shoulder down so he could take Kari's hand. "I'm sorry, Brandi, but we have plans. I'll see you around." He looked down at Kari and gave her an apologetic look. "Come on, Kari. Let's go."

"Lead the way. I'm starving."

Together, the two couples left Brandi behind and headed for the parking lot.

* * *

Ryan let out a sigh of relief when they stepped outside and into the players' lot. The look on Brandi's face when Kari had asked how she knew Ryan had been priceless. Ryan almost felt bad for deceiving her.

"I think we're in the clear," Ben said, glancing behind them. "I guess this is kind of redundant now that you two are practically dating, but, Ryan, this is my sister, Kari. Kari, this is Ryan Strobel."

Ryan released her hand and turned to face her. Her brown hair was pulled back in a ponytail that fed through the back of her Nationals ball cap, and her green eyes lifted to meet his. He sensed an innate confidence in her that made her pretty features even more attractive. "Thanks for helping me out back there. It was about to get very awkward."

"I had a feeling," Kari said. "It's nice to meet you, Ryan."

He was surprised when she took a step toward Ben's car without any further comment. She didn't mention their earlier ruse of going out to eat or seem interested in getting his phone number. He couldn't remember the last time he had met a woman who had acted that way, at least not while he was at the ball field.

"I'll see you tomorrow, Ryan," Ben said, reaching out to open the car door for his wife.

"Yeah. Tomorrow." Bewildered, he watched Kari continue toward the car.

Chapter 4

KARI HAD CONSIDERED STAYING AT home with Maya when Ben went to practice the next day. That decision changed as soon as she found out Maya had a doctor's appointment and had made arrangements to ride to the game with her friend Henry and his wife.

"Are you sure you don't mind coming early with me?" Ben asked as they drove past the Lincoln Memorial. "I can drop you off at the monuments, and you could take the subway to the game."

"It's okay. I'll have plenty of time to play tourist later, and I'd rather wait until Maya feels up to coming with me."

His eyes brightened. "Only a few more days of chemo."

Kari couldn't help but smile at her brother's expression. Never would she have guessed that her brother and best friend would end up getting married, but after seeing them together at Christmas and again over the past two days, she couldn't imagine either of them marrying anyone else.

"You know, you still owe me for setting you up with her."

"You hardly set me up." Ben shot her a you've-got-to-be-kidding-me look. "You let her move into my apartment without telling me."

Kari settled back in her seat. "You're welcome."

"You're unbelievable."

"Part of my charm."

"Speaking of which, thanks again for helping Ryan out last night."

"No problem." Kari turned to face him. "I have to admit, though, that was a strange way to meet one of your friends."

"But it was memorable," Ben countered.

"True." She let herself get distracted by the sights of the nation's capital. As they neared the ballpark, her thoughts returned to last night.

Ryan had played his part well in making it look like they were really a couple. As much as she didn't want to admit it, she had enjoyed that brief connection with him. Perhaps it was the casual companionship she had once enjoyed with Austin that she really missed. It was hard to believe it had been less than two weeks since she had taken such simple things for granted.

Now, the only consistent contact she had with a man other than her brother was the text messages Austin sent her every day.

As though on cue, her phone chimed.

She glanced down to see Austin's name on the screen with an incoming text message. *Please call me. We need to talk.*

Kari deleted the message.

"Is everything okay?" Ben asked, seeming to have felt the change in her mood.

"Yeah. I just wish Austin would get the hint and stop texting me."

"Maybe you should block his number."

"It might come to that." Eager to change the subject, she asked, "How long do you think it will take before your teammates try to get even with you for the shaving cream yesterday?"

"Actually, they already got even with Gavin. They thought he was the guilty party."

Kari couldn't help but laugh. "If the team got even with Gavin, I guess the real question is when Gavin will play a joke on you."

"I was wondering the same thing." Ben pulled into the parking lot and waved at the security guard. He slowed as he passed Ryan's car. "Looks like Gavin has already started."

Kari looked out the window to see the team's logo written in Oreos on Ryan's windshield. The left side of the curly *W* started at the passenger's side and streaked over in front of the steering wheel.

"He did a good job getting them to stick to the glass," Ben commented.

"Yeah. Once you open them up, the filling really sticks, especially in the heat," Kari said.

Ben shot her a sidelong glance. "And you know this how?"

"You taught me."

"Oh yeah." Ben parked and shifted to look at her. "I don't suppose you want to hang out here and guard my car, do you?"

"Not particularly."

"It was worth a try." Ben climbed out of the car. As soon as Kari was beside him, he added, "Of course, you realize you're going to have to help me clean up the mess when Gavin sabotages my car."

One eyebrow lifted. "Why would I have to help?"

"You're the one who put the shaving cream on the bases."

"Only because you asked me to." Kari fell in step with him. "You, of all people, should know it's dangerous to turn on your allies."

Ben looked back at Ryan's car. "Should I tell Ryan about his car?"

"That's up to you. I've barely met the guy."

Ben lowered his voice. "Don't say that too loud. For all we know, Brandi could show up again today."

"Why doesn't Ryan just tell her he's not interested in her anymore?"

"He's tried a couple times, but she likes the spotlight. The last time she showed up, photos started showing up of the two of them on Instagram, and the rumors circulated that they were back together."

"How did she get pictures of them together if they broke up?"

"She came with a bunch of us to dinner one night after one of our day games. Someone took a group picture, and Ryan was standing beside her. All of a sudden, he was dealing with the press asking about her again."

Her sympathy stirred. "Sounds like a pain."

"It was." Ben nodded. "So if anyone asks about you and Ryan . . ."

"I'm not talking to anyone about Ryan or anyone else on the team," Kari said. "That will keep everything simple."

"Makes sense to me. Let's hope it all stays simple while Brandi is in town."

* * *

Ryan sat on the bench in front of his locker and unlaced his street shoes.

Shawn Nills, standing beside him, turned to look at him. "I saw Brandi's in town." He buttoned up his uniform. "What's with that?"

"Not a clue," Ryan said. "I didn't invite her."

"That's not what she said to my wife."

Part of him wanted to know what stories she was spinning now, but he resisted going down that road again. He hated the way Brandi could twist his emotions even after six months apart. Standing firm in his decision to let the past go, he responded, "She can say anything she wants."

"Does that mean she isn't going to be your date to the concert tomorrow night?"

"Are you talking about the Midnight Express concert after the game?"

"Yeah. I thought you knew we're all getting extra tickets so we can bring our wives or a date."

Suddenly Brandi's presence made more sense. "Let me guess. Brandi told your wife she's going with me."

"Pretty much."

Ryan let out a sigh. How was he supposed to move on in life if she kept trying to pull him back into the past? He had no doubt if he took Brandi to the concert, they would have a great time. The problems would begin the next day when she started texting him all the time to make plans for a future he knew wasn't going to work between them.

Ben walked into the locker room and called out a general greeting to the dozen players already inside. Ryan thought of the way Ben had rescued him last night. Ryan still couldn't believe Kari had been willing to play along, especially to help someone she had never met.

"Hey, Ryan. Do you have a minute?" Ben motioned to him.

"Yeah, sure." He followed Ben to the far corner of the room. "What's up?"

"I hate to break it to you, but you have Oreos all over your car." Even though he'd said it apologetically, the corners of Ben's mouth twitched, and Ryan could tell he was fighting back a grin. "I thought you might want to clean that up before practice."

"Seriously?" He huffed out a breath. "How is it that you came up with the shaving cream idea and I'm the one who paid for it?"

"Gavin paid for it too."

"Gavin's probably the one who cookied my car."

Ben grabbed a handful of towels off a nearby table. "Come on. I'll help."

Ryan scooped up four water bottles, and the two men headed for the door.

"Where are you two going?" Coach Wheatley demanded.

"We have a little problem we have to take care of," Ben said. "We'll be right back."

"Team meeting starts in fifteen minutes. Don't be late."

"We'll be here," Ryan promised. As soon as they were out of hearing distance, he muttered, "I hope."

Ryan thought of Shawn's comment about the concert. "Are you and Maya going to the concert tomorrow night after the game?"

"Yeah, assuming she's up to it."

"What about Kari?"

"I'm sure she'll want to come." Ben pushed open the door and headed into the parking lot. "I guess I'd better see what I can do about getting her a ticket."

"If you'll let me tag along with you guys, she can have my extra one."

"Trying to make sure you don't have a ticket to give Brandi?"

"Something like that." He stepped past an oversized truck to see his car, the windshield still half covered in Oreos. Standing by the driver's side, Kari was plucking cookies off the car and dropping them into a plastic grocery bag.

"Hey, Kari," Ben called out to her. "I thought you were already inside."

"I didn't have the heart to have Ryan find this mess after the game." She pulled two more cookies off the windshield.

Ryan stared, not quite sure what to make of Kari's unexpected kindness. "That's really sweet of you."

"I don't know about that," Kari said, stopping long enough to look over at him. "I think it might be guilt for being the one who actually put the shaving cream on the bases."

"That's true," Ben said. "This never would have happened had it not been for Kari."

Her attention shifted to Ben. "I think I liked it better when I wasn't the person you were pointing the finger at."

"Especially since you're the one who put her up to it," Ryan added. He started removing cookies from the glass.

The three worked in silence, Ryan and Kari removing the gooey mess and Ben using the towels and water bottles to clean the rest of it off.

"I have to say, this is a lot more fun when we're putting the cookies on a car rather than taking them off," Kari said after a minute.

Ben squirted some more water on the windshield. "I agree."

"You've done this kind of stuff to people before?"

Kari looked up at him, genuine surprise reflected on her face. "Haven't you?"

"I can't say that I have."

"And yet you got roped into helping my brother with one of his practical jokes?"

"I'm pretty new at this kind of stuff," Ryan admitted. "But it was great seeing Lanski with shaving cream all over him, especially after he put peanut butter all over my shoelaces."

"Well, whoever did this will be sorely disappointed if they find out your car is clean before the game even starts."

"I really do appreciate your help," Ryan said. "By the way, Ben and I were talking about the concert tomorrow night."

"What concert?"

"A few times during the season, they have promotional concerts after our games," Ben told her. "Midnight Express is playing tomorrow night."

"Oh, I like them."

"I have an extra ticket if you want it," Ryan offered.

Kari looked at him, clearly not expecting the offer. "Are you sure?"

"Yeah, I'm sure," Ryan said. "But I was hoping you might act like you're my date again."

"I gather the ex is still hanging around."

"Yeah."

"In that case, it's a date," Kari said.

Before Ryan could process her choice of words, Ben turned around to look at them. "You're already dating my sister? She's only been here two days."

"We're only dating if his ex shows up," Kari corrected.

Not sure whether he should be relieved or disappointed by her response, Ryan opted for the first choice. "Exactly."

Chapter 5

KARI STOOD IN THE KITCHEN and sliced a cucumber while Maya sat on the stool beside her. "Do you want anything else to eat besides a salad?"

"No, thanks." Maya started to reach for a bowl, but Kari beat her to it. "You know, I really can take care of myself. You don't have to fix my lunch."

"You still have a few more days of chemo. It won't hurt you to take it easy and make sure your body is able to handle it." Kari finished their salads and carried them to the table.

Maya followed her into the dining room, carrying two glasses of water. As soon as they both sat down, Maya asked, "So what's the deal with you and Ryan?"

"What do you mean?"

"Ben said Ryan asked you to go with him to the concert tonight."

Kari shook her head. "No. Ryan offered to give me his extra ticket, and I agreed to pretend to be his girlfriend if his ex shows up."

"Ah." Maya took a sip of her water. "Have you heard anything from your ex?"

Her stomach curled at the thought of Austin. "He still texts me every day. You'd think he'd clue in by now that I'm not going to respond."

"I still can't believe he was engaged and never told you about it."

The stab of betrayal cut through her as though it had happened yesterday instead of two weeks ago. "I can't believe his family didn't say anything about it when I went home with Austin last Thanksgiving."

"That is odd," Maya admitted. "Maybe he really was going to break up with her, and his family thought he already had."

"Maybe." Kari stabbed a bite of tomato, considering. "Even if that were true, he should have told me what was really going on."

"I agree," Maya said. "Have you decided if you're going back to Vanderbilt?"

"I'm thinking of taking a semester off to decide."

Her fork already halfway to her mouth, Maya stopped to look at Kari. "Your parents aren't going to be thrilled with that idea."

"I know, but I can't stand the thought of having to deal with Austin and his father next year. If I keep going with pre-med, I would have to take his dad's class, and I'm sure Austin would be in it."

"Are you sure you want to do pre-med?" Maya asked skeptically. "That's a lot of school."

"I know, but every time I think about what you went through, I can't help but feel like I want to make a difference."

"You did make a difference," Maya said. "Not only did you help me through my early treatments, but you made sure I could stay in the medical trial." She paused, her rising emotions evident on her face. "I wouldn't be alive right now if it wasn't for you."

Kari swallowed hard against her own emotions. "You're alive because you had the right doctors. I'm just glad I was able to help you find them."

Silence hung in the air for a moment.

"Have you thought about going to school around here?" Maya asked.

"I thought I might check a few out while I'm here this summer." Eager to change the subject, she added, "Of course, I think we need to do some house hunting for you first."

"Ben has a day off tomorrow," Maya said, considering. "I'm not sure how excited he'll be to spend it driving around looking at houses though."

Kari's eyes lit with humor. "Sounds like we should narrow down the possibilities."

"My thoughts exactly."

* * *

Ryan tensed the moment he saw Brandi. The stage for the concert had been set up in the outfield of Nats Park, and one of the front sections had been reserved for the team and their guests. Ryan didn't know who had given her a VIP pass, but there she was, twenty feet away, her red hair artfully styled, her clothes looking like she had just stepped out of a magazine.

Sitting beside him, Kari reached over and put her hand on his arm. "Maybe you should talk to her."

He looked at Kari, amazed that she didn't seem the least bit upset that he'd been staring at another woman when technically she was his date. "I'm not sure what good that would do."

"It would help you understand why she's here. Go ahead. I'm right here so you can use me as an excuse if you need to get away from her."

"I guess that's true." Still, he wavered.

"Go on." She leaned closer and spoke quietly in his ear. "I'll go get us something to drink. That will give you an opening without looking like you're being rude."

Before he could agree, she stood and slipped past him. He watched her go, then looked back over at Brandi. Kari was right. He wasn't going to be able to stop thinking about her until he knew what she was really doing here.

Forcing his body to move, he stood and made his way past the dozen people between them. The music started right as he reached her, and he had to speak loudly so she could hear him. "Can I talk to you for a minute?"

She nodded and followed him away from his teammates and onto the lower concourse. With the concert starting, it was nearly empty. Ryan stepped beside a closed hot dog stand where they were afforded some privacy. "What are you doing here?"

"I came for the concert." She shifted her gaze toward the direction they had come from. "Rachelle mentioned it to me last week, and I thought it would be fun to come see everyone."

Well aware that Brandi was still friends with several of the players' wives, he said, "You told Celeste you were going to the concert with me."

"That's not exactly what I said." Her cheeks flushed slightly. "I just thought you might be willing to let me hang out with you since you didn't have a steady girlfriend. No one knew you were going out with Ben Evans' sister." Her voice took on an edge. "Are you really going out with Ben's sister?"

"Not that it should matter to you, but yes, I am going out with Kari."

"It does matter to me." Now she morphed into the sweet woman he had once loved. "I miss you. I was really hoping I would get here and find out you were still single."

"We've been through this before. We don't want the same things in life."

"Ryan, you're never going to find someone who wants all the same things you do," Brandi insisted. "Relationships are about compromise."

"And relationships end when you realize one person expects all the compromise to be on one side." He stepped back and shook his head. "I'd better get back in there."

She reached out and grabbed his arm. "Ryan, maybe you should think about the fact that you have a date sitting down there and yet you chose to come up here to talk to me."

"I am thinking about that." He looked down at his arm, staring until she reluctantly released him. "I think it showed a great deal of maturity for Kari to insist I come talk to you and clear the air." He started back toward the concert, then paused. "I hope you enjoy your time in Washington." He turned his back on Brandi, determined to make this the last time he let her play on his emotions.

Chapter 6

RYAN STOOD BESIDE BEN ON the sidewalk leading to the large house in a gated community and watched Kari and Maya lead the way inside with the Realtor. "How exactly did I get roped into coming with you today?"

"Misery loves company," Ben answered.

"I thought we were going car shopping, not house hunting," Ryan said.

"That was my plan," Ben grumbled. "I have Maya's car all picked out. Ten minutes at the dealership to pick it up is all I need."

"You want to pick it up after all of this house hunting?"

"Yeah." Ben sent him an apologetic look. "Sorry this is turning into an all-day thing."

"It's all right." Ryan fell in step beside him as they followed the women up the front walk. "I didn't have anything else going on anyway."

"And being with us makes sure you aren't home if Brandi tries to stop by."

"It's like you're reading my mind."

"Ben, look at this," Maya called out to him the moment they passed through the front entrance of the house. Hardwood floors spanned the entryway and continued into the living room to the left. On the right, a decent-sized study sat behind closed french doors.

Ryan followed them through the house, listening to Ben and Maya talk about the kitchen and the number of bedrooms. Even though Ben had put on a good show outside about not wanting to be here, Ryan could feel his excitement about the prospect of making a real home with his wife. He remembered wanting that and resented the memory immediately.

Kari stepped beside him. "They're so cute together."

"I don't think your brother wants to be considered cute," Ryan said dryly.

"I know, but they are. It's so cool to see them looking beyond Maya's treatments. I wasn't sure we would ever get to this day."

"What do you mean?" Ryan asked.

"When I helped Maya move out here last fall, we weren't sure she would still be alive by now."

Some of the bitterness from his own past relationship faded beneath the truth of what the couple in front of them had faced together. "What do you think? Is this the house for them?"

"Maya likes it, but we still have four more to look at today."

"Four more?"

"Well, yeah. It only made sense to check out several while we were in the area."

"It's a bit of a drive to the stadium."

"I mentioned that too, but they both want to get out of the city and have more space." She motioned to her brother. "Of course, as soon as Ben realizes having a yard includes mowing the lawn, he may reconsider."

"True." He glanced at the expansive backyard, a five-hole putting green situated to one side. "It's hard to believe Ben can afford something like this just because he's good at baseball."

"I'm sure you could too if you wanted."

"Yeah, but I don't have any reason to buy a house yet."

Ben stepped beside them. "I think we're ready to head to the next one."

They were nearly to the car when Ben's phone rang. He looked at the screen and said, "Sorry, I need to take this. It's the guy at the dealership." He hit the talk button. "Hey, Paul. Sorry, I haven't made it over there yet. My wife made another appointment for this morning. I was going to head over there this afternoon." Ben paused. "What time would I need to be there?" Another pause. "No, that's okay. I understand. I'll see what I can do to be there before then."

"Problem?" Ryan asked as soon as he hung up.

"Yeah. Apparently the dealership has a big training meeting this afternoon. If I want to pick up Maya's car today, I have to be there by one."

"Does Maya need to be with you?" Kari asked.

"I did want her to see the car before I finalize the paperwork," Ben said.

"You guys go ahead. I can look at the rest of the houses and check out the neighborhoods for you," Kari offered. "I'll even take notes to help you narrow down which ones you want to see yourself when we look at them again online."

"I don't know," Maya said. "I really wanted to see the other houses, and I feel bad abandoning you."

"I can go with her," Ryan offered, surprised to hear the words come out of his mouth. "I'm sure the Realtor can drive us and drop us off at either my apartment or yours."

"I'll check with her," Maya said, heading for the front door where Gretchen, the Realtor, was securing the key in the lock box.

"Are you sure you don't mind?" Ben asked.

"You guys go." Ryan waved toward Ben's car. "We'll be fine."

Maya approached them. "Gretchen said she's happy to drive you guys."

"In that case, we'll see you later." Ryan put his hand on Kari's arm. "Come on, Kari. We have some houses to see."

"See you guys later." Kari waved at Ben and Maya, then turned to Ryan. "You know, you really don't have to come with me."

"I don't mind," Ryan said. "It'll be good practice for when I do decide to buy a place."

"In that case, let's go. Only four more houses to see."

* * *

The first two houses didn't impress Kari or Ryan. One was ridiculously large but felt more like a museum than a home. The second was located on a main street, and Kari knew that wouldn't suit her brother or Maya.

"The next two houses are across the street from each other on a cul-de-sac," Gretchen told them. She pulled up to the gate at the community entrance and keyed in the code. She looked over at Ryan. "I believe two of your teammates live in this neighborhood."

Kari looked at the first few houses they passed, with their expansive yards and mature trees. The houses in this neighborhood appeared to be custom built and didn't follow the same uniformity as the first few places they had visited.

"Let's start with this one first," Gretchen said, parking the car in front of a colonial-style home.

Kari liked the look of the outside, the stone front giving it character. They followed the Realtor inside, and she felt a sense of home she hadn't experienced anywhere besides the house she had grown up in. She couldn't explain the source of the emotion and wondered if Ben would feel the same sensation.

A staircase to her left led upstairs, a stunning chandelier hanging above them in the center of a two-story foyer.

Kari wandered through the large great room, appreciating the way a long breakfast bar separated it from the kitchen. Four ladder-back stools lined the family side of the counter, and an oblong table occupied the dining area.

They circled through the rest of the main floor, finally coming to a hallway on the far side of the great room.

"What's over here?" Kari asked.

"This house has a full in-law suite." Gretchen led the way down a hall flanked with windows overlooking the back patio until they reached a door.

Ryan reached out and opened it for them, and Kari stepped through first. She had expected to walk into a bedroom, but she found herself standing in a miniature version of the great room/kitchen combination she had seen in the main part of the house. Crossing through the rooms, she discovered a master suite, the bedroom nearly as large as her parents', and a bathroom that rivaled the master bathrooms they had seen in a few of the other houses they had viewed today.

"Does this suite have a private entrance?" Ryan asked.

"It does." Gretchen motioned to a door in the kitchen area. "That door leads to a one-car garage. The main house has a three-car garage on the other side of the main kitchen."

Kari snapped a few pictures with her phone. "How many more bedrooms are there?"

"Five."

Ryan looked over at her. "Are you ready to see the upstairs?"

"Yeah. Let's go."

Together they walked back into the main section of the house. Gretchen waved in the general direction of the stairs. "I'll let you take a look while I call about the next house."

Ryan led the way up the stairs. They found an upstairs living area with three doors opening into it. One by one, they entered the various bedrooms, Kari taking pictures of each one.

"What do you think?"

"I really like this one."

"Me too. It's definitely my favorite so far." He shrugged his shoulders. "Not that my opinion really matters."

"Of course it matters." Kari wandered through the master bedroom and opened one of the closet doors. When she found it empty, she went to the other closet and repeated the process to find it empty as well. "It looks like there isn't anyone living here."

"I've heard they leave furniture in these big houses so they'll show better," Ryan said. "Or maybe whoever owns it has so many houses they don't keep their clothes here."

"I think it's more likely the owner has already moved out," Kari said. "That's pretty nice, since Ben and Maya would probably have some flexibility to move in sooner than later if they want."

"True." He started for the door. "Should we go look at the last one?"

"Sure." Kari snapped one last photo of the master bedroom and followed him downstairs.

The door was already open, Gretchen standing on the porch with a phone to her ear. She put her hand over the phone and spoke quietly. "I'm just getting the alarm code before we go across the street. If you want to head over there, I'll be right behind you."

"Okay." Kari and Ryan made their way to the curb, their pace slowing when they saw a man approaching with a black lab.

Across the street, Kari noticed two women standing in front of the house next door to the one for sale, and another man was standing in the center of the cul-de-sac while his son rode on his tricycle.

"Looks like a family-friendly street," Kari commented.

"Yeah, it does."

The man with the dog stopped and greeted them. "Are you two checking out the neighborhood?"

"I guess you could say that," Ryan responded.

"I'm Phil Atkins." Phil extended his hand.

"Good to meet you." Ryan shook his hand. "I'm Ryan Strobel, and this is Kari Evans."

The man's eyes widened. "I thought you looked familiar. You play for the Nationals, right?"

Kari sensed Ryan's reservation, but he somehow managed to keep his voice light. "Yeah. I gather you're a baseball fan."

"Big time." He waved eastward. "Domingo Hernandez and Shawn Nills live on the other side of the neighborhood, but I can't say that I've ever met them."

"They're both good guys," Ryan said. "So tell me, how do you like living here?"

"It's great. My wife and I moved in five years ago."

Kari listened to the man chat about the positives of the neighborhood and asked her own questions about traffic and the other neighbors. The more she listened, the more she was convinced that this might be exactly where Ben and Maya needed to live.

Gretchen approached them and interrupted the conversation. "I'm sorry about that. It took a few minutes to get hold of the right person."

"Lead the way," Ryan said before turning to the man beside them. "Nice chatting with you."

"Yeah, you too. I hope you decide to move onto the street. It really is a great neighborhood."

"Thanks."

They headed across the street, and as soon as they reached the door, Kari leaned closer to Ryan. "You realize that guy thinks we're a couple."

"Yeah, probably."

"And that you're the one house hunting," Kari added.

"Yep."

Kari chuckled. "I guess he'll find out that's not the case when you don't move in."

"Exactly."

Gretchen unlocked the door and deactivated the alarm. Ryan and Kari went inside, and again, Kari felt a sense of home. As with the other house, she suspected the furniture had been staged, but that didn't diminish the warmth and the attractive use of space.

Ryan wandered through the dining room located to their right and into the kitchen area. "I kind of like this one too."

"I was thinking the same thing." Kari crossed to a window overlooking the backyard. "Maya is going to love this."

"What?" Ryan moved to stand beside her.

"A tennis court." Kari motioned to the left. "Maya is an amazing tennis player. It's her favorite sport."

"Sounds like we need to take more pictures."

"I agree," Kari said, "but I have a feeling I'll be back here soon with Maya to show it to her in person."

Ryan turned to look at her. "I think you're right."

Chapter 7

"Ryan, I am so sorry about yesterday." Ben dropped down in the seat next to him, a look of apology on his face that was out of character for him.

"It was no big deal. Kari and I looked at houses. She took lots of pictures. End of story."

"Not exactly." Ben pulled his cell phone from his pocket. "I'm guessing you haven't seen Twitter today."

"No. Why?"

"Like they say, a picture is worth a thousand words." Ben opened the screen, tapped it a couple times, and turned it so Ryan could see the image displayed there.

Ryan leaned closer to see a photo of Kari and him standing next to a For Sale sign. "So someone snapped a picture of me and Kari yesterday. What am I missing?"

"Read the caption." Ben handed the phone to him so he could take a closer look. He scrolled up enough that he could read the words that preceded the photo: *Ryan Strobel and girlfriend, Kari Evans, out house hunting. Could there be a wedding in Ryan's future?*

Ryan handed the phone back with a shrug. "I guess it's true that single guys on the team can't even talk to a woman without someone blowing things out of proportion."

"I really am sorry about this," Ben said, clearly worried that Ryan would be upset. "I know you don't like to have your personal life all over social media."

"It's not like you or Kari had anything to do with it." His eyebrows drew together. "Who did post that?"

"I've never seen the name before."

"It must have been one of the neighbors. Kari and I talked to some guy walking his dog, and we introduced ourselves."

"Which explains how they had Kari's name."

"Yeah." Ryan considered how annoyed he would have been had this happened with Brandi. Had he grown a thicker skin over the past six months? Or had his mistrust of Brandi made him suspicious that she was somehow involved every time his name hit the Internet? "Has Kari seen this yet?"

"I don't think so. I only found out about it because Dayna in the front office showed it to me."

"How is Kari going to feel about it?"

"Honestly, she'll probably laugh it off," Ben admitted. "I'm glad you're about to do the same."

"Do you think I should at least call her and let her know about it before she gets ambushed coming to the ballpark?"

"That's not a bad idea."

Ryan pulled out his phone and started to scroll through his contacts only to realize he didn't have Kari's number. "What's her number?"

Ben retrieved her number on his phone and held it out so Ryan could put it into his phone.

Ryan dialed the number, and Ben stood. "I'm going to get changed. Let me know if I need to apologize to her too."

"Will do," Ryan said.

A moment later, Kari's voice came over the line. "Hello?"

"Hey, Kari. It's Ryan."

"Oh, hi, Ryan. What's up?" Though her words were casual, he sensed she was surprised to hear from him.

"I just wanted to give you a heads up. Our little shopping spree yesterday made it into my Twitter feed."

"You lost me."

Ryan explained how a photo of them had been posted on social media with both of their names mentioned. "I wanted to make sure you knew about it in case you come to the ballfield and get cornered by any reporters."

"You know, it's pretty sad that you can't go looking at houses without someone making a big deal about it."

"I know. I was just saying the same thing to Ben."

"Well, I appreciate the warning," Kari said. "I assume these things normally blow over pretty fast."

"I'm not really sure. Brandi always tried to turn them into a big deal, so I have no idea what happens when the posts get ignored."

"I guess we're about to find out," Kari said. "Good luck at your game today."

"Are you coming to watch?"

"Yeah. Maya and I are driving over in her new car. She's pretty excited about it."

"I'll bet." He smiled at the thought. "I guess I'll see you after the game."

"Okay. See you later."

Ryan hung up and was halfway through getting dressed when he realized he expected to see Kari after his game. For the first time since meeting her, he entertained an alarming thought. Did she have a boyfriend?

* * *

Kari grinned at Maya as they made their way to their seats. "I think you enjoyed driving yourself for a change."

Maya's eyes lit up. "I can't tell you how good it feels to have that kind of freedom again."

"How are you feeling?"

"I'm doing well, actually. Today was just my Nuelasta shot. One more chemo dose tomorrow and I'll be done."

"I'm so happy for you," Kari said, slowing when they approached their seats and found several women standing in the aisle.

A stunning blonde-haired woman turned to face them, her face lighting in recognition when she saw Maya. "Hey, Maya. How are you doing?"

"Good, thanks." Maya shifted her attention to Kari. "Kari, this is Celeste Nills. Her husband, Shawn, plays right field. Celeste, Kari is Ben's sister."

"It's good to meet you," Kari said, extending her hand.

"You too." Celeste narrowed her eyes. "Wait, aren't you the one who is going out with Ryan?"

Not sure if this woman was one of Brandi's friends, Kari said, "Something like that."

"I have to tell you, none of us had a clue Ryan was serious about anyone. Every time we turn around, it seems like he's with someone new."

"How long have you and your husband been married?" Kari asked, deflecting the attention back onto Celeste.

"Six months." Her face lit up. "We got married last off-season."

Maya put her hand on Kari's arm. "Kari, do you mind if we sit down? I think driving over here zapped my energy."

"No problem." Kari sidestepped Celeste. "It was nice meeting you."

"You too. I'm sure I'll be seeing you around."

"You can count on it." Kari took Maya by the elbow and helped her the rest of the way to their seats.

After they sat, Maya lowered her voice. "I'm sorry about that. The wives and girlfriends are all really nice, but during the season, everyone is anxious for something to talk about. I'm afraid you've become a hot topic of conversation the last couple days."

"It won't last once everyone realizes I'm not really dating Ryan."

"I'm sure you're right." Maya glanced around. "I don't see Brandi here. Maybe she finally gave up and went back home."

"I hope so, for Ryan's sake." Kari settled back in her seat and put her feet on the one in front of her. "Now, tell me, what do you think of the houses I was telling you about?"

"I think the two of us need to go look at the two you liked tomorrow. I'm really excited to see the one with the tennis court."

"I thought that one would catch your interest."

"I can't even imagine what it would be like to be able to play in my own backyard."

"Are you sure you don't want to wait for Ben to have another day off before you go look?" Kari asked.

"That won't happen for a while. The team goes out of town at the end of the week," Maya told her. "I thought we could go see the two houses you liked the best and help narrow down our options. If I think Ben will like them, I can go see them again before he goes to practice day after tomorrow."

"That works." Kari grinned at her. "Now that you have a car, all sorts of possibilities are open to you."

"I know." Maya's dark eyes lit up. "It's so exciting."

Chapter 8

RYAN COCKED THE BAT ABOVE his shoulder, his focus on the pitching machine. His movement was fluid as he swung through to the ball, connecting with it and sending it into the net at the back of the batting cage. At his coach's signal, he moved aside to make way for the next player in line.

He saw Ben waiting a short distance away and crossed to him. "How did the house hunting go? Did you and Maya go this morning?"

"We did. Maya's with the real estate agent now, writing up an offer."

"Really?" Ryan said. "That was fast."

"Not really," Ben said. "We'd been out looking a couple times before, and Maya had already done a ton of research online to help narrow down where we wanted to live. And, of course, I talked to Shawn and Domingo about the area and the commute."

"That's great. Congratulations," Ryan said. "Which house did you decide on?"

"The brick-front colonial you and Kari looked at. The one on the cul-de-sac with the tennis court."

Ryan rested his bat on his shoulder. "It's a beautiful home."

"It is. I have a feeling Maya and Kari are going to spend the whole summer shopping for furniture."

"I'm sure they'll love every minute of it too."

"Probably," Ben agreed. "Those two make shopping a sport."

"Have they been friends for long?"

"Since high school. Kari introduced me to Maya."

"So what's the deal with Kari?" Ryan shifted his bat again and tipped it against the fence. "You said she's staying here all summer?"

"I think that's her plan." Ben shrugged. "She had a pretty bad breakup last month and needed to get away. From what Maya told me, she's thinking about transferring schools, so it's possible she'll end up here permanently."

Ryan pondered this new information.

Ben's voice took on a suspicious tone. "Why do you ask?"

"Just wondering." Ryan leaned back against the fence. "You know how I called her a couple days ago about that picture on Twitter?"

"Yeah." Ben selected a bat from the nearby rack.

"Did you know she hasn't called me once?"

"So?"

"Ben, it hasn't been that long since you were single. You know how most women are with us, especially during the season." Ryan straightened again and held his hands out, exasperated. "I've still got a half dozen women calling me from our last road trip."

Ben cocked his bat and took a practice swing. "A lot of women like to be in the spotlight."

"And that's another thing. That picture on Twitter of me and Kari? Totally faded out of sight."

"Mostly out of sight," Ben corrected.

"What do you mean?"

"You know that website that lists baseball players and their girlfriends and wives?"

"Yeah. What about it?"

"Dayna in the front office mentioned that Maya was on there now."

"That makes sense. You married her last fall."

"Yes, but up until this week, Brandi was on there too," Ben said. "The picture of you and Kari is on there now."

"Hey, if Kari managed to get Brandi off that site, I probably owe her dinner, at the very least."

"Is this your way of asking if I mind if you date my sister?"

"Maybe," Ryan said. He had to admit, he was intrigued with the idea of going out with a woman who wasn't chasing him. A beautiful, fun, energetic woman. "Would it bother you if I asked her out?"

Ben fell silent for a moment. "It's not up to me who she dates, but I can tell you, I'm sure you're a huge improvement over the last guy."

"What was wrong with him?"

"He lied."

"That's never good." Ryan felt a sense of relief to find that Kari didn't have any other men vying for her attention at the moment. "Did you guys have any plans tomorrow night?"

"Actually, I was planning a nice dinner at home for Maya to celebrate the end of her chemo treatments. She had her last one yesterday."

"Maybe I can convince Kari to go out to dinner with me. Unless you wanted her to celebrate with you too."

"I'm sure Maya and I can manage on our own if Kari wants to go out with you."

"Has she said anything about me?" Ryan asked, trying to sound casual.

"I'm her brother. She doesn't tell me that kind of stuff." Ben put his hand on Ryan's shoulder. "I hate to break it to you, but you may have to resort to the old-fashioned way of asking a woman out and actually call her."

"I can do that."

* * *

Kari leaned forward in her seat and tried to remember to breathe. The game remained scoreless, a surprise in itself considering the batting averages of both teams. Now, in the bottom of the tenth inning, Gavin stood on first base, and Ben stepped into the batter's box.

"I'm afraid to watch," Maya said from beside her.

"I know what you mean," Kari admitted, yet her eyes stayed glued on her brother.

The first pitch whizzed by him, low and away. Ball. The second, inside but in the zone. Strike.

Kari could almost feel her brother's impatience. He was ready to put this game to bed. The pitcher wound up, and to everyone's surprise, Ben squared around to bunt.

The ball spun down the third-base line. A great move by the pitcher was good enough to throw Ben out, but now Gavin stood on second.

"You can look now," Kari said. "Ben sacrificed Gavin to second."

"Looks like it's up to Ryan."

Kari watched Ryan stride toward the plate from the on-deck circle. He took a deep breath, looked down at his bat, and then dug his lead foot into place in the front of the batter's box.

Kari suspected his ritual was so ingrained that he didn't even realize he followed a specific routine, but after watching him play for the past few days, she could already anticipate each movement.

After a moment of setup, Ryan planted his back foot. The pitcher wound up, Ryan cocked his bat above his shoulder, and the crack of wood against ball followed an instant later.

Kari jumped to her feet automatically. Her eyes followed the ball until she lost it in the lights. Then she saw the scramble of fans in the left-field section.

The roar of the crowd was instant and loud enough that Kari couldn't make out the announcer's words.

"Now, that's what I call a good game," Kari said, finally dropping back into her seat.

"I was starting to think no one would ever score."

"I would hate to be a pitcher facing this team, with Ben and Ryan going back to back in the lineup."

"They're both hoping this year they'll win the championship. Last year was tough on them, losing in the first round of the playoffs."

"Oh, I remember," Kari said, all too aware of how hard it had been on her brother that he had been the last out. "Did you want to head straight home, or do you want to wait to see Ben first?"

"Do you mind if we wait for Ben?"

"No, it's not a problem." She motioned to the steady stream of fans filing out of their seats and heading for the exits. "The traffic is going to be insane getting out of here anyway. We might as well wait for it to clear out."

"Thanks." Maya put her hand on Kari's. "I really am glad you're here. It's so much more fun to watch the games with someone."

"Have you made any friends from Ben's team?" Kari looked around at the other players' wives and girlfriends.

"Some of them are nice enough, but it's not the same as having someone who knew me before I was the miracle cancer survivor."

Kari heard her friend's weariness, and for once, the emotion didn't stem from disease. "You're not just a cancer survivor."

"I know, but sometimes it feels like that's all people see," Maya said. "Hopefully that will change now that my treatments are over."

"We really do need to celebrate."

"Ben said the same thing. Since he has a four o'clock game tomorrow, we decided to order dinner in afterward and hang out at home."

"That wasn't exactly what I had in mind, but if it's what you want." Kari considered the size of her brother's apartment and the fact that Ben and Maya hadn't had a lot of privacy since she arrived. "Maybe you and Ben should have some time alone. Tomorrow night might be a good time for me to get out and see some of the town."

"You don't have to do that," Maya insisted. "We both planned to have you join us."

"We can talk about it tomorrow," Kari said, not convinced.

* * *

Ryan followed Ben out of the locker room, the palms of his hands sweating. Where had that come from? He rubbed his palms on his slacks, grateful when he visually swept the area and didn't see Brandi.

Maya and Kari stood to the side with a couple of the wives. Ben led the way, a grin on his face when he scooped Maya up and gave her a kiss. "How do you like the new car?"

"I love it," she said, her face aglow with laughter. "It was so nice driving myself for a change."

"And how did it go with the Realtor?"

"Great. We just have to sign the paperwork tomorrow, and she'll put in the offer," Maya said. "She seemed optimistic that the owner will accept it."

Maya and Ben continued to chat about their upcoming housing purchase, and Ryan closed the distance between himself and Kari.

"I wasn't sure you girls would hang around now that Maya has a car."

"We wanted to congratulate you both. That was one heck of a game," Kari said. "You did great."

"Thanks." He shifted his weight from one foot to the other. "Hey, I was wondering if you had any plans tomorrow night."

"No, not yet." She took a step away from her brother and whispered, "I was actually trying to come up with some reason to get out of the house though. I wanted to give Maya and Ben some time alone."

"Would you be up for going out to dinner with me tomorrow night?" he asked, perfectly willing to take advantage of the opening she'd given him.

"I'd like that." He saw a brief flash of surprise on her face, followed quickly by her smile.

"Great," Ryan said, relieved. "If it's okay with you, we can leave from here right after the game."

"That's perfect." She glanced over at her brother. "It will be nice for them to have a little privacy before the team goes on the road."

Ryan thought over his upcoming schedule. Thirteen days on the road in four different cities. "Any preference of where you want to eat?"

"I don't know what's around here. The only times I've been to DC, I flew in and out within a couple of days. I really haven't seen much of the city."

"I guess I'll have to surprise you, then."

"I guess you will."

Chapter 9

THE NEXT NIGHT, KARI STOOD beside Maya in what had become their usual spot outside the clubhouse door. She wasn't sure what to expect today, especially from Ryan. This was the first time since she'd arrived that the Nationals had lost.

The nerves in her stomach jumped, and she tried to remind herself that she didn't have anything to be nervous about. After all, Ryan probably asked her out as a favor to Ben to get her out of the house. If Ryan was in a bad mood after their loss, they could always cut their evening short, and she could go to a movie instead.

As though reading her thoughts, Maya asked, "You didn't make plans with Ryan just to get out of the house tonight, did you?"

"No, of course not," Kari said. "He asked. I said yes."

"I know you pretended to be his girlfriend to help him out, but are you interested in him that way?"

"I hadn't thought about it until he asked me out." Her shoulders lifted. "He seems like a nice guy, but I don't know him very well."

"I guess today will be a good chance to get to know him better." Maya glanced at her watch. "And it's not often that they're done before seven."

"I guess so." The clubhouse door opened, and a few of Ben's teammates walked through. Kari sensed the frustration of the man nearest her and the easy-going manner of the player beside him. She wondered which type of baseball player Ryan would turn out to be.

Would he be able to let the losses go and look to tomorrow? Or would he fixate on what went wrong to help him learn from past failures? She always considered her brother to be a combination of the two.

The stream of weary athletes emerging from the locker room continued until finally Ben and Ryan walked out.

"Hey, Kari. Are you ready to go?" Ryan asked.

"Yeah." She turned to Maya. "I'll see you later."

"You have your key to my place, right?" Ben asked.

"I do. I'll text Maya when we head home."

"Have fun," Maya told them, taking Ben's arm and leading him toward the player parking lot.

"Sorry today's game wasn't one of our better ones," Ryan said as they headed for the exit. "It wasn't our day."

"No one's perfect," Kari said, grateful that he seemed to be taking the loss in stride. "The other pitcher was definitely on tonight."

"Yeah, unfortunately for us," Ryan agreed. They made their way to his car, and he opened the door for her.

"Thanks." Kari slid onto the leather seat.

He pulled his cell phone free of his pocket before taking his spot beside her and set it in the cup holder. Kari glanced down to see a text message on his screen from someone named Madison. His phone chimed, this time a text popping up from Desiree. Ryan ignored both, his attention on her. "What do you normally do when you aren't watching baseball games or helping your brother look for houses?"

"Study mostly," Kari admitted, not sure what to think about the stream of messages from other women. Of course, she couldn't say much, considering that Austin continued to text her at least once a week. Reminding herself this was a first date, she forced herself to relax. "It still feels weird to get home every night and realize I don't have any papers to write or required reading to catch up on."

"What are you majoring in?"

"I'm pre-med."

She expected him to express the same reservations Maya had brought up earlier, but he didn't seem fazed by her declaration. "Have you narrowed down where you want to go to med school?"

"George Washington University would be my first choice, but for now, I'm more concerned with where I want to finish my undergraduate degree."

"Ben mentioned something about a bad breakup." Ryan glanced over at her. "Do you mind if I ask what happened?"

"Not much to tell." Kari swallowed the bitterness to keep it from coloring her words. "I dated Austin for six months. We broke up when I found out he had been engaged to someone else the whole time."

"Oh man." Ryan shook his head. "He's lucky you let him live."

"I thought so." The dry humor pushed away what was left of her negative mood. "Tell me about you. Where are you from? Where's your family?"

"I grew up in Woodbridge, which is about forty-five minutes south of here." His eyes brightened. "When I was a kid, I used to sneak onto the roof of our apartment building and use binoculars so I could watch the P-Nats play. It was a dream come true when I got drafted into the organization."

"The P-Nats?" Kari repeated.

"The Potomac Nationals. They're one of the minor league teams that feed into the Washington Nationals."

"Gotcha." She waited until he navigated through a busy intersection before she asked, "What about your family? Are they still in Woodbridge?"

"It's just my mom, but she's still in the same apartment I grew up in." He raked his fingers through his hair. "I keep trying to convince her to let me buy her something in a nicer neighborhood, but she's being stubborn."

"Or she doesn't want to change," Kari said. "I have to imagine she feels a strong sense of community if she's lived there for over twenty years."

"I suppose, but I don't really understand why. Her neighbors change over every year or two. The only one who's been around for any length of time moved into a nursing home about three months ago."

"Have you tried talking to her since then?"

"Yeah, but so far she isn't budging." He turned a corner, and Kari looked up to see the Lincoln Memorial and the Vietnam Memorial a short distance away.

"It's hard to believe so many monuments are clustered so close together."

"Have you done any sightseeing since you got to town?"

"No. My parents and I went to the Washington Monument the first time we came to watch Ben play, but I've only been to that one and the World War II Memorial."

"Do you want to stop and sightsee for a little while before dinner?"

"Would you mind?" Kari asked. "If you're hungry now, we could come back later."

"We're already here." A block away, a car pulled onto the street. "And it's not often you can find a parking space this close."

"It must be a sign."

"It must be."

* * *

Ryan hadn't been to the monuments in years. Growing up a short distance from DC, he had visited many times with his mom and on various school field trips. Seeing everything through fresh eyes was an experience he enjoyed much more than he had anticipated.

After a visit to the Lincoln Memorial, they wandered down the path to the Vietnam Memorial. He looked at the names carved into the black granite. Not for the first time, the tribute to fallen military men brought up uncomfortable memories. "I always think about my dad when I visit here."

Kari turned to him, and he realized she hadn't pried earlier when they had been talking about his family. Most people asked where his dad was or why he wasn't in the picture.

"Is your dad military?"

"That's what my mom said." He fell silent, relieved when she didn't press. Perhaps it was because she respected his privacy that he was willing to share the truth, or at least what little truth he knew himself. "My parents met when my father was going through training at Quantico. They only knew each other for a few months before they got married."

"What happened?" Kari asked.

"Mom got pregnant. A couple months later, Dad shipped out to his flight school."

"And?"

"And that was it." A twinge of regret bubbled up, along with the wish that he knew what it was like to have a father in his life. "My mom was supposed to follow him to Florida, but when it came time to move, my dad showed up with divorce papers instead of a U-Haul."

"Do you have any idea why?"

"No." Ryan shook his head. "All I know is my mom rarely talks about him."

"Has he had any contact with you?" Kari asked.

"I've never met him."

"That's sad, but it's his loss."

Ryan's eyes met hers. "That's exactly what my mom always says."

"Sounds like she's a smart woman."

"She is," he said. "She's worked as a nurse's aide for twenty-five years, but I swear she knows more than most of the nurses she helps."

"Why didn't she ever go back to school and get a nursing license?"

"That's another one of those questions I've never understood the answer to." He reached out and took her hand, guiding her back toward the car. Her skin was warm and smooth beneath his own calloused hand. "Enough about me. Tell me about your family."

"We're pretty boring. I lived in the same house in Cincinnati from the time I was born until I left for college. Same with Ben and my older sister."

"I'm surprised you aren't thinking about moving back to Ohio to finish college."

"I thought about it, but the truth is that I really don't want to live there anymore," Kari said. "Don't get me wrong. I loved growing up in the Midwest, but I'm ready to be out on my own."

He reached into his pocket and retrieved his car keys, then glanced over at her. "You do realize you're living with your brother, right?"

She chuckled. "Yes, that's true, but it's only for a few months until I decide where I'm going to school. Even if I stay in the area, I'll find a place of my own."

"With the house they're buying, you could probably live with them, and they wouldn't even notice."

"It was big, wasn't it?"

"Yeah. Too bad the tennis court wasn't in the backyard of the house across the street. That second master bedroom was pretty much its own apartment."

"True." She waited for him to open the car door for her. "But staying with them would be too easy. I don't want to live off someone else. I want to take care of myself."

Ryan found the sentiment endearing. "That's a good way to live your life."

"I'm glad you think so."

* * *

Family, food, music, hobbies. Kari felt like she and Ryan had talked about everything under the sun by the time he pulled into a parking space in front of her brother's apartment building. The one thing they hadn't talked about was baseball. Or the three women who had continued to text him throughout dinner, even though he hadn't answered any of them.

"Thanks so much for everything tonight," Kari said. "I had a really good time."

"Me too." Ryan turned off the car and circled to open the door for her. He offered his hand, and she accepted automatically.

Not unlike the first time he had taken her hand tonight, she felt a jolt of attraction that she hadn't experienced when she had first met him. Or perhaps she had felt a connection but hadn't wanted to admit it. After all, at the time, he wasn't interested in her except as an escape from an awkward situation. She found herself wondering if tonight would lead to more time together.

As soon as she stood beside him, Ryan closed the door and locked the car. "I assume you have a key to the building."

"Yeah. Maya loaned me hers." She pulled her key free and unlocked the outer door.

Ryan pulled it open wide. "I'll walk you up."

Nerves fluttered in her stomach when he took her hand once more and they started toward the elevator.

"You know how you and Ben were talking about practical jokes you played when you were kids?"

"Yeah. What about it?"

"I was hoping you could help me come up with something to get one of the guys on the team."

"Oh, I'm sure we can think of something." They stepped into the elevator, and she pushed the button for Ben's floor. "Is Ben going to be in on it too?"

"Probably. Pulling anything on this guy is the ultimate challenge. He's quite the prankster."

"I'll see what we can come up with," Kari said with a grin.

The doors slid open, and Ryan led her into the hallway. She was surprised when they saw her brother standing outside his door, a screwdriver in his hand.

"Ben? What are you doing?" Kari asked as she and Ryan drew closer.

"Fixing the doorbell."

"What's wrong with it?" Ryan asked.

"One of the wires came loose."

"And you're fixing it at eleven o'clock at night because . . . ?" Kari asked, feeling very much like a sixteen-year-old returning from a date to find her dad waiting for her on the front porch.

"Because I leave for L.A. tomorrow morning, and Maya wanted it fixed before I go."

"Does it really matter if it works or not? People can knock instead of ringing the bell."

"They can, but I don't think you would be any happier than Maya if I let the bell ring all night," Ben countered. "It got stuck when the delivery guy came with the dessert I ordered. That was twenty minutes ago."

"Okay, I'll admit I wouldn't want to sleep through a constant doorbell." A little annoyed at the lack of privacy, she turned back to Ryan. "Thanks again for dinner."

"You're welcome. I'll talk to you later."

"Good night." Kari opened the door and glanced over her shoulder at Ryan before slipping inside. Once she closed the door behind her, she wondered if she really would talk to him again soon. After all, he had ignored the texts of a half dozen women since she'd met him. Would she be any different?

Deciding to remember only the positives about their evening, she dropped her purse on the kitchen table and headed for her room. Even though she normally talked to Maya about everything, tonight she found she wanted some time to let the memories linger without sharing them with anyone else.

Chapter 10

"HAVE YOU TALKED TO KARI lately?" Ryan asked Ben when he stepped beside him on the field to stretch. In the distance, the setting sun cast shadows over Dodger Stadium, the overhead lights already on.

"Yeah, last night. Why?"

"I was just wondering," Ryan said, hoping he sounded casual. The truth was he hadn't talked to her since their date four nights ago, and the silence was driving him crazy. She had his number. Why hadn't she called him?

"Did she tell you Maya set the closing date on our house?" Ben asked, oblivious to Ryan's dilemma.

"No. When is it?"

"In three weeks." Ben stretched his arms above his head.

"That fast?" Ryan asked, mimicking Ben's movement.

"Yeah. The owner wasn't living there, so all we're waiting on is the financing."

"That's great. Has Maya maxed out your credit cards yet buying furniture?"

"No, thankfully." Ben stretched his arm across his chest and held it for a count of ten. "Maya is actually more of a treasure hunter, especially when Kari is around."

"What do you mean?"

"They like to go to thrift shops and used-furniture stores."

"Are you okay with that?"

"Absolutely. They sent me a bunch of pictures from this one store in Phoenix called Furniture Affair. It sells furniture that used to be in model homes. It's actually cheaper to buy some of their stuff and have it shipped than to buy new in DC."

"Don't they want to see the furniture before they buy it?"

"Yeah. They're going to meet us in Phoenix on Tuesday so they can check everything out, and they'll stay for our series against the Diamondbacks."

"Is Maya up to traveling?" Ryan asked.

"She says she's feeling great," Ben said, but Ryan sensed his concern. "If it was her by herself, I would worry, but since Kari is with her, I'm sure she'll be fine."

"It will be good to see them."

Ben looked over at him. "Is there something I should know about you and Kari?"

"What do you mean?"

"I mean, you went out with her before we left, but she obviously didn't tell you she's meeting the team in Phoenix," Ben said. "I thought your date went well."

"It did." Ryan lifted his leg, holding his ankle to stretch out his quad. "And?"

"She hasn't called me since."

"Have you called her?" Ben asked.

"No."

"Any particular reason?"

"I just figured if she wanted to talk to me, she would call."

Ben laughed. "Hate to break it to you, Ryan, but Kari isn't the type to chase a guy. I doubt she'll call first. She's old-fashioned enough to expect you to call her."

Ryan let Ben's observation sink in. "Then you think I should call her?"

"That's up to you, but if you want to talk to her, that's the only way it's going to happen," Ben said. "Unless you wait a couple more days until we see them in Phoenix."

"I guess I'll call her after the game."

"Ryan, what time is our game tonight?"

"Seven. Why?"

"And what time is it in DC right now?"

Ryan did the math. "Ten."

"It's going to be after midnight in DC by the time this game is over. You might want to wait another day to call her."

Ryan held in a sigh. "Maybe I'll wait until tomorrow."

"Good idea."

* * *

"Why don't you call him?" Maya asked as they sat on her living room couch and watched the Nationals take the field.

"Because every other girl he's dated calls and texts him constantly. I don't want to be like that." Kari didn't want to admit that she was thinking about Ryan more than she was comfortable with, especially since they had been out on only one date.

"Kari, you aren't at all like the other girls he's dated."

"How can you tell?" Kari asked. "I've only gone out with Ryan once."

"Yeah, and he asked you out."

"So?" Kari looked at her friend and saw a combination of amusement and exasperation on her face.

"So he doesn't ask women out."

"What do you mean?"

"I mean, the women he dates are usually people he meets after games or at parties. They ask him out, not the other way around."

"And he's okay with that?"

"You do realize that women ask men out all the time, right?"

"Yeah, but asking a guy out is one thing. Chasing one isn't my style," Kari said, not sure how to describe her hesitation. "It just feels weird to me."

"Only because you aren't the type to chase a guy," Maya said. "Which brings us back to my point. You aren't like the other women he's dated."

"That may be, but I'm not going to change that and start calling him," Kari insisted. "If he wants to talk to me, he can pick up the phone and call."

"If you say so, but you could at least send him a text and wish him luck in his game tonight."

On the television screen, a ground ball headed right for Ryan. He made the play, throwing to second for the first part of a double play. "I think it's a little late for that."

"Then you can wish him luck tomorrow."

"We'll see." Kari shifted back in her seat and put her feet on the coffee table. "For now, I'm going to see how many innings I can get through before I fall asleep on your couch."

"You know as well as I do that you won't be able to sleep until the game is over."

Kari looked over at her, acknowledging the truth to her statement. "Okay, you're right, but it's because I know you'll stay up anyway, and I don't want you to get lonely."

Maya put her feet up beside Kari's. "Whose turn is it to make the popcorn?"

"Mine," Kari said. One of the Dodgers hit a double, and she straightened as the action unfolded on the TV. "I'll make it during the commercial."

"That's what you always say."

Kari looked over at her. "Can you blame me?"

"Not at all."

* * *

The ringing of her phone woke Kari from a deep sleep. The thought that it could be Ryan calling sent a thrill through her and caused her to fumble for the phone.

The number wasn't one she recognized, and she cleared her throat before hitting the talk button. "Hello?"

"Hey, Kari. It's Austin."

Her teeth clenched together. "This isn't your number you're calling from," Kari said, irritated on principle.

"You weren't taking my calls."

"That's right. I'm not taking your calls." She had hoped since Austin hadn't called or texted for a full week that he had finally given up on her. The hurt he had caused didn't slice through her as sharply as it once had, but the embarrassment that had resulted from his deception hadn't faded.

"I need to talk to you," Austin insisted.

"Ironically, I don't need to talk to you. Good-bye, Austin." Kari shifted the phone away from her ear and hit the end button.

Immediately, the phone rang again.

Kari hit ignore, set her cell back on her bedside table, and rolled over in bed.

The phone rang again. Again, Kari silenced it. She considered turning it off, but the seed of hope that Ryan would call prevented her from following through.

What was wrong with her? The man she wasn't interested in wouldn't leave her alone, and the one she wanted to talk to wouldn't call. Somehow she needed to find a way to reverse the situation.

She stared at the ceiling for a few minutes through three more calls from Austin. Deciding sleep wasn't going to happen, she headed for the bathroom, leaving her phone behind.

Might as well get the day started. Maybe by the time Kari was showered and dressed, Austin would have given up on his quest to talk to her.

* * *

Ryan woke to the sound of a text message. He rolled over and reached for his phone, a ripple of anticipation flowing through him. He didn't have any reason to think the text was from Kari, but that didn't keep him from hoping.

He picked up the phone and rolled onto his back as he looked at the screen. Robin. *I heard you're in town. Let's get together.*

The memory of a date last month during a series against the Angels came to mind. Ryan texted back. *Sorry, but I have a girlfriend, and I made plans with her.* His finger hovered above the send button.

Kari would hardly consider herself his girlfriend, but there had been enough on social media to make it look that way. Besides, it wasn't fair to Robin to lead her on since he had no intention of seeing her again.

Mustering his courage, he pressed send. He then scrolled down to his next unread message. Stacey from Colorado offering to meet him in Phoenix.

Ryan sent a similar response. *Sorry, I started dating someone a while ago. She's meeting me in Arizona for the series.* This time he didn't hesitate before he pressed the send button.

He checked the time and did the math. Nine o'clock in LA meant it was already noon in DC. He scrolled through his contacts and dialed Kari's number.

"Hello?" she answered as though she wasn't sure who was calling.

"Hey, Kari. It's Ryan."

"Ryan, how are you doing?" Her voice shifted now to her usual friendly tone. "Have you figured out which time zone you're in yet?"

"Barely," he admitted. "In fact, your brother saved you from getting a middle-of-the-night phone call last night. I was going to call you after the game until he reminded me that we have a three-hour time difference right now."

"Well, we'll be in the same time zone soon enough," Kari said. "Did Ben tell you we're going to meet up with you guys in Phoenix?"

"Yeah, he said something about that," Ryan said. He mustered his courage. "I thought maybe you would let me take you out after one of the games."

"I'd like that if you're up for it." He heard the enthusiasm in Kari's voice, followed by concern. "You must be exhausted."

"The first day or two of a road trip are always rough, but you get used to it." He swung his legs over the side of the bed, looking across the room to the window. It took him a moment to remember what city he was in.

They chatted for a few minutes, Ryan sharing some of the antics that had occurred among his teammates since they had last talked. One thing led to another, and before he knew it, thirty minutes had passed, and his room phone interrupted them.

"Hold on a sec," Ryan said, lifting the receiver. "Hello?"

"Good morning, Mr. Strobel. This is the wakeup call you requested."

"Thank you," Ryan said and promptly hung up the phone. "Sorry about that. It was my wake-up call."

"I think you're already awake."

"For a change," Ryan admitted. "I guess I'd better get going. I'll call you later."

"Sounds good. Have fun tonight."

"I'll do my best."

"That's all anyone can ask for."

Ryan hung up the phone, Kari's last words echoing through his mind. He found it odd that she hadn't wished him luck today but instead had focused on his enjoyment of the game. He stood up and crossed to the window, pleased to see the sun shining through a scattering of clouds. His mood lighter than it had been in days, he headed for the shower. Today was going to be a good day.

Chapter 11

TUESDAY FELT LIKE IT COULDN'T arrive fast enough. Kari had spoken to Ryan every day since he had called her before Saturday's game, and each conversation had been a little longer than the one before.

She worried that she now looked forward to his calls, expected them even. In the back of her mind, she wondered how many other women were waiting on Ryan to call them.

"I'm not sure which of us is more excited to see the guys, you or me," Maya said as a taxi took them from their hotel to the stadium.

"I don't know what you mean," Kari said, relieved when the driver pulled up by the main entrance.

Maya paid the driver and both women climbed out, handing their tickets to the gate attendant. She let the conversation drop until they were nearly to their seats behind the visiting team's dugout. "You realize this is me you're talking to. Your best friend. The one who bought you a whole cheesecake the night you and Joey Bartell broke up."

Kari grimaced. "I was sick for three days."

"Yeah, but you forgot all about Joey." Maya sat down. "What do you think, Kari? Is Ryan the type of guy you would get sick on cheesecake over?"

"I'm trying not to think about him that way." Kari sat beside her.

"Why not? He's a great guy, good-looking, and the two of you seem to get along well."

"Yeah, but how many other girls is he getting along with right now?"

"What do you mean?"

"It seems like every time we talk, I can hear him get another call or text. When we went out together, three different girls were texting him. I think he's dating around, and I don't want to get too attached if I'm just one of many."

"Have you talked to him about it?" Maya asked.

"We've been on one date. Don't you think it's a little early to be having a relationship talk?"

"I guess, but you've been a little more involved than just one date. You talked to him three times yesterday."

"Yes, but he knew I was coming out here today. For all I know, I might not hear from him at all the next time he goes out of town."

"Talk to him," Maya insisted. "One date or not, you're going to drive yourself crazy not knowing where you stand."

"I'm not having that conversation yet," Kari said, even though she knew Maya was right. Every time she talked to Ryan, butterflies fluttered in her stomach. Just the sound of her phone ringing could send her heart into overdrive. Yet those memories of their evening together, of the other women's names illuminating his phone screen, left her wondering if he would start ignoring her calls and texts as soon as he got bored of her.

Annoyed at where her thoughts had taken her, she shifted in her seat. "Do you want me to get you something to drink?"

Maya studied her for a moment, and Kari was relieved when she let the subject of Ryan drop. "I'd love a water bottle."

"I'll be right back." Kari retreated upstairs to the concourse, where the crowds were starting to filter in despite an hour remaining until game time. She purchased their drinks and headed back to Maya, her eyes sweeping over the others seated in their section. She noticed Celeste walking toward them, her expression brightening when she saw them. "Hey there. I didn't know you guys were coming to Phoenix."

"We thought it would be fun to catch up with Ben," Maya said.

"Just Ben?" Celeste's eyes sparked with humor as she turned her attention to Kari. "I saw you and Ryan leaving together the other night."

"We just went out to dinner," Kari said, trying to downplay her growing attraction. "No big deal."

"He made it seem like a big deal to Brandi. She was hoping to get back together with him again."

"Again?"

"Yeah." Celeste checked her ticket and sat in the seat in front of Maya. She shifted so she was facing Kari. "They dated for a few weeks around Christmas, but that was the last time I'd heard of them being together until she showed up in DC."

"Ryan did seem pretty surprised to see her," Kari admitted.

"She planned it that way. She and Rachelle had been talking for weeks about the perfect time for her to come visit," Celeste said. "She wasn't happy when she showed up to find Ryan had a new girlfriend. Rachelle felt so bad she begged the front office for an extra ticket to the Midnight Express concert."

Kari briefly debated confiding in Celeste that their relationship wasn't as old as Ryan let on, but she wasn't sure she could trust the information wouldn't go beyond them. She'd met the woman only a handful of times. Instead, she said, "I guess it's true. Timing is everything."

"Speaking of which, here come the guys," Maya said.

Kari lifted her hand to shield her eyes from the sun, despite the ball cap and sunglasses she wore. She saw several of the players emerge from the bullpen, but Ryan and Ben weren't among them. Slowly, more Nationals appeared, and finally Ryan stepped out of the dugout, his glove in his hand. He turned and looked up into the stands as though searching for something. Then his eyes met hers, and he gave her a quick wave.

Her smile was automatic. She waved back and reminded herself that she didn't want to get too involved with him.

In front of her, Celeste chuckled. "I can see why Brandi left. It's pretty obvious when you see the two of you together, Ryan is definitely over his ex."

Kari didn't respond. Ryan might be over his ex, but did that mean he was ready to be involved with someone else, or did he need more time before he settled down again?

As he jogged out onto the field behind two of his teammates, she decided to enjoy herself. She had flown across the country to see her brother play. If she got the added benefit of going out with an interesting and exciting man, so much the better.

* * *

Ryan settled into the back of the cab beside Kari and handed the driver the address.

"Where are we going?" she asked.

"I heard about a fun restaurant I thought we should check out."

"Fun, huh?"

"Yeah, fun." He took her hand in his, lacing his fingers through hers. "Trust me."

"Okay." She shifted in her seat so she could face him more fully. "You do realize I'm going to get spoiled if you keep taking me out like this."

"I hope you don't mind." The thought struck Ryan that when he had dated Brandi, she had always insisted on going out. With Kari, he suspected she wouldn't care one way or another if they went to a restaurant or chose to hang out in a hotel lobby and order pizza. "Maybe we should see if Ben and Maya want to go out to dinner with us tomorrow after the game."

"That would be fun." Her expression brightened. "It's so great seeing Maya have enough energy to do things again."

"Yeah, it really is. I can't imagine how hard that must have been on you and Ben when she was going through treatments."

"It was pretty terrifying," Kari said. "A lot of good came out of it though."

Ryan looked at her like she was crazy. "Good came out of her having cancer?"

"It was because of her treatments that she and Ben got to know each other, and she and I both decided to change our majors because of what she went through."

"That's right. You mentioned you wanted to go pre-med."

"Yeah, and Maya wants to go into nursing."

"Maybe the two of you will team up and work together some day."

"You never know," Kari said, clearly considering. "Of course, it's pretty overwhelming thinking about trying to get into medical school."

"It'll happen for you."

"You're the only person who is totally accepting of my plans. Why is that?"

"I don't know." Ryan considered her comment and contemplated the oddity of how much he wanted to see Kari achieve her dreams. "Maybe it's because I ended up in a profession that most people tell you won't ever happen. I figure if you work hard enough, you'll make your dream come true."

"I hope you're right."

The cab pulled up in front of a restaurant. Ryan paid the driver and helped Kari out of the car. They approached the door, walking inside to find the hostess dressed as Wonder Woman, her magic bracelets reflecting beneath the overhead lights.

"Reservation for Strobel," Ryan told her.

She drew out two menus. "Right this way."

They followed her past Billy the Kid and Joan of Arc to their table. "Your host will be with you shortly."

"Thank you."

They were barely in their seats when Abraham Lincoln approached. "Hello, kind sir. Madam. Welcome to the White House. May I offer you a beverage?"

"Just water for me, thanks," Kari said, not able to fight back her grin. "Same for me."

"May I tell you about some of the specials our White House chefs have prepared for your enjoyment?" He paused long enough for Ryan to give his consent. He then went into an elaborate explanation of each dish, acting as though they truly were still in Washington, DC, and had been invited to dine with the president of old.

After they made their selections and were left alone, Kari leaned forward. "When you said fun, I shouldn't have doubted you. This place is a riot."

A Pokémon trainer walked by carrying a tray of drinks, each cocktail contained in a ceramic kitchen sink. Ryan grinned at her. "Oh, we may have to try one of those."

"I don't drink, but if we can get a nonalcoholic version, I could go for a strawberry daiquiri."

"I think that can be arranged."

An hour and a half later, they walked outside, each holding a miniature kitchen sink as a souvenir of their evening together.

"Thank you so much for tonight. That was an experience," Kari said.

"A good one, I hope."

"A very good one. I kept thinking Honest Abe was going to break character, but by the time we were ready to leave, I was starting to think we really were eating at the White House."

"Me too." Ryan glanced at his watch. "You have to be exhausted. Come on. Let's get you back to the hotel. I have a feeling you and Maya are both going to want to sleep in tomorrow."

"I'm sure you're right. I assume you have to be to the ballpark early?"

"Yeah. It's an afternoon game, but it will be nice to get done early enough to have dinner at a normal hour."

"I'll talk to Maya in the morning about coming with us."

"And I'll hit up Ben. Although I have a feeling we aren't going to be able to top tonight's adventure."

"You may be right."

Chapter 12

RYAN HAD FORGOTTEN HOW ENJOYABLE an evening could be when he didn't spend 90 percent of it trying to get to know his date. He and Kari had laughed and joked with Ben and Maya over Chinese food, plotted against Gavin, who had managed to fill Ben's shampoo bottle with honey, and debated whether the lead singer for Midnight Express was dating the drummer.

"The drummer is cute," Kari said, turning to Maya. "Don't you think so, Maya?"

"Very cute." Maya crunched on a piece of her fortune cookie. "If I wasn't married, I would totally go out with him."

"Oh, really?" Ben's eyebrows lifted.

"Don't worry, honey. No one holds a candle to you," Maya said with a grin.

"That's better." Ben pushed back from the table. "Are you guys ready to go?"

"Sure." Ryan stood and picked up the two takeout boxes. He glanced over at Kari, who was staring down at the little slip of paper from inside her fortune cookie, her brow furrowed. "What's wrong? What does your fortune say?"

"Nothing." Kari looked up, her cheeks reddening.

"Let me see," Maya said, snatching it out of Kari's hand.

"Give it back. It's nothing."

Maya turned her back on Kari so Kari's longer reach wouldn't allow her to grab it away. Maya read the words on the slip and immediately laughed.

"What?" Ryan asked, his curiosity humming.

"I've never seen one like this before," Maya said, her voice filled with amusement when she read it out loud. "And I quote, 'Only a kiss can make your day better.'"

"Why didn't I get that one?" Ben complained.

Ryan ignored him, finding the opening too irresistible to pass up. He shoved the leftovers into Ben's hands, took two steps to close the distance between him and Kari, and scooped her into his arms. Her hand lifted to his chest, and he saw the surprise and embarrassment in Kari's eyes. That didn't stop him. In one fluid movement, his hand cupped the back of her head, and he lowered his lips to hers.

He heard a burst of laughter from Maya, and then everything faded away. What should have been innocent fun sent a spark through him that caused him to pull back long enough to see the shock in Kari's eyes.

He'd never been one to resist temptation, and he wasn't about to start now. His lips met hers again, and again the sensation set his pulse hammering. He had to fight to remember they were in a public restaurant, that this wasn't the place for this, but he couldn't help but let his lips linger on hers a bit longer.

When he forced himself to pull back, he stared down at her flushed cheeks. Trying to keep his voice light, he said, "My day definitely just got better."

Ben tapped him on the shoulder. "You do realize that's my sister you're kissing, right?"

"Yeah," Ryan said, pleased that his voice sounded casual. He caught the big-brother protective vibe emanating from his friend and faced it head on. "Sorry, Ben. That was an opportunity I couldn't pass up."

He let his gaze linger on Kari and slid his hand down to link his fingers with hers. "I think we're ready to go now."

Together they went outside and climbed into the rental car, Ben driving them the short distance back to their hotel. As soon as they walked into the lobby, Ryan said, "Do you guys want to grab some dessert at the hotel restaurant?"

"Ryan, we just ate," Ben said.

"That was fifteen minutes ago," Ryan said without missing a beat. "Besides, I'm not ready to lock myself in my room yet."

"I think I need to go upstairs and get some rest," Maya said.

"I'll come with you," Ben said, taking Maya's hand in his.

"What about you, Kari? You aren't going to make me eat alone, are you?"

"I could go for some dessert," Kari said.

"Great." Ryan put his hand on her back to guide her toward the restaurant. "We'll see you guys later."

"Stay out of trouble," Ben warned.

"Will do," he said, but his focus was once again on the woman beside him.

* * *

Kari's head was still spinning. The memory of Ryan's lips on hers wouldn't leave her brain, and she felt like she was underwater and didn't know how to get back to the surface for another breath.

His hand caressed her shoulder as he escorted her to their table in the hotel restaurant, and she had to remind herself that she had known him for only three weeks.

Sure they had talked every day for nearly a week, and they had gone out a couple of times, but that hadn't prepared her for the unexpected kiss or the flood of warmth that had seeped through her.

They reached their table, and Ryan waited for her to sit before sliding into the booth across from her.

Kari accepted the menu the hostess offered her, and she tried to recapture the ease of conversation she had previously enjoyed with Ryan. "Any idea what you want?" Kari asked.

"That depends on what you order."

"Why does it depend on me?"

"Because I figured if I order something different, we can share."

"I don't know if I'm hungry enough for a whole dessert." She looked over the menu and pointed at one of the selections. "There's a sampler here. Do you want to split that?"

"Sounds good." A moment later, the waitress appeared and took their order. When they were once again alone, he reached out and took her hand in his. "I hope I didn't embarrass you in front of your brother."

"I wasn't embarrassed," Kari said, trying to find a way to put her feelings into words. "I think confused would be a better description."

"Confused," he repeated as though trying to understand her meaning.

She gathered her courage. "I got the impression that you were dating a lot of different people. I guess I'm not exactly sure what to expect with you."

"What made you think I was dating around?"

"Ryan, your phone is constantly going off, and it isn't your teammates texting you."

His eyes lit with understanding. "It's true that after Brandi and I broke up, I dated a few women, but I never went out with any of them more than once."

"Why not?"

"No interest." He winced. "I know that sounds bad, but all of them made me feel like they were more interested in my job than they were in me."

Kari remembered Ben's ex-girlfriend and the problems he had experienced for the same reason. "I can see how that could be a challenge in your profession."

"It might seem like I'm the type to go out with a lot of women, but that's really not me. The truth is I'm only interested in dating one person, and that's you." He turned her hand over, tracing his finger along the center of her palm. "Are you okay with that?"

Her stomach jumped at the prospect, and she appreciated that Ryan was so straightforward in what he wanted. Looking toward her future, she nodded. "Yeah, I am."

"I should probably warn you that dating for me isn't easy during baseball season. I usually have to be at the ballpark by one, and I rarely leave before eleven."

"Ben's my brother, remember? I know how crazy your schedule can be," Kari said. "And at least I'm not taking classes right now."

"That's true, but I feel bad that our time together will largely be dictated by my job."

"You'll have to deal with my schedule in the fall, so that will make us even."

"Sounds fair to me." He leaned across the table and once again pressed his lips to hers. A shiver ran through her, along with surprise that a brief kiss could send her world spinning. She tried to convince herself that it was the newness of being with Ryan that left this churning inside her, along with an unexpected longing for more.

His fingers skimmed along her jaw, sending another ripple of pleasure through her. He settled back into his seat, his eyes meeting hers. "I should probably warn you, kissing you could become a habit."

"A good habit," Kari said, surprising herself.

"Yes. A very good habit."

Chapter 13

RYAN REMINDED HIMSELF TO PLAY it cool when he entered the visitors' clubhouse on Thursday. Enough of his teammates had seen him with Kari that he didn't want to deal with their speculation of how things had gone on their date, especially with Ben in the same room.

He still wasn't sure what had come over him when he had kissed Kari in the restaurant, but it was a moment he was sure he would never forget. He hoped she wouldn't forget it either.

Fighting the smile that wanted to break free, he took a deep breath and walked through the door a few steps behind Gavin. Ryan was nearly to his locker when he heard Gavin's voice laden with irritation.

"You've got to be kidding me." Gavin stared at his locker for a long moment before turning to glare at Ben and then Ryan. "I know one of you is behind this."

"What?" Ryan asked innocently.

"Where's the key?" Gavin demanded.

"What key?" Ryan approached the open locker and looked at where Gavin's jersey hung on a hanger. A bicycle lock ran through one sleeve of his jersey and out the other and locked in front. "That's creative. I wonder who came up with that."

"Oh, come on. I know you and Ben did this. Just give me the key already."

"I don't have the key." Ryan shrugged his shoulders. "Sorry, Gavin, but it really wasn't me this time."

Gavin shifted his focus. "Ben, hand it over."

"Don't look at me," Ben said, holding his hands out to his side. "I'm innocent."

"If you guys didn't do this, who did?" Gavin demanded.

"I'm telling you, someone is setting us up," Ben said. "Right, Ryan?"

"For sure."

"How am I supposed to put on my uniform when it's got a chain running through it?"

"Anyone have any bolt cutters?" Ryan suggested, stripping off his shirt.

"Someone is going to pay for this."

"Seems to me, Ben paid yesterday," Ryan reminded him. He shifted his gaze to several teammates who were standing across the room snickering.

"That wasn't me," Gavin insisted in the same tone Ben and Ryan had used moments before. "

Don't you think it's about time we stop letting these guys pit us against each other?"

Gavin's eyes narrowed. "You think some of the guys are pranking us so we'll go after each other?"

"You have to admit, it's working," Ben said.

Leaving Gavin to stew over the possibilities, Ryan and Ben returned to their own lockers and proceeded to change into their uniforms.

"How did everything go with my sister last night?" Ben asked.

Ryan noticed the protective vibe and decided it would be best to face it head on. "Is this going to be one of those 'don't mess with my sister' talks?"

"I didn't realize you were thinking of her that way." Ben leaned over to lace up his shoe.

"I talked to you about this before our road trip, and you knew I took her out." His eyes narrowed when he thought of that first date. "You were standing out in your hall on purpose when I brought her home that night, weren't you?"

"I figured things were still casual between you two," Ben said, irritated. "But things were sure looking serious last night."

"Oh, come on, Ben. So I kissed her. It's not like your sister has never gone out with anyone before."

"She's never gone out with one of my best friends," Ben countered. He straightened and squared off to face him. "I'd hate to have to break you into little pieces, but if you hurt her, that's exactly what I'll do."

Ryan absorbed the words and their sentiment. His admiration for Ben hiked up another notch. "I've always wondered what it would be like to have a brother or sister. I think I would have liked that absolute loyalty you and Kari have."

"Did you hear what I said?" Ben asked.

"Loud and clear."

Their manager walked in, his eyes landing on Gavin, who was sitting on the chair by his locker in his pants and a T-shirt. "Why aren't you dressed?"

"See for yourself." Gavin pointed at the locker.

"That explains this." Jack reached into his pocket and drew out a ring box. He handed it to Gavin, who flipped it open to reveal a key.

"Where did you get this?" Gavin demanded.

"Some girl left it at the front desk."

"I knew it." Gavin whirled around to face Ryan. "I knew it."

"What? Why are you looking at me?"

"I know you have the hots for Ben's sister. Are you roping her into doing your dirty work?"

Ryan stepped forward until he was toe to toe with Gavin. "Show some respect. That's no way to talk about her."

Gavin flicked a look at Ben. "Looks like things are getting serious."

"Watch yourself, Gavin," Ryan said evenly.

"Break it up." Jack stepped between Gavin and Ryan and nudged Ryan back. "You have a phone call. You can take it in the office."

"Me?"

"It's about your mom."

At first Ryan wondered if he was about to be the butt of another prank. Then he keyed into the word *about*. A wave of panic and concern swept over him. Turning, he rushed from the room and into the manager's office where the phone receiver lay in the middle of the desk.

Ryan snatched it up, worry pulsing through him. "Hello? This is Ryan Strobel."

"Mr. Strobel, this is Dr. Michaels from Potomac Hospital. Your mother was in an accident on her way home from work today."

"Is she okay?" He had to force himself to ask the question, his grip tightening on the phone.

"She's stable," Dr. Michaels assured him. "Her knee took the worst of the damage. We plan to operate to repair the torn ligament tomorrow."

Relief came first, followed by more concern. He did a quick calculation of his schedule for the next twenty-four hours. "What time?"

"Eleven."

"I'll do everything I can to be there," Ryan said. "Can I talk to her?"

"She's resting now, but I can have the nurses give her a message."

"Just have her call my cell phone," he said, frustrated that he couldn't speak to her himself.

"I will."

"Thank you, Doctor." Ryan turned to see Jack behind him. "My mom was in an accident. I need a few days to go see her."

"Sorry, Ryan, but we can't spare you right now."

"Jack, I'm all she has."

"The travel folks already looked into flights tonight. The only commercial option would be a red-eye that doesn't leave until midnight, and then you'd be stuck in Detroit for three hours. If you stay and play with us, you'll still get home earlier."

"And then? We have a game at home tomorrow night."

"I'll give you the next few mornings off, but that's the best I can do."

Resigned, Ryan nodded. "I do have one more request."

"What's that?"

"I need my phone with me in the dugout in case my mom calls."

"Give your phone to Frank," Jack said, referring to the bench coach. "He'll monitor it for you and make sure you don't miss the chance to talk to her tonight."

"Thank you."

"Now go get ready. We still have a game to play."

* * *

"Does Ryan seem off to you?" Kari asked. She couldn't put her finger on it, but something about how he was playing the game didn't seem quite like him.

"Not that I've noticed." Maya shifted her attention from Ben at second base to Ryan, who stood near third. "Why?"

"I don't know. He doesn't seem like himself out there." Kari watched the shortstop relay a routine ground ball to first base for the third out. The Nationals jogged into the dugout, Ryan's pace a little quicker than his teammates'. It wasn't until he disappeared from sight that she realized he hadn't looked up into the stands like he normally did.

Kari thought of her time with Ryan last night, of the steps they had taken from casual dating to a relationship. A knot of tension formed in her stomach. Did Ryan regret the changes between them? Was her presence here creating a distraction for him?

Her fears continued to escalate as she watched the lead-off batter walk, followed by a sacrifice bunt. Ben strode to the plate, and Ryan stepped into the on-deck circle. Again, she noticed a tension in him that seemed uncharacteristic.

Ben hit a single, scoring Shawn from second, and Ryan took his spot at the plate.

Kari clasped her hands together, and she found herself holding her breath with each pitch. Four pitches was all it took for Ryan to strike out.

"I think you may be right," Maya said. "That isn't like Ryan to strike out so quickly."

Kari wanted to voice her fears, but Celeste's presence in front of them was enough to make her swallow her words.

Another quick out and the Nationals took the field once more. The next four innings seemed to crawl by, only two batters reaching base and no one managing to score. Ryan racked up another out, this time a grounder on the second pitch.

"I really hope they can pull off a win tonight," Maya commented. "It would be nice to go home on a positive note."

"I have to imagine tomorrow will be tough since they have to travel home tonight," Kari said. "I don't know how they're expected to get any sleep."

"They won't get much," Maya admitted. "As soon as the game is over, they'll be on the plane heading home while we get to sleep in a bed tonight before we catch our flight out tomorrow."

"I hate to break it to you, but we aren't exactly going to get a lot of sleep tonight either."

"Yes, but at least we'll sleep in beds rather than on a plane."

"I plan to do both." Kari looked down at Ryan again and wondered when she would learn what was bothering him. If the team really did go straight to the airport after the game, would she even get to talk to him before he left?

He bobbled a grounder, rushing to make a throw to first. The ball arrived a fraction of a second before the runner, and even the umpire was slow to signal the out.

As she watched Ryan struggle through the game, she decided she couldn't let him leave Arizona before she knew what was bothering him. As much as she looked forward to exploring the connection between them, she wasn't about to be one of the women chasing him when he wasn't interested.

Her stomach churned again, and she wondered how she was going to make it through the next four innings.

* * *

Ryan checked in with the bench coach in the middle of every inning, but it wasn't until the beginning of the seventh inning that he finally got the word that his mother was awake and able to talk.

"Go make your call," Frank said. "I'll come get you when you're up."

"Thanks." Ryan walked down the tunnel toward the clubhouse and dialed his mom's cell number. A wave of relief rushed over him when he heard her voice.

"How are you doing?" Ryan asked. "The doctor said you had an accident, but he didn't give me a lot of information."

"I'll be fine. Just some bumps and bruises."

"And a messed up knee, I heard."

"Don't you worry about me. The nurses are taking good care of me, and they already have me scheduled for surgery tomorrow."

"I heard. I'll be there as soon as I can."

"Now, Ryan, there isn't anything you can do here other than fuss and make me worry about you."

"Mom, I'll be there," Ryan insisted.

"How did your game go tonight?" she asked, apparently ready to change the subject.

"We're up one nothing in the top of the seventh."

"Then why are you calling me? If you're supposed to be working, you get back to it."

Ryan couldn't help the smile that crossed his face. Leave it to his mom to scold him for worrying about her. "Well, I am working, but my boss said I could take a break to make sure my mother wasn't dying in some hospital bed on the other side of the country."

"Now you're being melodramatic."

"Maybe a little," Ryan admitted. "It's good to hear your voice."

"You'll hear plenty of my voice when I see you tomorrow," she told him. "Now you go get back to your game so I can get some sleep."

"Yes, Mama," Ryan said obediently. "I love you."

"I love you too, son. I'll see you tomorrow."

Ryan hung up the phone just as Frank appeared at the edge of the dugout. "Ryan, you're up next."

"Coming." Ryan jogged up the ramp. He looked out at the bases to see Ben at the plate and Gavin on first.

Ryan barely had time to grab a bat before Ben drew a walk. "How many outs?" Ryan asked as he walked by Frank.

"One."

Without breaking stride, Ryan walked to the plate and took a deep breath. The worry and frustration of the last two hours bubbled up inside him as he dug his front foot into the dirt, planting it before completing his stance and raising his bat into the ready position.

The first pitch was a little inside, but Ryan didn't care. He was ready to hit something. A quick swing and a lot of pent-up frustration combined to send the ball sailing. The crowd moaned in unison as they watched it land in the Diamondbacks' bullpen.

Amid the moans, Ryan could hear a few cheers, and the thought that Kari was among the Nationals fans here popped into his mind. He rounded the bases, accepting his teammates' congratulations when he crossed home plate.

As he and Ben made their way to the dugout together, he glanced into the stands, slowing long enough to spot Kari. He lifted his chin up in acknowledgment before letting himself get swept into the dugout, where more high fives followed.

Chapter 14

KARI BARELY LET RYAN WALK out of the locker room before she closed the distance between them. The way he had looked up at her after his home run had helped ease her nerves, but she found herself driven to understand what had been different during the early part of the game.

"Is everything okay?" she asked.

"Yeah." He took her hand and continued forward.

"You seemed distracted during the game," Kari pressed, the hand holding hers going a long way to easing her worries. The wrinkle on his brow, however, convinced her everything wasn't what it seemed. "Are you sure you're okay?"

He nudged her to the side of the door and away from the small crowd of teammates gathering there. "I got a call right before start time that my mom was in an accident."

Kari squeezed his hand. "Is she okay?"

"It sounds like it. She has to have knee surgery tomorrow. My manager is going to let me have the morning off so I can go see her."

"I'm sure you'll feel better once you see for yourself how she's doing."

That truth reflected in his expression. "Things are probably going to be crazy for the next week or two until she's back on her feet. I'm sorry about that."

"Don't be," Kari insisted.

"I just don't want you getting mad when I don't have time to go out."

"Ryan, your mom's health is a little more important than taking me out to dinner or visiting monuments or whatever," Kari said. "And I'm happy to help if there's anything I can do."

"Thanks." His gaze shifted to the cluster of teammates behind her. "I'd better get going. The equipment manager is loading the bus now."

"Let me know how everything goes with your mom."

"I will." He took a step back and released her hand. She found herself disappointed that he didn't kiss her good-bye, but when she noticed several pairs of eyes focused on her, Ben's included, she decided he might have been wise to forgo that gesture.

Kari watched him go and offered a wave to her brother before he too joined the team and headed for the door.

"Is everything okay?" Maya asked after she stepped beside her.

"I hope so," Kari said, forcing herself to turn away from the men walking down the hall. "Ryan's mother was in an accident. He found out right before the game." Kari relayed their conversation to Maya as they headed for the parking lot where a hired car was waiting to take them to their hotel.

"I don't know how the guys do this," Maya said as she slid into her seat.

"Do what?"

"Fly all over the country and still manage to play baseball almost every day."

"They love it."

"I hope so, because it's exhausting."

"I agree," Kari said, then leaned her head back against the headrest.

* * *

Ryan opened his eyes when he felt the car coming to a stop. He had dozed on the plane and on the car ride to Woodbridge, but worry had kept him from ever falling into a deep sleep. That and the concern that Gavin would take his revenge on him for the last practical joke. Normally their prank wars were a fun way to blow off steam. Today, he most definitely wasn't in the mood.

The driver his team had sent for him pulled up at the hospital entrance and turned around to hand Ryan a business card. "Here's my number. Call me when you're ready to leave, and I'll pick you up."

"Thank you." He glanced at his watch. "I'm hoping to stay until about three, so feel free to go grab something to eat."

"Thanks." He climbed out and opened the door for Ryan.

Ryan headed for the hospital entrance and made a beeline for the information desk. "I'm here to see Susan Strobel. Can you tell me what room she's in?"

"Yes, just a moment." The receptionist punched a few keys on her computer and gave him the room number. Five minutes later, he navigated his way through the maze of hallways and entered his mother's room to find her chatting with Jenny Holladay, her longtime coworker and friend.

His normally active mother lay beneath a yellow blanket, her tall, athletic frame seeming frail under the glare of hospital lights. A bandage covered the right side of her forehead, and her right arm was in a sling. Her eyes opened when he moved toward her. "Ryan. You're here."

"I'm here." He waved at her arm. "It looks like it's not just your knee that got banged up."

"Dislocated shoulder. Hurts like crazy, but it'll be fine."

Jenny stood and crossed the room to give him a hug. "I'm glad you were able to make it. Whether she'll admit it or not, your mom's been hoping you'd come."

In her usual no-nonsense manner, Susan raised an eyebrow. "Oh, now, don't start going on like that, Jenny."

"I'll give you some time to visit." Jenny gave him a pat on the arm and continued toward the door. "Ryan, it's good to see you."

"You too, Miss Jenny." He watched her leave and then continued to his mother's bedside. He leaned down, pushed aside a lock of his mom's dark hair, and kissed the exposed side of her forehead. "Tell me what happened."

"The other driver ran a red light when I was on my way home from work. I didn't see him until it was too late."

"How is he doing?"

"Concussion."

"I guess we're lucky no one was hurt worse," Ryan said, trying to find the bright side. "What's the deal with your surgery?"

"Apparently I'm getting a knee replacement whether I want it or not."

"What do you mean?" Ryan lowered himself into the chair beside her bed.

"Dr. Kennedy has been after me to replace my knee for a few years. The damage to my knee cap made it a necessity."

"Mom, you aren't going to be able to stay in your apartment. You live on the third floor."

"I'll manage," she said.

"No. It's time you let me move you someplace else."

"I'll be fine," she said firmly. "The doctor already has me scheduled to go into a rehab center for a week after I leave the hospital."

"And I'm sure the doctor would agree that your recovery will be significantly more efficient if you don't have to deal with stairs, especially in the first few weeks." Ryan saw the stubborn set of his mother's jaw. "At least let me get you a hotel or something for a while. Or you can come stay with me for a few weeks."

"Ryan, you have a one-bedroom apartment, and you're hardly ever there. Besides, I don't want to move."

"You're being stubborn."

"So are you."

"I learned from the best," Ryan countered and earned a smile. He shifted his attention to the door when he heard movement behind him.

"Are you ready, Ms. Strobel? I'm here to take you down to surgery."

"Would it matter if I said no?"

Ryan stood. "You know, I've heard people say doctors make the worst patients. I'm starting to believe nurses are just as bad."

"I'm not a nurse," Susan countered.

"Close enough." Ryan put his hand on her arm. "Now, behave for the nurses. The sooner we get you into surgery, the sooner we can get you on your road to recovery."

"Fine," she said curtly. "But don't you go looking for houses or renting rooms or whatever it is you're thinking about doing."

Ryan shoved both hands in his pockets. In a childish gesture, he crossed his fingers. "I won't do anything without talking to you first."

"That's what I wanted to hear."

* * *

Kari was already sitting in Nationals Stadium when Ryan called. "Hey, how's your mom?"

"The doctor said the surgery went well. They plan to transfer her to a rehab center tomorrow or the next day."

"So she's going to be okay," Kari said, relieved.

"Looks like it," he said wearily.

"You sound exhausted." Sympathy stirred inside her.

"It's been a long day."

On the field below, several of the players walked onto the grass to begin their pregame routine. "Where are you?"

"I'm pulling into Nats Park now."

"You're cutting it close. The guys are already out warming up."

"I know," he said. "Hey, any chance Maya and Ben drove two cars today?"

"Yeah, why?"

"I was hoping they would let you borrow one to drive me home. The team hired a driver to take me to the hospital today, but I didn't have time to go home and pick up my car."

"Just a second." Kari lowered her phone and turned to Maya. "Can I borrow a car to take Ryan home tonight after the game?"

"Sure. You can take Ben's. He's been dying to drive mine again anyway."

"Thanks." She lifted the phone to her ear again. "All set. I'll meet you after the game."

"Thanks a lot. I appreciate it."

"I'll talk to you later. Try to have fun tonight."

"At this point, I'm just hoping to stay awake."

"I highly recommend it."

When the team took the field a short time later, Kari wondered if any of them were rested enough to be playing. She knew the pitcher had flown home a day earlier so he would have the advantage of a full night's sleep. When the Nats had committed two errors by the end of the third inning, Kari suspected the pitcher knew he had to carry the team tonight. She thought he was going to succeed in his quest until he stayed in one pitch too long and gave up a two-run homer in the seventh inning. When the final out was made, the Nationals were down 3–2.

After the game, Ben was among the first to emerge from the clubhouse. "Hey, Kari. Any chance you want to drive my car home tonight? I'd rather not drive if I don't have to."

"Actually, I was going to borrow it anyway to drive Ryan home."

"Why do you need to take Ryan home?"

Kari explained the situation, but that didn't change Ben's defensive posture.

"I'm sure Monroe can give him a ride. They don't live too far from each other."

"Ben, stop playing big brother," Kari said firmly. "It's not like Ryan and I are going out tonight. He needs to get home and get some sleep just as much as you do."

Reluctantly, Ben handed over his car key.

Maya took Ben's hand and tugged him toward the exit. "We'll see you later."

"I should be home in an hour or so." Kari focused on Maya. "Don't let him wait up for me. He's exhausted."

"Don't worry. I won't."

"She won't what?" Ryan's voice sounded behind her.

"Let Ben stay up to play big brother."

"If he doesn't feel comfortable having you drive me home, I can catch a cab."

"Don't be silly." Kari shook her head. "He wanted me to drive his car home anyway."

Clearly too tired to argue, Ryan fell into step beside her, a duffel bag over one shoulder and one hand pulling a rolling suitcase behind him.

"I really appreciate you being willing to take me home."

"I'm happy to do it." They walked in near silence to the car. Kari unlocked it and waited for Ryan to load his things into the backseat. When he slid into the passenger seat beside her, she motioned to the GPS on Ben's dashboard.

"Why don't you plug your address into that? Then you can go to sleep."

"I should argue with you, but I'm not going to." Ryan did as she suggested and started the GPS. He then shifted the seat back and closed his eyes. "Wake me if you get lost."

"Don't worry. I will."

Chapter 15

RYAN OPENED HIS APARTMENT DOOR to find a basket in the hall, a white card with his name on it tucked beneath the handle. He lifted it and walked back inside to inspect the contents.

Fresh fruit, protein bars, some water bottles and Gatorade, a mixture of other snacks, and a bouquet of flowers in a simple glass vase. Curious, he ripped open the card.

Consider this your hospital survival kit. The flowers are for your mom. I hope she feels better soon. Kari

Touched by the gesture, he pulled his phone from his pocket and texted her. *Just found your present. Thank you.*

The response was almost instant. *You're welcome. Enjoy your visit with your mom.*

Ryan selected a few items to take with him from the basket, leaving the rest on his kitchen table. Still thinking of the kindness of Kari's gesture, Ryan made his way to his car. He barely remembered the ride home last night, but now that he looked back on it, he found himself amazed that Kari had been so understanding.

One thing was certain: Brandi wouldn't have ever thought to tell him to sleep on the way home. He still couldn't believe he had been comfortable enough with Kari to give in to her suggestion, but the truth was he had fallen asleep almost instantly and hadn't woken until Kari had parked outside his building.

Annoyed at himself for comparing the two women, he climbed into his car, tucked his snacks into the cup holders, and settled the bouquet in the passenger seat, strapping it into place with the seat belt.

An hour later, he made his way into the hospital and deposited his apple core and protein-bar wrapper in the trash can by the front door. Carrying the bouquet of flowers, he headed inside and took the elevator to his mom's floor. He was a few doors from her room when he saw Dr. Michaels.

"Ryan, I was just about to call you."

"Is everything okay?"

"We want to keep your mom here at the hospital for another day," he said. "The swelling in her knee hasn't gone down as much as we would like, and she's struggling to get up and around."

"I don't imagine that went over well when you told her."

"No, it didn't." He spoke in a hushed tone. "My concern is her living situation once she leaves here. I've ordered a week at a rehab facility, but I understand she lives in a third-floor apartment. She shouldn't be doing stairs for at least six weeks."

"I talked to her about letting me put her up somewhere else, but she's resisting," Ryan admitted. "She's used to taking care of herself. This isn't going to be easy on her."

"For her to be released, we need to know she will be in a safe living environment, especially since she lives alone."

"I'll talk to her."

"You might want to let her tell you about all of this. She isn't likely to take it well if she thinks we're ganging up on her."

"I gather you've known my mother for a long time."

"I've been working at this hospital for fifteen years."

"Which means you've been working with her for that long," Ryan said with understanding. "I'll tread lightly."

"I appreciate that." Dr. Michaels took a step down the hall. "And good luck."

"Thanks." He continued into his mom's room to find her awake, her lunch tray in front of her. He didn't even want to think about how his breakfast time coincided so closely with her midday meal. "How's the patient today?"

She looked up at him. "Tired. Sore."

"That's not surprising." He set the flowers on the windowsill.

Her dark eyes warmed. "Those are lovely. Thank you."

"I'm just the deliveryman," Ryan said. "Those are actually from a friend of mine. She knew I was coming to see you today."

"She? Do you have a new girlfriend I don't know about?"

"I'm working on it." He lowered himself into the seat beside her.

"Where did you meet her? She's not one of these girls who follows you around after your games, is she?"

"No, she's not anything like that. In fact, she's the sister of one of my teammates," Ryan told her. "I actually met her when I was trying to avoid Brandi."

She wrinkled her nose with distaste. "When did you see Brandi?"

"She showed up a few weeks ago, hoping to get back together. Kari helped make things a lot easier than if I'd had to face her on my own."

"Is this the same Kari who had her picture with you all over Instagram?"

"Since when do you follow me on Instagram?"

"Since I got tired of everyone at work telling me what was going on with my own son."

"Mom, I call you at least once or twice a week."

"Usually on your way to or from an airport." She wagged a finger at him. "And I'm not that easily distracted. Is Kari your Instagram girl?"

"I think it was Twitter, but yes, she's the one in those photos." Ryan pulled his phone out and retrieved a selfie he had taken of the two of them in front of the Lincoln Memorial. He held it out to show his mother. "That's her."

"She's pretty."

"Yeah, she is." He stretched out his legs, not sure if his mother was about to lecture him on women or share her approval. Rather than wait to find out, he asked, "Has the doctor said when you get to transfer to rehab?"

"That sounds so bad," she said with a wince. "It's like I have a drug problem or something."

"Mom, you barely even take Tylenol. I don't think anyone would ever think you have a drug problem," he said dryly. "What did the doctor say?"

"Something about waiting for the swelling to go down a little more." Disgust hung in her voice. "They act like I can't take care of myself."

"Mom, you were just in a car accident. I think you should let people take care of you for a bit." Ryan mustered his courage. "Which brings me back to where you're going to stay when you get released."

"I'm going home."

"Mom, be reasonable. You'll need help, and you won't be able to do stairs." He could see her digging in her heels and took another approach. "Okay, if you insist on staying at your place, at least let me hire someone to come in and take care of you." She opened her mouth to protest, and he held up a hand. "You have a choice. Either stay somewhere else for a few weeks until you can do stairs comfortably, or have someone stay with you so you don't have to do stairs."

"Have I told you lately that you're being stubborn?"

"Yesterday."

"Just checking."

Chapter 16

RYAN DIDN'T THINK HE COULD keep up the pace much longer. After three days straight of visiting his mom before his games, exhaustion was setting in, and his teammates were starting to notice the impact.

He had barely finished dressing for the game when Jack approached. "Ryan, I'm starting Monroe today. I think you can use a few innings off."

Ryan didn't argue.

"How is your mom doing?"

"They're transferring her to the rehab center tomorrow morning."

"I thought that was supposed to happen yesterday."

"It was. The doctor had some concerns so he held her for another day."

"I know you want to be with her, but you can't keep up this pace."

"Jack, I don't know what to do," Ryan admitted.

"Tell you what. You give me the next two days, and then I'll let you have Thursday off. We're flying to New York that day, but I'll have the front office make arrangements for you to come up on Friday morning before our game. That will give you some extra time to get things settled if you need it."

"Thanks, Jack." As compromises went, it was a good one.

"And make sure you get some rest tonight. No using the time off to go hang out with some girl."

Ryan's eyes narrowed. "Have you been talking to Ben?"

His brow furrowed. "No, why?"

"Just wondering." As soon as his manager walked away, he pulled out his cell phone and texted Kari. *I'm not starting today. And I think my manager grounded me.*

Grounded you? came the response. *You have to explain that one.*

Something about not going out so I can get enough rest.

That's not grounding you. That's common sense.

Ryan thought about his coach's restrictions and opted for another possibility. *Breakfast tomorrow?*

I'd love to, but will you have time?

Yeah. I'm not going to be able to visit my mom tomorrow.

Text me when you get up, and we can make plans.

I'll talk to you after the game. He switched screens and called his mom, annoyed when he got her voice mail. "Hey, Mom. I just wanted to let you know I won't be able to get work off for the next couple days, but I'll be down to visit on Wednesday morning."

Knowing his mom wasn't the best with technology, he texted the same message to make sure she got it.

Still not sure how he felt about sitting the bench, Ryan changed his clothes. One way or another, he needed to support his team, and if that meant cheering for a few innings, that was what he would do.

* * *

Fourteen innings. Of all nights for the manager to try to give Ryan some time off, this apparently hadn't been the best choice. Their starting pitcher had struggled from the beginning of the game, giving up three runs before the first inning concluded. By the bottom of the fourth, the pitcher was sitting on the bench, and Ryan was back in at his usual spot at third.

The Nationals had come from behind to tie the game in the bottom of the eighth, then fallen behind in the eleventh only to tie it up again. A squeeze play in the fourteenth inning had finally made the difference and ended the four-hour and thirty-seven-minute game.

"Hey there." Ryan crossed to Kari, his weariness evident on his face.

"How are you doing?" Kari asked. "You didn't get a lot of rest tonight."

"Yeah. I guess Monroe wasn't as ready to come in as the manager thought."

"He didn't do bad," Kari said unconvincingly.

"It was a tough night to throw in a bench guy." Ryan slipped his arm around Kari's shoulders and followed behind Ben and Maya.

"It was a long night for all of you."

"That's the truth."

"You know, if you aren't up for going out in the morning, I'll totally understand," Kari said.

"Kari, I've hardly seen you in days," Ryan said. "I think we both need a couple of hours to relax together."

His words and the insistent tone behind them both touched and amused her. "You do realize that a month ago you didn't even know me, right?"

Maya and Ben walked outside, but Ryan stopped short of the door. "Yeah, but now I know what I was missing." He lowered his lips to hers and moved his hand to rest on her waist. She felt herself sliding into the kiss and the warmth of his embrace. She had missed this. She had missed him.

How was that possible when they had known each other for such a short time?

He pulled back and tucked a lock of hair behind her ear. "I guess I'd better walk you to your car before Ben comes looking for you."

"I guess so." Her head still spinning from the kiss, she let him lead her outside. "Any idea where you want to go for breakfast tomorrow?"

"I have a couple of thoughts." Ryan looked at his watch. "How about I pick you up at eleven?"

"Eleven? Do you normally eat breakfast that late?"

"After a night game, that's pretty normal for me."

"Will that be cutting things too close for you?" Kari asked. "What time do you have to be at the ballpark?"

"Not until two. If it's okay with you, I thought you could come with me to work so we'll have more time together." He slowed when they were a few yards from Ben's car. "Unless you don't want to hang out at Nats Park before the game."

"That's fine. I normally come early anyway."

"I know. I like being able to see you in the stands." Ignoring Ben's presence beside the driver's side door a few feet away, Ryan leaned down and gave her a brief kiss. "I'll see you in the morning."

Kari reached out and held up his hand so they could both see the watch he wore on his right arm. "Ryan, I hate to break it to you, but it's already morning."

"Oh yeah." Ryan reached out and opened the back door for her. "I'll see you in a few hours, then."

"Get some sleep," Kari said, hoping he would do just that.

"I will." He helped her into the car and said good-bye to Ben.

As they started to pull away, Ben glanced at Kari in the rearview mirror. "Should I be worried that you're spending as much time with Ryan as you are with me?"

"The only thing you should be worried about right now is the fastest way home," Kari said. "We're all exhausted."

"I know I am," Maya agreed. She put her hand on Ben's shoulder. "Honey, I think tomorrow you should win your game a little faster. You need your rest."

"Right. I'll be sure to tell my team you want a short game tomorrow."

Maya turned to look at Kari. "See how easy that was?"

"We'll see tomorrow if he's really paying attention."

* * *

Ryan led Kari to a grassy area overlooking the Potomac River, a takeout bag from the local bakery in his hand. He had spoken to his mother that morning and replayed some of the same arguments about getting her the help she needed. Now, with Kari's hand warm in his, he realized how much he needed this time away with her where he didn't have to be anyone but himself.

He heard Kari's cell phone chime and was oddly pleased that she didn't bother to see who was texting her.

"What a great spot," Kari said, stopping to look out at the various boats on the water, the skyline of Washington, DC, visible on the other side of the river. "What city are we in right now?"

"This is old-town Alexandria. My apartment is technically in Arlington, but I love this area."

"Why don't you live here, then?"

"My place is a little closer to work, and when I first moved up here, I was only planning to keep the apartment during baseball season." They found an empty bench and sat facing the water, a sense of contentment settling over them.

"Are you living up here year-round now?"

"I was. With my mom's surgery, I'm wondering if I'm going to have to reconsider that idea, but I can't imagine going back to living in the tiny place I grew up in."

"Still no luck convincing her to move?" Kari asked.

"None. In fact, she's insisting that she won't move somewhere else even temporarily while she recovers," Ryan said with frustration. "She can't do stairs for at least six weeks, but her apartment is on the third floor."

"And there isn't an elevator?"

"Nope." He opened the paper bag he held and took out a wrapped breakfast sandwich. He handed it to her before retrieving one for himself. "I can make sure she gets into the apartment okay, but I don't know how she's going to manage the basics. She's not the type to want to stay shut in."

"Have you thought about having someone stay with her?" Kari asked. "When Maya was first going through chemo, she hardly ever went out."

"I thought about hiring in-home care for her, but when I talked to her about it, she wasn't very excited about the idea." Frustration stewed inside him. "If it was during my off-season, I could take care of her myself, but right now, there's no way."

"I could do it."

"Kari, I couldn't expect you to do that." Surprise reflected in his voice and was undoubtedly written all over his face. "You came here to spend time with your brother and Maya, not babysit my mother."

"Ryan, I'm here trying to figure out what I want to do next in life. I can research colleges from anywhere as long as I have Internet access." She looked at him. "She does have Internet, doesn't she?"

"Yes, she has Internet."

"And I'm planning on going into medicine. It wouldn't hurt for me to get a little practice taking care of someone."

"It sounds like you already had plenty of practice with Maya." What she was offering was too much. Or maybe he wasn't quite ready to take their budding romance to the next level. He wasn't sure he wanted to go through the emotions of seeing his mother disapprove of yet another girlfriend. Even with Brandi and their two years together, he had never felt like his mother had really accepted her as a part of his life.

"Taking care of Maya was mostly making sure she made it to her doctor appointments and putting food in front of her. I have a feeling your mom's recovery will be heavier on physical therapy."

"I just can't ask you to do that. I know you're going to want to help Maya and Ben move into their new place." Ryan shook his head. "Besides, if you're at my mom's place, that means I'll hardly get to see you."

"I guess that's true." A wrinkle formed on her brow. "Of course, you are getting ready to go on a three-week road trip."

"Starting in New York," Ryan said. He surprised himself when he added, "I was kind of hoping you would come up for the series."

"Maya and I were talking about it, but we thought it would make more sense to wait until your series in Philadelphia. It's closer, and the hotel rooms are a lot cheaper."

"I'll pay for your hotel room."

"I can't let you do that."

"Why not?" He shifted to face her.

"I don't know. It just feels weird to have you pay for something like that."

"Kari, I'm asking you to follow me because of my work so I can spend time with you," he said, pointing out the obvious. "It's hardly fair to expect you to pay for that."

"It still feels weird."

He stared at her. Here she was, a college student who wasn't currently working, and yet she was insisting on paying her own expenses. "You know, you really aren't like anyone else I've ever dated."

"Is that a good thing?"

Unable to resist, he leaned forward and pressed his lips to hers. "Yeah. It's a good thing."

Chapter 17

SHE COULDN'T PUT IT OFF any longer. Kari sat at Ben's kitchen table with her laptop, a notebook, and a pencil. She had been in DC for nearly a month and hadn't yet looked into the local colleges. She opened an Internet browser and started her search with the universities Ben and Maya had mentioned to her: Georgetown, George Washington, George Mason. Apparently George was a more popular name around here than she'd realized. She spent two hours comparing programs, expanding her search to Mary Washington University and University of Maryland.

Her head was spinning with possibilities by the time Maya came in and put a plate of naan and buttered chicken in front of her, along with their tickets to the upcoming game.

"You need to eat something before we head over to Nats Park."

"I was wondering if maybe I should skip tonight," Kari said, even though she had been looking forward to seeing Ryan. "I really need to spend some time visiting campuses and deciding if I'm really going to transfer from Vanderbilt or not."

"The team leaves town for three weeks on Friday morning. You'll have plenty of time to visit schools while they're gone."

"We'll only have three days before we meet them in Philadelphia."

"And we can make school visits a priority," Maya countered. "It actually makes sense to do it then anyway. Ben and I close on our house two days after we get back from Philadelphia."

"How are you going to manage that if he's still traveling with the team?"

"He signed a power of attorney so I can sign for him."

"Doesn't that make you nervous, buying a house by yourself?"

"Yes, which is why he has an attorney coming with me to look over everything first."

"Smart." Kari wavered, looking at the notes she had made this morning. "I guess I could start visiting schools tomorrow."

"Why don't you check out George Washington tomorrow since Ben will be home and it's literally right down the road? Then on Friday, we can drive out to George Mason. I wanted to drive by the new house anyway and take another look at the area."

"That would work."

"Good." Maya picked up a piece of naan off her own plate and took a bite. "Now hurry up and eat. We don't want to get stuck in traffic on the way to the game."

"Maya, this is DC. We always get stuck in traffic on the way to the game."

"Okay, I don't want to get stuck and end up being late."

"That I can understand." Kari took a bite of her lunch. "Have you decided for sure where you're going to go to school?"

"I was looking into it some more, and I think I'm going to start out getting my associates degree from the community college. They have a great nursing program, and then I can transfer to a four-year university," Maya said. "That will give me a little more time to be sure where I want to go, and the scheduling from the community college is a little more compatible with baseball season."

"Sounds complicated."

"Not really. With the location of the new house, I'll probably end up at George Mason." Maya tucked a leg up underneath her. "You know, you're always welcome to stay with us while you're in college."

"You guys need your space."

"Have you seen our new house?" Maya asked pointedly.

"Yes, but that doesn't change the fact that you're newlyweds. Plus, I really don't want Ben playing big brother every time a guy asks me out."

"Seems to me you're only interested in one guy asking you out," Maya countered. "Is it safe to say you're over Austin?"

"I've been over him," Kari said. "If it wasn't for his dad teaching there, I'd probably go back to Vanderbilt for my last two years."

"But then you'd have a thousand miles between you and Ryan."

Just the thought of having so much distance between them left her heart heavy. She tried to push aside her growing attraction in an attempt to be practical. "Maya, Ryan's a lot of fun, but there's no way of knowing if we'll last past the summer. I don't want to make my decisions based on a guy."

"I don't think Ryan should be the only thing you consider, but I think you should factor him in. I've seen the way he looks at you."

Kari looked up from her food. "How does he look at me?"

"Let's just say it's pretty obvious you matter to him."

Her heartbeat quickened at the thought.

She let her gaze shift to the pile of notes about colleges and the baseball tickets beside them. Her internal debate was short-lived. She couldn't deny that she wanted to go tonight and that her primary reason was so she could see Ryan. The question was whether she was letting the Nationals' third baseman matter enough to influence her decisions about her distant future or only her immediate one.

* * *

Something was off with his mother, but Ryan couldn't put his finger on what it was. For the past two days, when he spoke to his mom on the phone, she sounded like herself, but some of the things she was saying didn't make sense.

He supposed it was possible that one of his mom's friends was getting married in the hospital, but he couldn't figure out why anyone would choose that as a venue for such a special day. And her talk about going shopping for something to wear was definitely out in left field. She'd worked in hospitals her entire adult life. Surely she knew she couldn't just check herself out, go to the mall, and check herself back in.

He walked into the rehabilitation center late Thursday morning with the hopes of finding some answers. Dr. Michaels met him at the door.

"Doctor. I didn't expect to see you here."

"Do you have a minute?" Dr. Michaels asked.

"Yeah, sure. Is everything okay?" Ryan's sense of unease hiked up a notch when the doctor didn't answer, instead leading him down a hall and into an empty office.

"Please, sit down." Dr. Michaels motioned to a chair even as he leaned against the front of the desk.

Ryan didn't want to sit, but he complied in an attempt to speed up the flow of information. "What's wrong?"

"I've been concerned that the swelling in your mother's knee hasn't been going down. It looks like there may be some blood pooled there that is keeping the new joint from healing properly."

"What does that mean?" Ryan gripped his hands together.

"It means I'd like to go in and operate again. The procedure shouldn't take long, but it needs to happen as soon as possible."

"Do whatever you need to, Doctor. I just want her to get better," Ryan said. He replayed the doctor's words through his mind and asked, "Exactly how soon is 'as soon as possible'?"

"Two o'clock. An ambulance will be here shortly to transfer her back to the hospital."

"Is her condition serious?" Ryan asked.

"I don't think so, but I don't want to wait to find out what we're dealing with."

"I thought you just said you know what we're dealing with."

"I'll know more after I open that knee back up." His voice was grim. "In the meantime, you'll need to wear a gown, gloves, and mask if you want to see her."

"Why all the precautions?"

"We've seen some indications that she may be suffering from hallucinations. Emergency protocol demands that we treat her as though she's suffering from an infection until we rule out the possibility." He pushed away from the desk and took a step toward the door. "I need to go prep for surgery. If you go to the front desk, they can let you see your mom before we transport her."

"Doctor," Ryan called out before the physician could escape the office completely. "How long until I know what's really wrong with her?"

"A few more hours." His voice held compassion. "I know it isn't easy, but try to be patient. I'll let you know as soon as I have any information for you."

"Thank you." Ryan watched him go and rolled his eyes heavenward as he fought against a wave of fear and concern. He took advantage of the privacy of the office for a few minutes before he forced himself to approach the front desk.

Donning the protective gear took several minutes. When he finally walked into his mother's room, he found her staring across the room, glassy-eyed.

"Hey, Mom. How are you feeling?"

"I'm ready to go home," she said, her voice weak.

"I know you are, but the doctors need to run a few tests before they can let you out of here."

"I don't need any more tests. I have to get home. I have to take care of Fibi."

"Fibi?"

"My dog. You know Fibi."

Ryan stared at her, unsure how to react. He did indeed know who Fibi was, but the little toy poodle from his mother's childhood had been gone for more than thirty years.

He was saved from further debate when the ambulance attendants arrived, also dressed in protective gear, and began to prepare her for transport.

Ryan stepped out of the room, and one of the nurses approached him. "Dr. Michaels said they are taking her straight to pre-op, so you might want to get something to eat before your mother goes into surgery. It's going to be awhile before you get to see her again."

"Thanks," Ryan managed to say. He stripped off the protective clothing and headed for the exit.

When he reached his car, he climbed inside and started the engine. He rolled down the window to let some of the heat escape only to turn the engine off again. What was he supposed to do now? His stomach was in too much turmoil for him to think about eating, and he didn't want to sit around a hospital waiting room for the next four hours.

He wasn't sure how long he sat staring, but after several minutes, he saw the front doors of the rehab facility open and the ambulance attendants wheeling his mother outside.

He watched them load her into the back of the ambulance, one of the attendants climbing into the back with her while the other took his place behind the wheel.

At a loss of what else to do, Ryan started the engine again and pulled out of his parking space. Without another destination in mind, he followed the ambulance, praying that the doctor would have good news for him before he went completely insane.

Chapter 18

KARI NAVIGATED THE HOSPITAL CORRIDORS until she found the correct surgical waiting room. The text from Ryan earlier had been simple and concise, but that hadn't prevented her from reading between the lines. His mother was having surgery again, and he was scared.

She pushed the door open to find him prowling the room as though he were afraid to sit still. It wasn't until he completed his lap of the room that he noticed her presence.

He pulled up short, surprise illuminating his face. "Kari, what are you doing here?"

"I thought you might want some company." She held up a water bottle and a sandwich from a local sub shop. "And I figured you probably hadn't eaten."

"I can't eat anything."

"You aren't going to do your mom any good if you run yourself into the ground," Kari said in a fair imitation of her mother. "Any news yet?"

"No. They should be taking her into surgery now." He sat in the center of a row of empty chairs. Kari sat beside him and handed him the sandwich.

She suspected he took it only because it would be rude not to. He peeled back the paper and took a bite as though on autopilot. After he swallowed and took a second bite, he looked down at the meatball sub smothered in melted provolone.

"How did you know I like meatball subs?"

"Just a guess." When he continued to stare at her, she added, "You had spaghetti and meatballs when we went out to dinner once. I figured a meatball sub would hit the spot."

"Thanks."

"You're welcome." Kari sat quietly beside him while he ate. She was glad he didn't seem to feel obligated to make conversation when he was clearly so distracted.

When he finished his lunch, he got up to throw away the trash and begin his pacing again. Every few minutes, he sat beside her, but she didn't try to stop his constant movement. She recognized the restlessness and the worry that went with it. Determined not to make any demands, she watched and waited, her own impatience increasing as the minutes passed.

Over an hour after her arrival, Dr. Michaels walked into the room.

"Well?" Ryan asked anxiously.

"I'm afraid the news isn't all good."

"What do you mean?" he asked as Kari put her hand in Ryan's.

"Your mother has an infection called MRSA. That's what's causing the swelling in her knee."

"How bad is it?" An edge of panic sounded in his voice.

"We cleaned out what we could of the infection and put a drain in. We're also starting her on heavy antibiotics." He drew a breath. "We're waiting for some test results to come back, but it appears the infection is in her blood."

"How serious is that?"

"I'm not going to lie to you. It can be very serious," he said gravely. "We're keeping her here at the hospital until we're sure she's stable, but at this point, the best medicine besides the antibiotics is rest."

"How long?" Ryan managed to ask. "How long until we'll know if she'll be okay?"

"It's hard to say. If she responds quickly to treatment, we may know as early as tomorrow. Some patients take a week or more before we are able to get the infection under control."

"And some patients don't make it," Ryan said flatly.

"Unfortunately, there are some who don't make it," Dr. Michaels confirmed.

Ryan swallowed hard.

Sensing that he couldn't form words, Kari stepped forward. "How long until Ryan can see her?"

"She'll be in recovery for at least an hour. The nurses will let you know when she is moved into a room."

"Thank you, Doctor," Kari said.

Dr. Michaels nodded at them and left the room.

Grateful that the waiting room was nearly empty, Kari followed instinct and slipped her hands around Ryan's waist. She didn't say anything. What was there to say?

He returned the embrace, holding her tightly against him as though she were a life preserver and the only thing keeping him from drowning.

Several minutes passed until finally he released her and lowered himself into a chair.

"Do you want me to text Ben? He can let your manager know what's going on."

Ryan's lips pressed together in a hard line, but he nodded his consent.

Kari retrieved her phone from her pocket and sent her brother a text. She then reached over and put her hand on Ryan's. He laced his fingers through hers, and together they settled back to wait for another eternity.

* * *

Ryan stood at his mother's bedside, his frustration bubbling over. For two days, he had stayed in his childhood home, spending almost every waking moment in his mother's hospital room. His manager had given him a couple of days off, but tonight he had to go home so he could be ready to catch an early-morning flight to Philadelphia.

Though the doctor believed he had cleaned out the infection, Ryan's mom's lack of improvement had prompted a second surgery yesterday. They were still waiting to see if the combination of the surgery and antibiotics was successful in overcoming the problem.

"I wish I could stay longer," Ryan said, already going over in his head whether he could manage one more night in Woodbridge.

Kari stood behind him, and he was grateful for her constant presence over the past few days. She had commuted back and forth from Ben's apartment in DC, but except when he was sleeping, she seemed to always be here. He couldn't remember a single meal he had eaten in the past three days that she hadn't provided for him, and somehow she had turned into the conduit for communication between him and his manager.

Despite Kari's help, his mother had yet to acknowledge her presence, even though Ryan had attempted to introduce them several times. He didn't know whether his mother really was so out of it that she didn't recognize Kari's presence or if she didn't want to deal with acknowledging he had a new girlfriend.

Jenny Holladay was also a frequent visitor and currently sat in the chair beside his mom.

Kari put her hand on Ryan's arm. "Ryan, I'm happy to stay here with your mom while you're traveling."

Even though Kari had lowered her voice, Susan mumbled grumpily. "I don't need a babysitter."

Ryan looked over at Jenny sitting in the corner, and a look of understanding passed between them.

"I have the next few days off," Jenny said, offering him the assurance he needed that his mother wouldn't be alone.

Despite that knowledge, guilt weighed heavily on him. "Mom, I wish I could stay."

"Go play your baseball," she insisted. "I'll be fine."

His emotions in turmoil, he had to swallow before he spoke. "I'll call you tomorrow."

"It was nice meeting you, Ms. Strobel," Kari said. "I hope you feel better soon."

No response.

"Come on, Kari." Ryan took her gloved hand in his own and tugged her out into the hall. As soon as they were outside, they discarded their protective gear and threw it into the disposal container located outside his mother's door. Ryan started down the hall, and Kari caught up to him.

"I really don't mind staying with her," Kari said. "It might be easier for you to know you can call and check on her anytime."

A lump formed in his throat, and he tried to swallow it. He knew how bad MRSA could be. Add septicemia to the equation and the infection could turn deadly. How could he walk away right now?

He reminded himself of the doctor's words: the best medicine for his mother was rest. If he was here, he couldn't do anything but cause her more worry and drive the hospital staff crazy while he paced her tiny room.

"Jenny will keep me up to date," Ryan finally managed to say.

"Hey." She took his arm and stopped walking. He looked down at her as she held out her arms and drew him to her. "She's going to be okay."

Ryan's arms tightened around her, Ryan drawing strength from her embrace. He closed his eyes against the tears that formed, determined to keep them at bay. A minute passed before he managed to swallow the better part of his emotions.

When he drew back, she looked up at him with her bright green eyes. "Is there anything I can do for you?"

"Come with me to Philadelphia."

Her lips turned upward slightly. "Ben already reserved a room for me at the hotel where the team is staying."

Relieved beyond words, he shifted, slipping his arm around her shoulders as they continued down the hall. When they got to the parking lot, he walked her to her car. "I can't tell you how grateful I am for everything you've done the last few days."

"I'm glad I was able to help." She stood on her toes and reached up to kiss him. "I'll see you after the game tomorrow night."

"Text me when you get to Philly."

"I will." She started to reach for her door handle, but he beat her to it and pulled the door open for her.

Before she could climb into the car, he put his hands on her shoulders and turned her to face him. Her eyes lifted to meet his, and he saw the weariness reflected there. Not once had she mentioned being tired or commented about the long drive between Washington and Woodbridge, and yet he suspected she had gotten less sleep than he had.

Touched beyond words by her selflessness, he pulled her into his arms and held on, a rush of warmth flowing through him. "You really are amazing, you know that?"

She looked up at him, but her eyelids were heavy. He touched his mouth to hers, a ripple of pleasure chasing away his own weariness. His pent-up emotions flowed into the kiss until it drained him and all that was left was her. He could feel himself sinking into someplace unknown and forced himself to pull back.

"Drive safe," he said, finally letting her get into her car.

"You too." She fastened her seat belt as he closed the door, and she looked at him one last time before putting the key in the ignition. He stepped back and started toward his own car parked a few spaces away.

He dug out his keys and hit the unlock button, but he couldn't help but look over his shoulder once more to where Kari was pulling out of her parking spot. He stood there for several minutes, not moving until she had turned onto the road and disappeared from sight.

Chapter 19

THE CITY OF BROTHERLY LOVE wasn't happy with their Phillies tonight. Boos echoed through the stadium when Ben's bat connected with the ball and sent it sailing over the center field wall.

Kari looked down at the jersey she wore bearing her brother's number and their last name on the back, tugged her red Nationals cap a bit lower and leaned closer to Maya. "We aren't going to get lynched when we leave here, are we?"

"I think we might want to let the crowd thin out before we try to leave."

Kari looked up at the scoreboard. Top of the ninth: Phillies 4, Nationals 9. She supposed she would be frustrated too if her team had managed to score four runs but was still out of grand-slam range of winning.

A pitching change followed Ben's home run, and the new pitcher succeeded in getting Ryan out on a long fly ball that nearly made it out of the park.

Fifteen minutes later, the game was over. Kari and Maya listened to the final disgruntled boos from the diehard Phillies fans who had stayed to the bitter end.

"Just think," Maya said, her voice barely loud enough to be heard. "We have two more nights of this."

"Are they any better when they win?"

"I'm not sure." She reached down and tugged on her own jersey, which was identical to Kari's. "I think we might want to change if the guys decide they want to go out tonight."

"After the beating they took in New York, I think they might want to stay in," Kari said, all too aware that the Mets had swept the Nationals during the first three days of their road trip. Of course, her only real connection with the team while they were in New York was through the news outlets and texts from Maya. She had spoken to Ryan's manager a few times, but those conversations had centered on Ryan's mom and how Ryan was holding up rather than the box scores.

Now, instead of communicating with Ryan's team, she was receiving messages for him from his mom's friend, Jenny. The latest didn't give any new information other than Susan's appetite had increased a bit. Kari hoped that was a sign of improvement.

She still wasn't sure what to think of Susan's reaction to her in the hospital, or rather her lack of reaction. Either the woman really didn't like her, or she was too out of it to notice her. She hoped it was the latter.

"Come on," Maya said, tapping her shoulder. "Let's go find the guys and get back to the hotel."

"I'm right behind you." They made their way downstairs to the restricted part of the clubhouse, showing their passes to security as they went through.

"Good game tonight," Maya told Ben when he and Ryan approached them.

"Thanks." Ben slung his arm around his wife's shoulders and tilted his head toward Ryan. "It was good having Ryan back in the lineup."

"It was good to be back," Ryan said, although Kari wasn't sure how true his words were. She saw the distracted look in his eyes and put her hand in his.

"I got a text from Jenny a little while ago. Apparently your mom is eating better today."

"That's always a good sign," Ben said. He retrieved a business card from his pocket and handed it to Maya. "Here. This is the phone number for the driver who's going to take you to the hotel. I didn't want you guys to have to find a cab."

"Thanks." Maya leaned in and gave him a kiss on the cheek. "We'll see you over there."

Kari started to follow her, but Ryan caught her hand in his before she could take a step.

"Thanks for being here tonight," he said.

Her eyes lifted to his. "I wouldn't have missed it."

* * *

Two straight wins over the Phillies, his free time spent with Kari, and numerous phone calls to the hospital for updates on his mom—Ryan was enjoying himself and going crazy at the same time.

He was halfway to breakfast on his final day in Philadelphia when his phone rang, Dr. Michaels' name illuminating the screen.

"What's the latest?" Ryan said the moment he hit the talk button.

"Good news," the doctor said, the relief obvious in his voice. "We operated on your mom's knee again last night to clean out more of the infection, and we're finally seeing the improvement we were hoping for."

Ryan stopped walking, taking a moment to absorb the doctor's words. "That's great."

"She's still got a long road ahead of her, but if all goes well, she'll be able to transfer from the hospital back to the rehab center in about a week."

"And then?"

"One to two weeks in rehab and then home." For the first time since Ryan answered the phone, he heard reservation in the doctor's voice. "I have to tell you, though, I can't release her from rehab until I'm sure her home environment won't be detrimental to her health. She's going to need someone to stay with her, and getting her in and out of a third-floor apartment simply won't work."

"I can look into hiring someone to stay with her," Ryan said. "As for the apartment, she has it in her head that once she gets inside, she can just stay there until she's better."

"To get better, she will need extensive physical therapy, and that will mean leaving the house three times a week, not to mention follow-up appointments with me."

"So she has to move."

"She has to live somewhere else for at least two to three months, maybe longer."

"I'll figure something out," Ryan said.

"Good luck."

"Thanks for all your help, Doctor. I really do appreciate it."

"You're welcome. I'll have my nurse follow up with you on her progress."

Ryan hung up the phone, relief and concern merging together. Part of him looked forward to when his mother returned to her normal, independent self, the person who would fight against leaving her home. Another part of him prayed she would recognize her limitations and let him help her find a new place to live.

He reached the hotel lobby and found Kari already waiting for him. He glanced around to find she was alone. He took advantage of the situation and leaned down to greet her with a kiss. "Good morning."

"Good morning." Her hand slipped into his. "Any word on your mom today?"

"Actually, the doctor just called." Ryan related the conversation as they made their way into the hotel restaurant. As soon as they were seated, he asked, "I don't suppose there's any way I can convince you to come with me to Kansas City."

"I'd love to come, but Maya is closing on her house in a couple of days. I promised I would help her move."

"Is that happening already?"

"It is." Kari opened her menu. "I'm kind of surprised they didn't try to move in last week while the team was in Washington. The owner offered to let them do a rent-back agreement so they could move in early, but Ben didn't want to push things that quickly."

"A rent-back agreement?" Ryan asked.

"Yeah. I guess it's when you're buying a house and you basically rent it until the legal transfer happens."

Ryan considered the possibilities, and a plan began to form.

Their waitress approached and set water glasses in front of them. "Are you ready to order, or do you need a few more minutes?"

Without looking at his menu, Ryan gave her his order and waited for Kari to put in her request. As soon as they were left alone again, he asked, "Do you or Maya still have the phone number for the real estate agent who took us house hunting?"

"I'm sure Maya has it. Why?"

"Can you get it for me?"

"Yeah. I'll text it to you tomorrow after I get back to Maya's place." She looked at him quizzically. "You aren't thinking of buying your mom a house without her consent, are you?"

"Not exactly, but I think I may have an idea that will help her out without getting me into too much hot water."

"Are you going to share?"

"Let me see if it will even work first," Ryan said, afraid to voice his thoughts aloud. "But I promise, if everything falls into place, you'll be the first to know."

Chapter 20

KARI CARRIED AN ARMFUL OF Maya's dresses into the house and headed for the master bedroom. To keep her from doing too much lifting, Ben had banished Maya to the kitchen, where she was currently organizing her cabinets.

Kari hung the clothes and headed back outside to where Ben was standing at the curb talking to one of the movers. "Hey, Kari, do you care what kind of pizza I order?"

"Anything's fine." She glanced across the street and noticed the For Sale sign in front of the other house they'd looked at now had an Under Contract sign above it. "Looks like you're not going to be the only new neighbors on the street."

"That must have just happened. That sign wasn't there yesterday." He started toward his new house. "I'd better go call in the pizza order."

"And make sure Maya isn't doing too much," Kari added.

"That too."

Kari continued to unload Maya's car, which consisted mainly of her closet. She was down to a box full of shoes when she noticed a familiar car pull into the driveway of the house across the street.

Ryan climbed out and waved. Kari set the box of shoes on the backseat and shut the car door. She started across the street as Ryan came toward her.

"I think you parked at the wrong house. Ben and Maya bought that one."

"Yeah, I know."

"Then don't you think you should move your car? I don't know if the new owners of this one will be thrilled to have you park here."

"I'm sure the new owner won't mind," Ryan said.

"How can you be so sure?"

"Because I'm the new owner. Or at least I will be at all-star break."

"Wait. What?" She reached out and put a hand on his arm.

"I'm the new owner."

"You bought a house?" Stunned, she shook her head, trying to comprehend his words. "When did this happen?"

"I signed the paperwork last night when I got back from Kansas City." He put his hand in his pocket and retrieved a key ring. He held it up to reveal the single house key. "Want to come check it out with me?"

She glanced back at her brother's house and the steady stream of movers walking inside. "Yeah, I'd love to see it again."

"Come on." He took her hand and led her to the house, then unlocked the door and pushed it open.

When he stepped back, Kari thought he was moving to let her go first. She gasped with surprise when he pocketed the key and scooped her into his arms, cradling her against his chest.

"What are you doing?" she asked, unable to contain her laughter.

"Isn't this tradition? The guy is supposed to carry the girl over the threshold?"

"That's for when you get married."

Ryan stepped over the threshold. "Close enough."

"Hardly." Kari shook her head with amusement. "You've only known me for a month."

"I swear it's been longer than that."

"Okay. Thirty-six days."

His eyebrows lifted as he kicked the door closed. "You've been counting?"

"I know the date, and I can do math. It isn't that complicated."

"That's right. You're going to be a doctor. You're smart like that."

"Counting to thirty-six isn't exactly brain surgery," she insisted. "Are you going to put me down?"

"I guess so." He set her on her feet only to pin her against the door. His eyes dark, he lowered his lips to hers. As though he had craved this during their days apart, he drew her closer, a hum of approval echoing from somewhere deep inside him.

He changed the angle of the kiss, his hands shifting to caress her shoulders.

She might have been floating on a cloud. The heady sensation of being treasured seeped through her, overwhelming her. Had she really known Ryan for only five weeks? Here in his arms, she felt like it had been forever and found herself hoping for a future that would last far beyond this moment.

All too aware that they were in his house alone, Kari lifted her hand to his chest and pushed until his focus was completely on her. Her voice was husky when she spoke. "I'm starting to understand why my brother keeps showing up when we're together."

"Don't you trust me?"

"I don't trust that it's a good idea for us to be in a house alone."

He seemed to consider her words. "You're probably right."

She stepped sideways to free herself of his embrace. "I should go help Maya."

"If I promise to keep my hands to myself, will you walk through with me?" Ryan asked. "I have to decide by Wednesday what furniture I want to keep."

"Can I really trust you?"

He took his time in answering, waiting until their eyes met before he did so. "Kari, I promise you'll always be able to trust me." The sincerity of his voice was absolute.

"In that case, lead the way."

* * *

Ryan bit into a piece of pizza and leaned back against Ben's kitchen counter. Maya had texted Kari only minutes after they had started looking through his new house, and they had decided to eat lunch before finishing their walk-through.

"I can't believe you're going to live across the street," Ben said, a paper plate in one hand and a slice of pepperoni pizza in the other.

"I can't believe he bought a house," Maya added, taking up position beside her husband.

"I can hardly believe it myself, but it made sense," Ryan said. "My mom won't let me buy her a place of her own, and this house has a great in-law suite. I figure she can stay there while she recovers, and after that, we'll see how it goes."

"How is she doing? Have you seen her since you got back?" Kari asked.

"I FaceTimed her this morning," Ryan said. "I'm going down to see her this evening. I thought maybe I could convince you to come with me."

"Are you sure?" Kari asked hesitantly. "She would probably be happier if you went without me."

Ryan thought of how odd his mother had acted when she and Kari had first met. He wanted that to change. He needed it to change. "I want you to get to know her."

"If you're sure," she said.

"I'm sure." He reached out and gave her hand a squeeze.

Maya took a drink from her water bottle. "Do you think your mom would want to stay with you after she gets better?"

"Not a chance." Ryan shook his head. "She wants to take care of herself, but I like that she'll have a room up here when she visits."

"She lives an hour away. I doubt you'll get her to visit much," Ben said.

"You never know," Ryan said halfheartedly. In truth, he couldn't explain why he had followed impulse and bought such a large house. It wasn't logical. What was he going to do with six bedrooms, especially once his mom was healthy again?

"You know," Ben said. "I think that open space in your backyard would be perfect for a batting cage."

Ryan couldn't help but smile. "I had that same thought."

"We'd better get back to unpacking," Maya said, throwing her paper plate into a trash bag on the floor.

"I can help you with the kitchen," Kari offered.

"I'm fine. Go ahead and help Ryan with his place. It sounds like he's going to need it."

"Thanks, Maya. Holler if you need me."

"I will."

Ryan tossed his trash into the garbage bag and led Kari through the kitchen and out the front door.

"I've never been inside your apartment," Kari said as they crossed the street. "How much furniture do you have that you'll want to keep?"

"I don't have much. I have a recliner I like, and my bed is new."

"Then we're really just looking at the furniture in the new house and deciding what you like enough to keep."

"That's the plan." He pulled open the door and waited for her to walk inside.

Kari led the way into the living room. She stared at the matching couches positioned there and then slowly turned around as she studied the room. When she turned to face him, a sense of home washed over him.

As though his body had a mind of its own, he closed the distance between them and lowered his mouth to hers for a sweet and gentle kiss.

The scent of potpourri lingered in the air and mixed with the raspberry from her shampoo. His fingers framed her face, his thumb stroking beneath her jaw where he could feel her pulse jumping.

When he drew back, he saw the confusion on her face, and he wondered if he would ever get back on level footing with Kari around. "This house suits you."

She looked a little off-balance herself. "It's a beautiful home. The important question is whether this house suits you."

"Apparently it does."

She pulled free of his embrace. "Come on. We have work to do before we go visit your mom."

"She's going to like you, you know."

"She didn't seem to like me the last time I saw her."

"She'll like you," he repeated.

* * *

"Are you sure about this?" Kari asked as Ryan led her through the hospital hallway. It was one thing to come with him before to see his mom. She had been doing that to support him. This felt entirely too much like being put on a display for his mother, a mother she wasn't sure approved of her.

"It'll be fine," Ryan insisted. He pushed open the door to his mother's hospital room, and Kari tugged her hand free before she followed him inside. "Hey, Mom. How are you feeling?"

Kari stood awkwardly beside him and noticed the way Susan's gaze shifted to land on her. Those dark eyes were no longer clouded with confusion. Instead, they narrowed with suspicion.

"Who are you?"

"This is Kari Evans," Ryan said, motioning Kari forward. "She came with me to see you a couple weeks ago, but you probably don't remember. You were pretty sick at the time."

"It's nice to meet you again," Kari said, not sure how else to properly greet her.

"You're the one who sent the flowers," Susan said now.

"Yes."

Ryan motioned for Kari to sit in the single chair situated beside his mother's bed. Though his mother's gaze was less than welcoming, Kari sat. "How are you feeling?"

"I'll feel better when I'm free of this place."

Ryan took position behind Kari. "The doctor said he's going to approve your transfer to the rehab center on Wednesday."

"I just want to get out of here." She looked past Kari and spoke directly to Ryan. "Jenny left yesterday for California to visit her grandkids for the next month. I've been bored to tears."

"At least she was able to visit a lot while I was on the road," Ryan said, obviously looking for the bright side.

Susan shifted her gaze to Kari. "Did you go with Ryan on his road trip?"

"I was able to watch him play in Philadelphia," Kari said, quickly adding, "My brother plays with Ryan, so I went with his wife to watch that series."

"I see."

Silence hung in the air for several long seconds. Never a fan of confrontation or the silent treatment, Kari felt her heart beat rapidly in her chest. "Ryan, I'm going to give you and your mom some time alone. I'll meet you in the lobby in a little while." Kari stood. "It was nice seeing you again, Ms. Strobel. I hope you have a speedy recovery."

Susan nodded in response but didn't speak.

"I'll be down in a few minutes," Ryan told Kari.

"Take your time." She put her hand on his arm. Whether Susan liked her or not, the woman deserved to have her son's support. "Seriously, you came a long way to see her. Take all the time you need."

"Thanks."

Chapter 21

IRRITATED BY HIS MOTHER'S BEHAVIOR, Ryan sat in the chair Kari had vacated and leaned forward to rest his elbows on his knees. "Okay, spill it. What's with you? You hardly said hello to Kari, and you're acting like she's some used-car salesman trying to swindle you."

"I'm still recovering. That's all."

"You've spent the last two days telling me that you're well enough to go home, and you certainly have shown that you're capable of having a polite conversation when you want to." He waved toward the door. "You were being downright rude to Kari."

"I don't like her." Susan crossed her arms and stared at her son.

His voice raised a decibel. "You don't know her."

"I know she doesn't let you do anything without her." Fire lit her voice. "Jenny said she was with you every time you came to visit me."

"Do you even remember her coming with me?"

She shook her head.

"Well, I remember. She put everything on hold to sit here in a hospital room with someone she didn't even know because she was worried about me," Ryan said, driven to defend Kari. In truth, he didn't know how he would have gotten through the stress of the past two weeks since his mother's accident without her support. "The only reason she came with me today was because I asked her to."

"Which only proves my point. You're in the middle of baseball season, your mother is in the hospital, but your focus is on that girl."

"That girl is one of the kindest people I've ever met," Ryan shot back.

Her eyes narrowed, and he suspected he was about to get a don't-talk-to-your-mother-in-that-tone-of-voice lecture. "Exactly how serious are you about Kari?"

"What do you mean?"

The edge to his mother's frustration melted away, and he saw a glimpse of the woman who had supported him through Little League, broken windows, and algebra. "Seems to me you didn't get this riled up when I first met Brandi."

"You weren't this hard on Brandi."

"Oh, sure I was," she insisted. "I just don't think Brandi cared if she made a good impression on me, and she certainly didn't care whether I liked her or not."

Ryan's tone turned cold. "Kari isn't anything like Brandi."

"I can see that."

"And yet you've decided not to like her."

She pursed her lips, but then her demeanor softened. "I might be persuaded to change my mind."

"I hope you do."

"Now, on to more important things." She lowered her voice. "You've got to talk to the doctor about getting me out of here. I am going insane."

"Mom, you had a serious infection. You're going to need medical care when you do go home."

"I can take care of myself."

"So you keep telling me." Ryan started to bring up the new house but decided against it. One thing at a time. "In the meantime, is there anything you need while you're still in the hospital?"

"I wouldn't mind something to read. Daytime television isn't terribly entertaining."

"I'm sure I can come up with something." He stood. "I'll run down to the gift shop and see if they have any magazines down there."

"You don't have to worry about it today. Are you coming back to visit tomorrow?"

"Yeah. I'll be back in the morning, but then it will probably be a couple days before I can make it back down."

"Is Kari coming with you tomorrow?"

"I don't think so. She was going to visit a couple of colleges in the area. She's thinking about transferring."

"What is she studying?"

"Medicine."

Disbelief registered on her face. "That little thing thinks she's going to be a doctor?"

"That's her current plan."

"Maybe if she was my doctor, she'd let me out of here."

Ryan chuckled. "I'm sure she would just to get some peace around here."

"I should rest." She shifted her position to get more comfortable.

"I love you, Mom."

"I love you too." She waved toward the door. "I'll see you tomorrow."

* * *

Kari sat in a chair in the hospital lobby and used her phone to search through college websites. She was trying hard not to take Susan's cold reception personally, and any distraction right now was a welcome one.

Twenty minutes passed before she came to the conclusion that if Ryan's mother had chosen to dislike her so quickly, she probably didn't approve of any women Ryan dated. That helped smooth away the sharpest edge of disappointment but didn't take away the negative sensation completely.

"Hey, Kari." Ryan's voice broke into her thoughts, and she looked up to see him approaching. She tucked her phone into her purse and stood. "I'm sorry about my mom. She's always been overprotective, and being trapped in the hospital for so long hasn't helped her mood."

Though Susan's disapproval stung, reliving it wouldn't help either of them. Instead, she asked, "Did you tell her about your new house?"

"Not yet."

"Why not?" Kari asked as they headed for the door. "I would think your good news would make a nice distraction."

"I don't think she's going to see it as good news, especially since that's where I expect her to live for the next couple months."

"Ah." They got into the car, and Kari twisted in her seat to face him. "Have you figured out what you're going to do about home care yet?"

"I left a couple of messages with the company the doctor recommended, but so far I've been playing phone tag. My schedule isn't the best when it comes to dealing with office hours."

"Do you want me to try to get some information for you?"

"Kari, you've already done enough."

She heard the weariness in his voice and noted that he didn't say no. "Give me the phone numbers of the places you want information from, and I'll see what I can find out tomorrow while you're at practice," she said. "And if that doesn't work, I can ask Maya's friend Henry. He works at the hospital. I'm sure he knows what companies are worth talking to."

"You really are too good for me. You know that, right?"

The thought that his mother didn't agree crossed her mind, but she swallowed those words. "I hope you keep thinking that."

"I doubt you could do anything to change my opinion. You're one of a kind."

The words and the sentiment behind them left her speechless. Ryan pulled up to a red light and reached out to give her hand a squeeze. "Since you're being so generous with your time, any chance you would be willing to come with me to my apartment before I drop you off at home? I thought I could pack a few more things so I could sleep at the new house tonight."

On the surface, the request seemed innocent enough, but remembering how he had welcomed her to his new home, she hesitated.

"No hidden agenda. I promise. You can even keep the door open," he said as though reading her thoughts.

"I'm happy to help."

"You really are one of a kind." He squeezed her hand again. "And I mean that in the best possible way."

"Thank you."

* * *

She kept the door open. Ryan almost laughed out loud when they entered his apartment and she deliberately pushed it against the wall. When she looked around the messy apartment, her eyebrows lifted.

"I would think if you can afford to buy a new house, you would have invested in a cleaning service."

"They come tomorrow." Ryan picked up a suit jacket that had fallen to the floor.

She started toward the kitchen. "Do you want me to pack some of your food while you pack clothes?"

"Yeah, that would be great." Ryan started for the hall. He had already pulled his suitcases out of his closet, but except for meeting with the Realtor to sign his paperwork, he hadn't been home long enough to pack.

He opened his closet, stared at the contents, and decided packing was overrated. He lifted a dozen items still on their hangers and carried them into the living room.

Kari poked her head around the corner. When she saw his arms full, she grinned at him. "It looks like you pack the same way I do."

"It seems silly to throw everything into a suitcase when I have to hang it all up again anyway."

"Exactly." She ducked back into the kitchen, and he could hear the refrigerator door open and then close.

He brought out another armful of clothes and set it with the first, returning to his room, where he dumped the contents of his dresser into the suitcase. The first two drawerfuls fell in neatly, but the contents of the third spilled onto his bed. He pressed down on the messily packed clothing and zipped his first suitcase shut.

He loaded the second suitcase with the escapees and several pairs of shoes. As soon as he was satisfied that he couldn't fit any more into his luggage, he dragged the suitcases down the hall and parked them by the front door.

"How's it going?" he asked Kari when he entered the galley kitchen.

She pointed to several grocery bags on the tiny kitchen table. "I got most of the refrigerator cleaned out, and I loaded up a few things from the pantry."

"That's great. I'm going to start putting stuff in the car. I'll be right back."

"I can help you." Kari picked up three of the grocery bags and followed him to the door.

Ten minutes later, they were in the car, heading to his new house. He thought of the open spaces and the six bedrooms. "Do you think it's crazy that I bought a huge house when it's just me who will be living there?"

"It won't be just you," Kari said without missing a beat. "And no, I don't think it's crazy. Everyone needs someplace they can call their own."

"Have you ever thought about what you want your home to be like when you settle down?"

"Not really. I guess I would want it to be like the house I grew up in," Kari said, clearly considering. "My parents always made everyone feel welcome. I liked that."

Ryan thought of how his mother had acted a short time ago and quickly pushed it aside. He didn't want to have his mother's voice in his head, not when it came to his relationship with Kari. "Have you made any more progress in deciding where you're going to go to school this fall?"

"Actually, I have," Kari said with a hum of excitement. "I thought I would have to sit out fall semester because I'm so late in applying, but George Mason has a visiting student program. It looks like I would be able to take classes while they process my application."

"When would you graduate?"

"A year from May."

He thought of her future plans and found himself aligning them with his own. "What about medical school? Is George Washington University still your first choice?"

"Either there or Johns Hopkins, but I doubt I'd have any chance of getting in," Kari said. "I'll have a better idea of my options after I take the MCAT."

"When is that supposed to happen?"

"I just got the study materials to start prepping for it." She brushed her hair behind her shoulders. "I don't want to think about that though. It makes me too nervous."

"Then let's think about more important things, like what to get for dinner."

"We have a bunch of your groceries in the backseat."

"Yeah, but I don't feel like cooking tonight." He thought for a moment. "Why don't you call Ben and Maya and see if they've eaten. If they haven't, we can get some takeout, and we'll have them over to my place to eat."

"Okay." Kari made the call and relayed information back and forth until they decided on where to pick up dinner. She hung up and made another call, this time to place their order with a restaurant located along their route.

"It looks like you're about to host your first dinner party in your new home," she said as soon as she hung up.

"We," he corrected. "We're about to host our first dinner party."

"Fine. We," she said agreeably. "And after dinner, you need to take it easy and get some rest. You've got to be exhausted."

"It's been a busy day." He reached over and put his hand on hers again. "Definitely one to remember."

Chapter 22

RYAN STRAIGHTENED HIS SHOULDERS AND prepared for the fight. He had visited his mother several times over the past week, but he hadn't yet dared bring up the fact that she wasn't going home when she was released. He had been so relieved to see her condition improving that he hadn't wanted to open the door to any negative emotions.

For the same reason, he hadn't asked Kari to come with him on the last couple of visits. Admittedly, his mother was always slow to warm up to the women he dated, with the possible exception of Lucy Peterson in the tenth grade. Of course, Lucy had also been the daughter of one of his mother's closest friends.

High school sweetheart aside, Susan Strobel had never viewed any of the women in her son's life as being worthy of her little boy. He might be six foot four, but by his mother's standards, Ryan would always be little.

He made his way into his mother's room at the rehab center to find her sitting in a chair rather than her bed. "Hey, how are you doing?"

Her expression brightened. "The nurses said I should get released tomorrow."

"That's great."

"You don't sound too excited." She studied him for a moment. "You didn't go out and do something crazy, did you? I told you I don't need you to buy me a house or condo or whatever it is you were looking at."

"Actually, I did buy a house, but not for you. I bought one for me."

She straightened in her seat. "You bought a house? Why didn't you tell me?"

"Because one of the reasons I decided on this particular house is because it has an in-law suite for you to live in until you've recovered."

"Excuse me?"

"Mom, whether you want to admit it or not, you can't stay at your apartment, not until you can do stairs by yourself." Ryan rushed on before she could voice her objections. "I hired someone to come help you when I'm working. This way we'll get to see a lot more of each other instead of me driving an hour each way only to be able to visit for twenty minutes when I get here."

She stared at him but didn't speak. Ryan wasn't sure what to think of the silence. Finally, she took a deep breath and spoke in a calm voice. "I appreciate what you're trying to do, but I don't want to be a burden on you."

"Mom, you could never be a burden, and I want to do this." A smile began to form on his lips. "And it's a really great house."

"Tell me about it."

"Six bedrooms, five and a half baths."

Her eyes widened. "So big?"

"Your room even has its own kitchen and living room."

"Ryan, are you sure about this?"

Relieved that she wasn't fighting him, he nodded with conviction. "I'm sure."

* * *

Kari stood in Ryan's driveway, the July heat thick with humidity, her backpack over one shoulder.

"You don't have to do this," Ryan insisted. "The medical transport service I hired can help get my mom settled."

"You aren't thrilled she's coming into your house the first time without you here," Kari said. "It's bad timing that you have to work tonight. The least I can do is hang out and make sure she has everything she needs."

"She tends to be a little overprotective of me, especially when it comes to women."

Kari cocked her head to one side. "Tell me something I don't know."

"Are you sure you're okay with this?" Ryan asked in his I-really-hope-you'll-say-yes tone. "You'll miss the game."

"I can watch it on TV." She motioned toward the open garage where his car was parked. "Go to practice. I'll be fine."

He leaned down and kissed her. "I really appreciate this."

"I know." She stepped toward the door.

"Wait, let me give you my spare key to make sure you don't get locked out." He dug into his pocket and pulled out a Washington Nationals key chain, a single house key attached.

Kari took it from him. "Remind me to give it back when you get home tonight."

"Hold on to it. It's always good to have someone else with a spare key."

Her eyebrows lifted. "In case you haven't noticed, I'm an old-fashioned kind of girl. I'm not the type who would have a key to a guy's house."

"And I love that about you," Ryan countered. "You can always leave it somewhere at Ben and Maya's house. It's just for emergencies."

"Okay, if you put it that way." She pocketed the key. "Have fun tonight."

"Thanks. And call if you have any problems. The phone numbers for the transport service and the home health aides are on the kitchen counter."

"I'll text you as soon as she gets here."

"Thanks. I'll see you later."

Kari watched him go before heading into the house. The relief from the air conditioning was instant. She toed off her shoes, tucking them into the coat closet located near the front door. She continued into the kitchen and set her backpack down on one of the barstools. Though she was sure Ryan had already prepared his mom's room for her, she couldn't help but go down the hall to check for herself.

Her lips curved when she saw a bouquet of daisies on the round table in the kitchenette. She noticed a throw rug on the tile floor in the kitchen area and crossed to pick it up. Remembering that such things tended to be tripping hazards for recovering patients, she rolled it up and looked around for somewhere to store it. During her search, she found two more throw rugs, one in front of the couch and another in the bathroom. Adding those to her stack, she put all three in the corner of the bedroom closet.

Satisfied that Susan's new living space wouldn't be hazardous to her health, Kari headed back into the living room. Ryan hadn't changed the space much since he'd moved in the week before, but, then, he hadn't been home long enough to do much more than unpack his clothes. She wasn't entirely sure he had even completed that basic task.

Together they had gone through the house and decided what furniture he wanted to keep. He hadn't been particularly fond of the western furnishings in the upstairs living room, instead replacing them with the pieces he had brought over from his apartment. They had cleaned out two bedrooms upstairs and removed all the artwork.

Kari had to admit she had been glad to see him make that decision. The modern pieces certainly hadn't been in either of their tastes, and she could envision a fun combination of his sports paraphernalia and classic photos and art to give his home character.

She indulged herself and wandered through the main living area, coming to stand by the french doors leading to the deck. The swimming pool looked inviting beneath the haze of humidity, and she considered that walking in the water might be good therapy for Ryan's mom when she got a little stronger.

Turning back to the kitchen, she forced herself to open her backpack and retrieve her laptop and MCAT prep book. Like it or not, if she was going to get into med school, she had to put some serious time into studying.

She read through the first three sample problems and was overwhelmed. So much to learn. So many more years of school.

The doorbell rang, and another kind of anxiety rose within her. Drawing a steadying breath, she squared her shoulders and walked to the door.

The moment she pulled it open, Susan looked up at her from her wheelchair, narrowed her eyes, and demanded, "What are you doing here?"

"I asked Ryan if I could come over and make sure you had everything you need," Kari said, rushing on before she could respond. "He felt bad that he had to go to work tonight."

Susan huffed out a breath and waved a hand to the man standing behind her. "Well, show me where I'm staying, then."

"Right this way." Kari held the door open wider and motioned toward the hall. Shifting her attention to the tall black man pushing the wheelchair, she said, "I'm Kari."

"Ronaldo. Good to meet you."

"It's down the hallway to the left."

Susan looked around the living room as they passed through. Clearly astonished, she turned to Kari. "My son really owns this place?"

"He will as of next Thursday. That's when he'll close on the house."

"It's a mansion."

"I know what you mean," Kari agreed. She started to mention her brother's place across the street but wasn't sure how Susan would feel about her living in such close proximity to her son. Instead she said, "Three of his teammates live in this neighborhood. That was how he found this house."

"All I can say is he'd better stay healthy."

Kari directed Ronaldo to the correct door.

"This is your room," Kari said, following them into the small living room.

"This is my room?" Susan looked up at her, her eyes wide.

"Ryan brought some things for you from your apartment, but if there's anything he missed, let me know, and I can drive down there for you."

"I'm sure I can manage."

"Ms. Strobel," Ronaldo said, interrupting their conversation. "I'm going to leave you right here for now while I go get your walker."

"That's fine." Susan motioned to the flat-screen television hanging on the wall. "Does that thing work?"

"It does," Kari said. "If you don't mind, I was hoping you would let me watch Ryan's game with you tonight."

Susan pursed her lips as though contemplating whether she could get away with saying no. "I suppose that would be okay."

Ronaldo returned a moment later carrying a walker. A woman in her midforties followed behind him carrying a large plastic bag and a backpack. The woman's curly hair was cut short, and her round face looked like it had adopted a permanent scowl.

"I'm heading out now," Ronaldo said. "This is Lois. She's the nurse who will be coming in to check on you."

When Susan didn't say anything in response, Kari stepped forward and extended her hand. "I'm Kari Evans, and this is Susan Strobel."

"Good to meet you," Lois said, brusquely shaking Kari's hand and then moving to the kitchen table. "I have Susan's medical supplies here. She's already had her antibiotics today, so I'll show you how to administer that when I come back tomorrow."

"I thought Susan's son hired you to stay with her during the day for the first week or two," Kari said, confused.

"Oh, no. I only come in two or three times a week to check on her."

"I see."

"I don't need round-the-clock nursing," Susan said, closing the door on the conversation. "I do need to flush out my PICC line though."

"Didn't they do that this morning?" Lois asked.

Susan sent Lois an irritated look. "Yes, but it needs to be flushed twice a day."

"Oh, once is plenty."

Seeing the fire in Susan's eyes, Kari stepped forward. "I'm sure it won't hurt to flush it out again. Besides, I'd appreciate it if you'd show me how."

"I have other patients." Lois's condescending tone grated against Kari.

"And it will only take you five minutes to show me how to do it," Kari said.

"Fine." Lois bit off the word and rummaged through the bag she had put on the table. Despite her confrontational posture, Lois went about the task with skill and precision. The tubes running from the PICC line, a direct-access port into the vein in Susan's arm, were shorter than Kari had expected. When Maya had had a PICC line during her early cancer treatments, the tubing had been long enough that she could flush it out herself if needed.

As soon as the task was completed, Kari showed Lois out. When she returned, Susan had slumped down slightly in her chair.

"You must be exhausted." Kari crossed to her. "Would you like to lie down? Or I can help you move into the lounge chair."

"I think I will rest for a bit."

Kari moved behind the chair and wheeled Susan into the bedroom.

"If you get me my walker, I can get into bed myself."

Kari did as she asked and proceeded to turn down the blanket and sheets to make it easier for her to get in. Worried that Susan's strength was failing her, Kari took her by the elbow as she shifted her body and pulled herself into the bed. Susan didn't object when Kari helped her reposition her legs until she was comfortable.

"Can I get you anything? Have you already had lunch?"

"I just need to sleep for a bit."

"Okay." Kari motioned to a bell Ryan had set on Susan's bedside table. "Let me know if you need anything. You can ring that if I don't hear you call."

Her only response was to close her eyes.

Kari left the room, deliberately leaving the door open. She made her way back to the kitchen and looked down at the phone numbers for the medical transport and home care services.

Certain that Ryan expected more extensive nursing services than what Susan had received, she picked up her phone. If he was going to have her living here, Susan was going to need a lot more help than a couple visits a week.

Chapter 23

Ryan climbed out of his car and rolled his shoulders to work out some of the tension settled there. Tonight's game had not gone well for him or for any of his teammates, and they were all ready to put it behind them and look to tomorrow. At the moment, what he really wanted was to collapse onto his bed and sleep for ten hours. If he was lucky, he might get seven.

The scent of tomato sauce greeted him when he opened the door leading from the garage to the kitchen. The light over the stove provided a soft glow in the otherwise dark kitchen. Though his stomach rumbled with hunger, he made his way down the hall to his mother's room. As in the main part of the house, only a single light was on, this time coming from the bathroom.

Ryan peeked into the bedroom to see his mother sleeping, a walker positioned beside her bed and a wheelchair pushed into the corner of the room. Satisfied that she was resting peacefully, he turned back to the main part of the house in search of Kari. With the way the lights were off, he supposed she might have gone back to Ben's house, but he had thought she would stay with his mom until he got home.

His question was answered when he reached the living room. Kari lay on the couch, a throw pillow beneath her head and an afghan tucked around her legs. Her dark hair curtained part of her face, and he recognized the sweatshirt she wore as one of his own. He felt himself softening, and he found himself yearning for something unknown.

Dark eyelashes fluttered, and she shifted, her eyes opening to meet his. She smiled lazily, and sleep hung in her voice when she spoke. "Hey there."

"Hey."

She moved to sit up, sliding her legs down to make room for him. "I don't know if you're hungry, but I left some dinner in the oven for you."

"Thanks. I'll get some in a minute." He lowered himself onto the couch beside her. "How was my mom tonight?"

"Tired, grumpy." She raked her fingers through her hair, only succeeding in messing it up more than it had been before she'd made the effort. He found he rather liked her rumpled look.

She tugged at the hem of the sweatshirt. "I hope you don't mind that I borrowed this. It got a little cold in here once the sun went down."

"I don't mind." He waved in the direction of his mom's room. "So everything went okay tonight?"

"Mostly. There was an issue with the nurse. She was only here for five minutes before she left. She's supposed to come back in the morning, but she said she was only planning to come two or three times a week."

"That can't be right," Ryan said. "I arranged to have someone here from noon to eight o'clock every day."

"I know. I called the home care service, and they said they would look into it." She stifled a yawn. "I wanted to make sure you knew about it though."

"Thanks."

"You're welcome." She started to rise, but he took her hand to hold her in place.

"I mean it, Kari. Having you here to make sure my mom was okay meant a lot to me."

Her eyes warmed. "I was happy to help."

He leaned forward and pressed his lips to hers. The now familiar sensation flooded through him. Pinpricks of pleasure danced along his spine, an unexpected wash of belonging seeping through him as he drew out the kiss.

Even in the darkness, he could see the flush in her cheeks when he drew back.

She glanced at the clock on the wall. "I didn't realize it was so late. I should get going."

"Stay another minute." He kept her hand in his, their eyes meeting as he studied her in the dim light. With his free hand, he brushed her hair back from her face, tucking a lock behind her ear. He saw her confusion and couldn't explain why he felt the need to draw out their time together. When he first got home, all he cared about was sleep. Now that was the last thing on his mind.

He thought of how she had integrated into his life so quickly, of her reaction today when he had given her his house key. He loved that he could trust her so completely, both in his home and with his privacy. A jolt shot through him when another thought tumbled through his mind. He didn't just love the characteristics he had discovered in Kari. He loved her. Completely.

"Are you okay?" She turned slightly as though trying to see him from a different angle.

Still stunned from his realization, he swallowed before asking, "Will you stay for a little while?" He needed to keep her here longer. "I hate to eat alone."

"I'm not hungry, but I'll sit with you while you eat."

They stood together, and Kari led the way into the kitchen. She picked a hot pad off the counter and retrieved a glass dish out of the oven. Ryan edged closer to see chicken breast smothered in spaghetti sauce. "Chicken parmesan?"

"Yeah. I hope that's okay. I thought your mom would enjoy having something that didn't taste like hospital food for a change."

"This is great."

"There's salad in the fridge if you want."

"No, this is fine." While she dished a piece of chicken onto a plate, he retrieved a cup and filled it with water. He sat at the table and took a bite of his dinner. "This is really good. Did my mom eat some?"

"A little bit. Her appetite wasn't the greatest."

"Did she give you the third degree about being over here?" Ryan asked, almost afraid to hear the answer.

"She was fine."

"Fine?" He looked at her suspiciously. "We're talking about my mother, the one who doesn't like any women I date."

"I think she was too tired to think about anything beyond sleep. We watched part of your game together, but she only lasted four innings before she dozed off."

"I owe you for this."

"No, you don't." She shook her head. "This is what friends are for."

"I'm really glad you came to DC this summer."

"Me too." She motioned toward the door. "But I really do need to go before I collapse."

Ryan pushed back from the table. "I'll walk you home."

"I'll be fine," she said. "Besides, you shouldn't leave your mom alone."

He walked her to the door. "I can at least watch you walk across the street."

She motioned to the sweatshirt she still wore. "I'll wash this and get it back to you."

"I'll see you tomorrow." He leaned down and kissed her good-bye. Standing in his doorway, he watched her cross the street and let herself into Ben's house. When she disappeared from sight, he put a hand on his heart; an odd sensation centered there. Was he really in love with her? And if so, what in the world was he going to do about it?

* * *

Kari knocked on Ryan's door, his now-clean sweatshirt tucked under her arm and a red gift bag dangling from her fingers. An unfamiliar car was parked in front of his house, and she hoped he had worked out the problems with his mother's medical care.

The door swung open, and her heart did a slow, slippery meltdown. Ryan stood on the other side of the threshold wearing a pair of shorts and a T-shirt. His hair was wet, as though he had just stepped out of the shower, and his feet were bare.

His face lit up with a smile. "I was hoping that was you. Come on in."

Kari followed him inside and held out the sweatshirt. "Here. I wanted to return this before it got mixed up with Ben's laundry."

"You only borrowed it yesterday. How did you have time to wash it?"

"It's almost noon. Don't you have to leave for your game soon?"

"I was just making sure my mom has everything she needs before I go."

"How is she today?"

Ryan shrugged. "Not very happy about the nurse staying with her, but I think she'll manage."

"I hope so." She held out the gift bag. "Also, I got you something."

"What is it?"

"Just a little housewarming present."

Ryan dug through the tissue paper and pulled out a ceramic trivet shaped like home plate. In script letters, it read *The best things in life happen at home.* "This is great. Thank you."

"You're welcome. I saw it in the store, and it felt like you." She took a step toward the door. "I should get going. I just wanted to return your shirt and make sure the nurse showed up today."

"Were you planning to go to the game early today?"

"I was thinking about it," she said. "Believe it or not, I seem to get more studying done at the ballpark than when I'm at the house."

"Do you want to drive over with me?"

"Sure, if you want." She kept her voice casual, even as she delighted in the prospect of spending more time with him.

"I do. It'll just take me a minute to finish getting ready."

Kari took a step toward the door. "I'll go grab my stuff, and I'll be back in a few minutes."

"Hey, before you go, I have something for you."

Her eyebrows drew together. "What?"

"I got you a Nat's jersey." Ryan retrieved a Washington Nationals jersey from the back of his couch.

"Thanks, but I already have a few at home."

"Yeah, but all of those say Evans on the back. I thought you might consider wearing my number to the game today."

Kari took it from him, turning it to see Ryan's last name stitched across the back. She grinned at him. "I love it. Thanks."

"You're welcome." He leaned down and gave her a quick kiss. "I'll see you in a few minutes." He took a step down the hall. "Just walk in when you come back. You don't need to knock."

"Okay." Kari headed outside, looking down at the gift Ryan had given her. She kind of liked the idea of wearing Ryan's name.

The memory of Brandi wearing a Strobel jersey wormed its way into her mind. She was sure there was a time when Ryan had offered his ex-girlfriend one of his jerseys. Kari stopped that thought in its track. Ryan was not a prize to be won.

A handsome man had asked her to go with him to his game, and she was going to appreciate every moment she got to spend with him. She had to remind herself of that when she walked into his house ten minutes later to find herself facing his mother and her nurse.

"Ms. Strobel. It's so good to see you up and around," Kari said.

"I'm in a wheelchair. That's hardly up and around."

Kari ignored Susan's edge. "How are you doing today?"

"I was doing fine until I came in here to find a woman walking into my son's house without even knocking."

She felt color wash into her cheeks. "Actually, I did knock when I came over a few minutes ago. Ryan told me to come in when I came back. He offered to give me a ride to the game."

"I see."

Hearing the disapproval hanging in the woman's words, Kari considered that she might prefer to see Susan when she was too exhausted to criticize.

Ryan walked down the stairs and approached them. "Hey, Mom. Good to see you out of your room."

"Thanks. I was getting a little claustrophobic."

Kari noticed how Susan's mood altered completely when she was speaking to her son, but she didn't comment.

Ryan turned his gaze to Kari, and instantly he grinned. "I like the jersey."

"Thanks. This really great guy gave it to me."

"I wonder who that was," he said. He looked back at his mom and leaned down to kiss her cheek. "I'll see you later." Then he looked up at the nurse. "My phone numbers are on the counter if you have any problems." He reached out, took Kari's hand, and led her to the door.

Chapter 24

RYAN FOLLOWED HIS MOTHER'S INSTRUCTIONS to begin her antibiotic infusion and wondered if he should consider hiring another nurse. Yesterday, a second nurse had come in the morning to take care of this task, but now that Lois was scheduled to come for the afternoons and evenings, the morning antibiotic infusion had fallen to him.

"You know, I really don't need anyone staying with me while you're at work," Susan said as though reading his thoughts.

"The doctor released you early on the condition that you have someone available to help you all the time for at least two weeks." He connected the antibiotic to her PICC line and shifted to sit in the chair beside her.

"The occupational therapist comes today. She'll tell you I can manage on my own."

"She'll also tell me that you can't drive yet. You have physical therapy tomorrow and a checkup with your doctor the next day."

"Which the medical transport service can take me to," she reminded him.

Ryan wondered if the transport service could also administer her antibiotics. His game on Saturday started at four o'clock, which would make things difficult for him to take care of her needs before he had to leave for the ballpark. Sunday's game was even earlier.

"What's going on with you and Kari? Are things getting serious?" his mother asked casually.

The truth, or at least a watered down version of it, spilled out before he thought to censor his words. "I think they're heading that way."

"I noticed you gave her one of your jerseys yesterday," she said. "Brandi had quite a few when you were together."

He frowned in concentration. "I never even thought about that when I gave it to her."

"And I have to say, I thought it was very rude yesterday when she walked into your house without knocking."

"She only did it because I told her to. I knew I would be getting ready when she came over, and I didn't want her to have to stand out in the heat while she waited for me to let her in." He gave her a pointed look. "Seems to me you haven't exactly been polite to her. Maybe you should stop nit-picking at her. If you give her a chance, I think the two of you will find you have a lot in common."

"I doubt that."

"You work in medicine. She wants to be a doctor."

"I don't exactly socialize with doctors."

"Give her a chance. Please?"

She studied him in silence for a moment. "You really like this one."

"Yes, I really do." He stood. "I'm going to go fix you some breakfast. I'll be back in a few minutes."

He went into the kitchen and pulled out a frying pan to make some eggs. His mind wandered as he turned on the stove and cracked two eggs into the pan.

His mother's comment about Brandi wearing his jerseys when they dated irritated him on principle. While technically he had given Brandi a couple of his jerseys, all but one of them were ones she had "borrowed" and never returned. Still, the fact remained that he had given Brandi her first jersey with his name on it, just as he had given one to Kari.

Was he trying to recreate the relationship he had once had with Brandi? A relationship he had hoped would lead to marriage and family?

He plopped a piece of bread into the toaster and shook the thought out of his head. Sure, there might be some similarities between the two relationships, but what he felt for Kari was so much more than what he had experienced with Brandi. Never in a million years would Brandi have given up going to a game to sit at home with his mother, and the only reason she had ever gone early to a game with him was if she knew she would have friends there with her.

Kari, on the other hand, never seemed to have any kind of hidden agenda. He knew she studied while waiting for the game to start, but she could just as easily have stayed home and accomplished the same thing with a lot less effort. No, Kari wasn't anything like Brandi. The only real similarity was that he had once professed his love to Brandi and he hoped to do the same to Kari. This time, however, he knew what the word really meant.

* * *

Kari waited on Ryan's doorstep and debated whether she should use his spare key to enter. He had asked her to ride with him to Nats Stadium, but apparently her timing had coincided once again with him getting ready to leave.

Another minute passed, and she rang the doorbell a third time. Ten seconds later, Ryan opened the door, breathless and shirtless.

"Sorry, I was in the shower. Have you been waiting long?"

"A few minutes," she managed to say, trying not to stare at his well-muscled chest.

"You could have just let yourself in."

"That didn't go over so well with your mom yesterday."

"Yeah, sorry about that." He motioned her inside. "Did I mention she's protective?"

"Once or twice."

He motioned to the jersey she wore, one bearing her brother's name across the back. "I think you're wearing the wrong number."

"I figured I can split my time between you two. Besides, the one you gave me needs to be washed."

"I guess I'll have to add to your collection."

"I think you already spoil me too much."

"Nah." He leaned down and gave her a kiss. "I'll be back in a minute. I need to finish getting ready and make my mom some lunch before we leave." He took a step back. "Can you do me a favor and let the nurse in when she gets here?"

"No problem." She waved toward the stairs. "Go finish getting ready. I'll make your mom something to eat."

"Thanks. There's still some of the leftover chicken parmesan in there. I was going to heat some up for her."

"Okay." Kari went into the kitchen and set about heating up Susan's lunch. She retrieved a bag of premade salad and added that to the plate, along with an individualized cup of ranch dressing left over from one of Ryan's visits to a restaurant.

After filling a glass with water, Kari debated briefly whether she should wait for Ryan to take it to her. A glance at the clock on the wall made the decision for her. Ryan was running late, and so was Susan's nurse.

Kari carried the food down the hall, adjusting the plate to sit on her arm so she could knock before entering Susan's suite.

"Come in."

Kari nudged the door open farther and moved the plate again so she would have a better grip. Susan was sitting on her couch, a book in her hand.

"Hi, Ms. Strobel. Ryan is still getting ready for his game, so I thought I would bring you your lunch."

"Oh, thank you." She set the book aside and motioned toward the kitchen. "There's a tray over there you can put it on."

Kari did as she was asked, setting the plate and cup on the serving tray that had been left on the kitchen counter. She then carried it to Susan. "Here you go."

"Is there anything else you need?" Kari asked after it was settled in Susan's lap. "I got you water, but I'm happy to get you something else to drink if you want."

"This is fine." She eyed Kari. "It seems you're here at Ryan's house nearly as much as he is."

Kari didn't see a point in disagreeing. "Lately, it does seem that way."

Susan took a sip of her water. "You aren't the type of girl who is trying to get a key to my son's house, are you?" Before Kari could answer the question, Susan continued. "You know the ones—first, they worm their way into a man's home, and before you know it, the guy gets used to her being there, and she ends up with a ring on her finger."

"As I already told Ryan, I'm not the kind of girl who is comfortable having a man's house key on my key ring."

"I can't tell you how glad I am to hear you say that." Susan gave a definite nod. "I might decide to like you after all."

Kari's lips quirked up. "I hope so."

"Thank you for bringing me my lunch."

"You're welcome." Kari heard the doorbell ring. "I'll be right back." She answered the door and showed Lois into Susan's suite. While Lois moved to the kitchen table to start organizing her supplies, Kari repeated her earlier question to Susan. "Is there anything else you need?"

"This is fine. Thank you."

"Okay, I'll see you later." Kari said good-bye to the nurse and then continued into the hall. As she made her way back to the front of the house, she felt as though a weight had been lifted off her shoulders.

Ryan was everything to his mom, and for the first time since meeting Susan, Kari finally felt like she wasn't a potential barrier between mother and son.

Ryan jogged down the stairs, his phone in hand. "Sorry I took so long. I got a call from Shawn, asking for a ride. His car broke down." He motioned toward his mom's room. "Did the nurse get here?"

"Yeah, your mom's all set."

"Great. Let's go."

"Maybe you should poke your head in real quick to say good-bye. I'm sure she would appreciate it."

"Kari, I'm already running late."

"It'll only take a second."

His expression changed to acceptance. "Okay." He jogged across the room and down the hall. Kari could hear the quick exchange with his mother, followed by his footsteps heading back toward her. "She's good. Let's go."

Once they were settled in the car, he turned to her. "Thanks for making me say good-bye. I think she was waiting for it."

"Glad to help."

"Yeah, that's always how you are," Ryan said. He pulled out onto the road. "I love that about you."

Chapter 25

KARI HURRIED ACROSS THE STREET to Ryan's house, one hand gripping her long skirt so she wouldn't trip. She had been nearly finished getting ready to go out to dinner with Ben and Maya when she received Ryan's text. *Can you come over right now? It's urgent.*

Slightly winded, she knocked on Ryan's door. Instantly, it swung open to reveal Ryan wearing a suit and tie.

"Oh, good. You're right on time."

"On time for what?" Kari asked, confused. "Your text said it was urgent."

"It is." Ryan motioned her inside, his demeanor surprisingly calm.

"What's wrong? Is your mom okay?"

"Everyone is fine."

Kari's eyes narrowed suspiciously. "Then what's so urgent?"

"Come with me, and I'll show you."

Curious, Kari followed Ryan through the house and onto the back porch. Her eyes widened when she looked out at the scene he had set. White Christmas lights twinkled in the dogwood tree to the right. Candlelight flickered from the center of the bistro table situated on the lawn a short distance away. The scent of grilled meat wafted on the faint breeze, and a picnic basket sat beside the table.

Kari turned to look at Ryan. "What's all this?"

"I wanted to do something special for you." Ryan took her hand. "I hope you don't mind that I asked Ben to keep you occupied this afternoon so I could get everything ready."

"This is all very sweet." She reached up and kissed him. "Thank you."

"You're welcome." He led her across the lawn and pulled her chair out for her.

She sat, amazed that Ryan had turned his backyard into such a romantic setting. He sat across from her and pulled a wine bottle from a bucket of ice.

"Sorry, Ryan, but I don't drink."

"I know. That's why I got sparkling cider."

Her smile was instant. "You're really something. You know that?"

"I'm glad you think so." He popped the top and poured. "I hope you don't mind a quiet evening at home."

"This is perfect." She lifted her glass. "And very thoughtful."

Clearly pleased with how well his surprise had been received, he retrieved a bowl from inside the picnic basket. "I hope shrimp pasta salad is okay. It's one of the few side dishes I know how to make that I can do ahead of time."

"It sounds wonderful."

"It's one of my mom's recipes."

"Did your mom help you make it?"

"She made sure I didn't mess it up," Ryan admitted. "In exchange, I promised to save her some steak. Speaking of which, dinner should be ready."

Ryan got up and crossed to the grill. A moment later, he returned and served her a steak and put another on his plate.

"Thank you."

Kari scooped them both some pasta salad, and as soon as she took a bite, she rolled her eyes in appreciation. "Mmm. This is good." She leaned forward. "You will share the recipe, right?"

"I might be persuaded, especially if you agree to go on a hike with me on Thursday."

Kari took another bite and considered. "I think I like it when you have days off."

Ryan took her hand. "Me too."

* * *

"You did what?" Ryan stared at his mother with disbelief. For the past few days, he'd finally found a routine that worked for him. He helped his mother with her infusions in the morning, drove with Kari to and from his games, and returned home to go to sleep and start the whole process all over again. Now his mother was sitting in her favorite recliner, telling him she had just blown that routine out of the water.

Susan repeated her statement from a moment before. "I fired her."

"Mom, you need someone to help take care of you, at least until you get through your antibiotic treatments."

"You've been helping, not Lois."

"Yes, and I leave on a road trip tomorrow morning," Ryan reminded her.

"Then I'll do them myself."

"How?" he asked impatiently. "You need two hands to do the infusions, and one of yours can't even reach the tubing."

"I can have the nurse change out the tubing for a longer set."

"The nurse you just fired?"

That caused her to pause. "I'll have the hospital staff do it for me. It will only take a few minutes to change it out."

"And your friends who work at the hospital live over an hour away." He dragged his hands through his hair impatiently. Banking down on his frustration, he took a steadying breath and tried to swallow the anger bubbling inside him. "Why did you fire the nurse?"

"The last two days when she had to do my antibiotics, she forgot to flush the PICC line out with saline before using it. When I reminded her, she said it was only necessary once a day." Susan held up a finger as she made her point. "I am in this situation because I have an infection. I don't need another one."

"I can call the home care service and ask them to send a replacement."

"I don't want a replacement. I'm tired of being treated like I need a babysitter," she said. "All I need is someone who can follow directions. It isn't that difficult."

"I can do it." Kari's voice silenced the room.

Ryan turned to see her standing in the doorway. Tonight he had planned to take her out on their first real date in weeks, but that prospect was yet another casualty of his mother's decision. He processed her words, still not sure he had heard her correctly. "You can do what?"

"I can help your mom while you're away."

"Kari, I can't ask you to do that," Ryan said, uneasy. "The home care nurse was going to stay here with Mom around the clock. It's a full-time job."

"And in case you haven't noticed, I'm between jobs right now," Kari said.

"Mom, will you excuse us for a minute?" he said, not comfortable continuing this discussing with his mother in the room. He didn't wait for an answer before he crossed the room, took Kari's hand, and led her out of his mother's suite and down the hall. He stopped to face her when they reached the living room, and he lowered his voice. "Kari, I can't let you do this."

"Ryan, I was supposed to do a medical internship this summer. That situation blew up in my face, and I lost out on the opportunity." She waved toward his mother's room. "Let me help you out. It will be a good experience for me too."

He wavered. In truth, he needed someone. "Would you be okay staying over here?"

"You do have a few extra bedrooms," Kari reminded him. "If it's okay with you, I'll stay in the guest room on the main floor. That way I'm not too far from your mom if she needs help."

His heart swelled as he was once again struck by her kindness. "I don't know how to thank you."

"You can start by convincing your mom that this is a good idea."

"She isn't going to make it easy on you."

"Ryan, I promise I will make sure her needs are met, and I'll respect her privacy as much as possible. If she doesn't like having me help her, she can rehire the nurse."

"I guess if I put it to her that way, she'll much prefer having you here." He gave her an apologetic look. "I'm afraid our plans for tonight aren't going to work out the way I had hoped."

"We can change them," she said easily. "You're going to be eating out for the next week straight. Instead of going out to dinner, let's make something in. That way your mom can join us. If you want, we can all watch a movie together."

"There's also a swimming pool in my backyard we haven't used yet."

She grinned. "I like to swim."

"Maybe you should go change into your swimming suit, and we can hang out here for a while before we go to the store."

"Sounds like a plan." She took his hand and gave it a squeeze. "And while I change, you can talk to your mom and make sure she isn't going to lock me out of the house."

"You have a key."

"Technically, Ben has your key, but either way, your mom doesn't know that."

He leaned closer and whispered in her ear. "We should probably keep it that way."

"Good idea."

* * *

Kari opened the box of medical supplies and read through the instructions. Ryan had left early that morning for the airport, and she had arrived in time to say good-bye and see him off, along with her brother.

With Susan watching, Kari followed her typical logic and lined up the supplies she would need on the table, beginning with the baseball-sized plastic bag full of liquid antibiotics.

"I hear you're studying to be a doctor," Susan said, breaking the silence.

Kari heard the derision in the words but didn't understand the cause. She glanced at Susan and nodded. "That's right."

She pointed at the medicine ball in Kari's hand. "You aren't doing that right. You have to flush the PICC line out with saline first."

"Yes, that's what it says here." Kari set the medicine down and opened the box of saline syringes.

"Do you know how to use one of those?"

"Actually, I do," Kari said, careful to keep her voice calm and neutral. The last thing she needed was to be at odds with the woman she had been charged with caring for.

"Doctors always think they know how to do everything."

"You're probably right," Kari said. "The truth is, most of what I know about medicine isn't from college. I learned how to flush a PICC line when my best friend was going through chemo."

Susan's eyebrows lifted. She didn't say anything for a moment, and when she finally did speak, she was sympathetic. "You're awfully young to have friends with cancer."

"I agree." Kari selected the syringe and gently took Susan's arm, resting it on the edge of the chair before working with the tube to insert the syringe. "Seeing Maya go through so many treatments at only twenty years old inspired me to pursue medicine."

Susan fell silent, watching closely as Kari completed the flushing process and hooked up the antibiotic treatment.

Once Kari finished her task, she set the medicine on the table, making sure it didn't pull at Susan's arm. "May I be frank, Miss Susan?"

"Please."

"I imagine a lot of doctors don't give nurses and nurses' aides the respect they deserve, but I'm not like that. I think I can learn a lot from you, and I really hope while I'm staying here that you will be willing to share some of your experiences with me."

Susan's eyes met hers. "How did you know I worked as a nurses' aide?"

"Ryan told me," Kari said, settling back in her chair. "He's very proud of you."

"He is?"

"Of course. You can hear it in his voice every time he talks about you."

"I wouldn't think he would have time to talk about me much with this busy life of his."

"Ryan told me about you on our very first date," Kari said, sensing an insecurity in Susan she hadn't previously noticed. "He talked about how you raised him alone and how you were smarter than most of the nurses you worked with."

"I don't know about that. I never got any of the advanced training they all have."

"That doesn't mean you weren't capable of it." Kari shifted in her chair. "Would you like me to turn on the television?"

"I think I'll read a bit."

"In that case, I'll be right back. I'm going to go get my study materials." Kari went into the living room, where she had left her backpack, and returned a moment later with one of her MCAT prep books.

Susan looked at the book and then at Kari. "If reading that book is how you spend your free time, we may have to plan a movie night, or you're going to be cross-eyed by the end of the week."

"Or we could do a movie day so we can watch Ryan play at night," Kari suggested.

"That would work too."

Chapter 26

RYAN SAT ALONE IN THE hotel restaurant, his phone in his hand. The Internet search of medical schools displayed on the screen didn't inspire much hope.

The likelihood of Kari getting into one of the local schools wasn't impossible, but the competition in all of them was fierce. What would he do if her best prospects ended up being across the country? And then there was residency—four years of it. He couldn't imagine the toll it would all take on her. And he thought his schedule was challenging.

He thought of his baseball contract and wondered if his agent would be able to make some changes to help him follow Kari to wherever she ended up in med school. It might not be the best situation for his career in the long run, but if he could be with her, it would be worth it.

"Hey, Ryan. Mind if I join you?" Ben asked.

"Grab a seat." Ryan motioned to the chair across from him.

Ben flagged down a waitress and put in his order. "Have you seen Monroe yet this morning?"

"No. Why?"

"Gavin and Shawn insisted on helping him with a haircut last night after the game. I have to say, blond hair and mullets don't always go great together."

"I'm just glad the practical jokes aren't aimed at us for now," Ryan said. "If we get lucky, the pennant race will slow them down for a while."

"That's what happened last year." Ben motioned to Ryan's phone. "What were you looking at?"

"Medical schools."

"Planning a career change?"

He rolled his eyes. "I'm not looking for me. I'm looking for Kari."

"How did you get roped into helping her? She hasn't even figured out where she's going to finish her bachelor's degree."

"I was curious what possibilities were in the area." He saw the speculation on Ben's face. "I know I've asked you this before, but you never really gave me an answer. How long did you and Maya date before you got married?"

Ben let out a short bark of laughter. "We didn't."

"Excuse me?"

"My first official date with Maya was to Liam and Rachelle's wedding."

"But I thought you got married before Liam."

"That's right." Ben let out a sigh and leaned forward. "Kari let Maya move into my apartment so she could get the cancer treatments she needed. I didn't know anything about it until I decided to move back from LA during the off season."

"Kari just handed over your keys to her?"

"And by doing so saved her life and gave me everything that is important in mine."

"I still don't understand how you got married without dating her."

"She was living in my place. I planned to live there too, but I wasn't about to live with a woman I wasn't married to."

"So you married her?" Ryan asked, stunned at this new revelation.

"So I married her," Ben repeated. "Looking back, I can say it's the best decision I ever made."

"Wow. That's quite a story."

"Yeah." Ben glanced around the room. "And I would appreciate it if you keep it to yourself. Not everyone would understand my decision."

The waitress arrived with Ben's food, and he picked up his fork, then glanced over at Ryan. "You and my sister seem to be getting pretty tight. I hardly ever see her any more unless you're standing next to her."

"Yeah. We've been hanging out a lot."

When Ryan didn't expound on his answer, Ben straightened in his seat and adopted the older brother posture he had probably spent years mastering. "Since my father isn't here to ask the question, I guess it falls to me. What exactly are your intentions toward my sister?"

"I'm in love with her."

Ben's jaw dropped. Clearly he hadn't expected such a direct response. "Does she know how you feel?"

"Not yet."

"Why not?"

"I don't want to scare her off," Ryan admitted. "We've only been dating two months."

"And?"

"And what? I was with Brandi for almost two years before we got engaged, and you saw how that turned out."

"It's not about how long you're together before you make the commitment," Ben said. "It's about making the commitment to the right woman."

Ryan studied his friend for a moment before he asked, "So you're saying you would be okay with it if I marched out and bought her a ring today?"

"Whether you're ready to buy her a ring is up to you. What I'm telling you is that if you're anything less than a gentleman with Kari, I'll break you into tiny pieces, pennant race or not."

Ryan's lips twitched into the beginnings of a smile. "Understood."

Ben pulled out his cell phone and sent a text. A moment later, Ryan's screen lit up, indicating he had received something.

"Why are you sending me a text when you're sitting at the same table as me?" Ryan asked.

"I forwarded you my dad's phone number." Ben picked up his fork again. "Just in case you decide to go ring shopping sooner than later."

Ryan opened the text and added the contact to his phone. He looked up at his teammate and said simply, "Thanks."

* * *

Kari stood in Ryan's kitchen stirring the curry chicken Maya had brought over.

"How is everything going?" Maya asked, sitting on one of the bar stools across from her.

"Not too bad. I finally figured out how to block Austin's number, so it's been nice and peaceful lately."

"Was he still texting you?"

"And calling," Kari said. "It was only happening about once a week, but with the craziness of helping Susan, I couldn't deal with him bugging me any longer. I swear all I've done this week is take Susan to doctor appointments. It's no wonder she still needs to nap in the afternoons."

"How are the two of you getting along?"

"Okay, I think." Kari shrugged her shoulders, not quite sure what to think of Ryan's mother. She didn't seem quite as determined to dislike her as she was before Ryan left on his trip, but she didn't appear to be quite ready to welcome her into her inner circle of friends either.

"At least she hasn't fired you," Maya said.

"True." Kari put the lid on the pan and turned down the burner. "Thanks for making this for us. It's so much easier to heat things up than to have to start from scratch. Ryan's kitchen isn't terribly well stocked, and the only time I've been able to go grocery shopping was while Susan was at her physical therapy appointment yesterday."

"It's not a problem. You know how much I love to cook, and it's been so nice to have the energy to be able to do it again."

"When are your next scans?"

"This Friday. I meet with the doctor next Tuesday. Any chance you would be willing to come with me? I'd rather not be alone when I get the scan results."

"Are you kidding? I'd love to," Kari said, not able to count how many times she and Maya had traveled this journey together. At least this time, they were optimistic the results would be in her favor.

"Will Susan be okay without you? We probably won't get back until after the guys leave for their game."

"I'll double check with her, but she's actually been doing great. She's already graduated to a cane, and her physical therapist said she might be able to go home as early as next month."

"That's great." Maya laid her hand on the counter. "I almost forgot to tell you. Lauren is coming to visit this weekend."

"What for?" Kari asked. Their college friend had been a constant part of their social circle during their freshman year. Maya had no way of knowing that Lauren was also good friends with Austin.

"She's been interning in New York and decided to come down to see us and check out the new house."

"Is she staying with you?"

"Yeah." Maya looked at her suspiciously. "Is there a problem between you two that I should know about?"

"No, nothing like that. I just haven't really seen her since Austin and I broke up," Kari said. "She was one of the people who was trying to convince me to give him another chance."

"If it's going to be awkward for you, I can have her stay somewhere else."

"It's fine. Really," Kari insisted. "Austin's old girlfriend did me a favor by showing me who he really is. Besides, if it hadn't been for him, I wouldn't have come here to stay for the summer, and I wouldn't have met Ryan."

Maya wiggled her eyebrows. "You really like him."

"Yeah, I really do. It's going to be weird, though, when I go back to school again and his season ends. It seems like our schedules are always going to be opposite of each other."

"Yeah, especially when you factor in the demands of medical school," Maya said, concerned. "Ten more years of school is a long time."

"I know." Kari's heart sank a little at the thought. When she had first decided to pursue medicine, the sacrifices required hadn't seemed like they would be a big deal. Now that she had Ryan in her life, she wondered what she was going to have to give up to pursue that dream.

Maya put her hand on Kari's arm. "Just remember. One step and one semester at a time."

"Right. One semester at a time."

Chapter 27

THIS WAS MADNESS. CRAZY. INSANE. That thought had circled through his mind over and over again, but it hadn't kept him from visiting three jewelry stores in the past two days, nor had it prevented him from repeatedly imagining possible conversations with Kari's father.

Technically, he had already met Kari's parents. The whole team had. Their attendance at several games the previous season had put most of Ben's close teammates on a first-name basis with Steve and Jane Evans. Somehow, it didn't seem appropriate to use Steve's first name now.

Ryan scrolled through his contacts, looking at the three names under Evans. He didn't know if it was logic or cowardice that caused him to hit the call button on Kari's name rather than her father's. He settled on common sense. After all, it was only logical to make sure Kari shared his feelings before he approached her father to ask for her hand in marriage.

The sound of her voice instantly lifted his spirits. "Good morning."

"Hey, what are you up to today?" Ryan asked.

"I'm taking your mom to a doctor's appointment in Woodbridge. Then we're going to meet Jenny for lunch."

"How is Mom doing?"

"Really well. She's not sleeping nearly as much, and she's getting around a lot better." Kari lowered her voice. "I think she annoyed the occupational therapist, though, when they were debating whether she needed to keep using a shower chair."

Ryan winced. "I think that was more information than I needed."

Her laughter rang out. "I didn't want you to feel like you were missing anything."

"I'm starting to think I'm never going to be able to repay you for all your help."

"I've already told you I don't mind helping. Besides, it has forced me to spend more time studying for my MCAT."

"How is that going?"

"Not so great," Kari admitted. "Every time I think I have something down, I go to quiz myself on it and I feel like I've never seen the information before."

"You'll get it."

"Maybe." Her sigh carried over the phone. "I did great when I was reviewing the stuff on medical testing and radiology, but I already know a lot about that because of Maya," she said. "Enough about me. How are you doing? I saw you had fun with Dobkin's slider last night."

He smiled. "Yeah, that was a good at bat."

"A good at bat?" she repeated. "I wasn't sure that ball was ever going to come down."

"Did you see the guy who ended up with it?" Ryan asked, excited.

"It was some guy in uniform, right?"

"Yeah. He had just gotten home from a tour overseas for the Marine Corps. The PR guys set it up for me to meet him afterward. It wasn't until then that I found out he had lost his leg when his vehicle hit a land mine. He wanted me to sign the ball to the kid of one of his buddies who didn't make it."

"That had to be a really memorable moment. I'm sure it meant a lot to them both."

"I may have signed a little more than just a ball."

Her amusement carried over the line. "Let me guess. A jersey, a bat, and a poster or two."

"Something like that," Ryan said, appreciating that Kari already knew him so well.

"What did you do for the guy who caught the ball?"

"Actually, he's going to be in Washington in the next week or two to visit the Pentagon, so the team is getting him tickets and VIP passes for one of our games."

"I hope I get to meet him. He sounds like a good guy."

"Yeah. It helps keep things in perspective when you meet these guys who sacrifice so much."

"It does," Kari agreed. "Hey, I'm sorry, but I've got to go. I need to help your mom get ready."

"Give her my love."

"I will." Kari hung up, and warmth filled him. He wondered if she had any idea that over the past two months, she had completely captured his heart.

* * *

Ryan walked into his house at seven o'clock Monday morning to find Kari standing at the stove and his mother sitting at the kitchen table in a fuzzy purple robe, a cane propped beside her. The welcoming scent of bacon, eggs, and toast beckoned to him despite his fatigue. Two rain delays had caused his game to go into the early morning hours, and he hadn't slept except in snatches on the flight home.

His mother was the first to greet him. "Good morning."

"Hey," Ryan managed to respond, bleary-eyed.

"I think he was hoping you would say 'good night.'" Kari lifted a spatula and scooped scrambled eggs out of a pan and onto a plate. "Ryan, do you want something to eat? I made plenty."

"Yeah, that would be great. Thanks." He left his suitcase in the entryway and dropped into the seat beside his mother. An instant later, Kari set a plate in front of him and another in front of his mom. "This smells great."

"I hope it tastes that way." She squeezed his shoulder. "Welcome home."

"Thanks."

Kari poured everyone drinks before she went back to the stove to fix a plate for herself.

Ryan took a bite, rolling his eyes with pure pleasure. "These eggs are amazing."

"She puts cream cheese in them," Susan said. Her tone didn't hold accusation but rather something akin to wonder. "Have you ever heard of such a thing?"

Ryan's only response was to take another bite. He finished half the food on his plate before he thought to ask, "How are you all doing?"

"I see the doctor today," his mother said. "If all goes well, I should be able to start working on stairs."

"Mom, that's great."

"Yeah. And I only have another week of antibiotics. Before you know it, I'll have my life back."

"I'm glad to hear you're improving." Ryan finished his food and went into the kitchen looking for more. He lifted the pan of eggs. "Is anyone going to want more of these?"

"I'm done," his mother said.

"Me too." Kari stood and gathered her dish as well as his mom's. "Go ahead and finish those off."

"Thanks." Ryan dumped the rest on his plate and sat back down.

Kari set about cleaning the kitchen while Ryan visited with his mother. He was trying to think of a way to steal a minute alone with Kari when his mother looked at her watch.

"Kari, we'd better get going." Susan used her cane to stand.

Ryan stood as well, hovering until he was sure she was steady on her feet.

Kari picked up her purse from the counter. "Ryan, is it okay if we use your car? It's easier for your mom to get in and out of than mine. We should only be gone for a couple hours."

"That's fine. I'm going to spend my morning sleeping."

Kari started to step toward him and stopped herself. He read her original intention and saw the blush rise to her cheeks when she realized she had nearly kissed him good-bye in front of his mother.

Not willing to let her escape so easily, he closed the distance between them. He knew his mother was watching them when he leaned down and kissed Kari. When he pulled back, Kari stared at him in disbelief.

Ryan glanced over at his mother and saw the speculation on her face, certain that she understood the meaning of the gesture. Kari might not know that Ryan hadn't ever kissed another woman in front of his mother, but his mom was most certainly aware of that fact.

Pleased with himself and with life in general, he started toward the stairs. "See you later," he called out. By the time he heard the garage door open, he already had his shoes off and was sprawled out on his bed.

* * *

Kari held the door for Susan as she hobbled into the waiting room at her doctor's office. She had to admit, she was impressed at how much Ryan's mom had improved over the past week.

Kari let Susan move at her own pace, and she waited patiently for the older woman to make her way to the receptionist to check in.

As soon as they were seated, Kari said, "While we're down here, is there anything you want me to get for you from your apartment?"

"I already had Jenny pick up a few things for me," Susan said. "I was halfway through a novel before the accident. I'm dying to find out what happens."

Kari chuckled. "That would be frustrating."

"I know. It's been so long, I think I may have to start the whole thing over."

The door beside the receptionist opened, and a woman in her thirties poked her head out. "Ms. Strobel."

Kari stood up and waited for Susan to stand. "I'll wait here for you."

"You can come back if you want," Susan said. "If you're going to be a doctor, you might as well learn all you can now."

"Are you sure?" Kari asked, taken aback by the offer.

Susan nodded and slowly started toward the examination rooms. The nurse went through the basic routine of checking weight, pulse, and blood pressure.

Once they were left alone to wait for the doctor, the minutes stretched out.

"When you're a doctor, I hope you organize your time better than this," Susan said. "It always seems like you never get seen until a half hour after your actual appointment time."

"I've noticed that too," Kari said. "Although you would understand what's going on behind the scenes a lot better than I would."

A knock sounded at the door, and Dr. Michaels entered. "Sorry for the wait." He moved to a computer on a desk and pressed several keys. "Let's take a look at your last X-ray."

Kari edged forward so she could see the screen where Susan's knee joint was displayed. She pointed to the top of the joint. "Is that where the artificial joint meets bone?"

"It is." Dr. Michaels explained the image to both of them.

Kari listened to the doctor discuss Susan's progress as he probed and prodded her knee.

"How much longer until I can move back home?" Susan asked as soon as he was done with his examination.

"It's still going to be a few weeks. My best guess is that by early to mid-August, you should be strong enough to handle the stairs," he said. "We'll have you finish out the antibiotic regimen we have you on, and once that is completed, we can take that PICC line out."

"I'm ready for that to happen," she said. "Now, I do have one more question for you."

"What's that?"

"Do you think it's necessary for me to have someone with me all the time?" Susan asked.

Dr. Michaels looked from Susan to Kari and back again. "As long as you are comfortable using your cane and you can avoid stairs, I think you should be fine on your own."

"Thank you, Doctor."

"You're welcome." He scribbled something on her chart and reached for the door. "I'll want to see you back in two weeks."

As soon as he left, Susan turned to Kari. "You heard him, right? I don't need a babysitter anymore."

"Miss Susan, I don't think you ever did," Kari said, choosing her words carefully. "But I appreciate you teaching me so much over the past few weeks."

"Well, it was nice to have some company when Ryan was gone," she said. "And you do make pretty good scrambled eggs."

"Why, thank you." Kari waited until they were in the car before she asked, "Where were you supposed to meet Jenny for lunch?"

Susan shifted to look at her. "Weren't you coming too?"

"I thought you might want some time alone with your friend."

"What would you do?"

"I don't know. Probably go grab a sandwich and study."

"Young lady, you need to spend a little time enjoying life." Susan gave a definite nod. "Do you like Mexican food?"

Recognizing the question as an offer of friendship, Kari nodded. "I do like Mexican food."

"Good. Then you're eating with us." She pointed at the upcoming intersection. "Take a right at the light."

"Yes, ma'am."

Chapter 28

RYAN COULDN'T BELIEVE IT. HE had spent the past week and a half looking forward to seeing Kari, and now that he had a night off, she wasn't anywhere to be found. He had texted her three times already, hoping he could take her out, but so far, he hadn't gotten any response, and his knock on Ben's door had gone unanswered. Where was she?

"You know, if you keep pacing that way, you're going to wear a path in the carpet."

Ryan turned to see his mother standing behind him, her cane in her hand.

"Hi, Mom. I thought you were still in your room."

She slowly made her way to the living room and gingerly lowered herself onto the couch. "Do you want to talk about it?"

"There's nothing to talk about. I was just trying to get hold of Kari, and she hasn't been answering my texts."

"Probably because her phone died today when we were using the GPS on it."

"What?"

"I got turned around on our way back from lunch. I know her battery was almost spent by the time we got home."

"Any idea where she went after you got back?" Ryan asked. "I haven't seen her since this morning."

"She said something about helping Maya, but I'm not sure what it was."

Ryan considered the new information and opened his phone again, this time sending a text to Maya. *Can you ask Kari to call me? I think her phone is dead.*

"You know, I don't remember ever seeing you like this over a girl before," Susan said as Ryan paced across the room again.

"It's just that I don't get many nights off during the season. I wanted to take her out."

"I don't think she'll care if you go out or stay in. I like that about her."

Ryan turned to face his mother. Sitting on the couch opposite her, he said, "I thought you didn't like her."

"I didn't know her." Susan readjusted herself on the couch, and Ryan was surprised to see her look of apology. "I know I was difficult when I was in the hospital and when I first got here. I wasn't myself, and I was worried about you getting into a serious relationship so soon after breaking up with Brandi."

"How did you know things were getting serious between me and Kari?"

"Mother's intuition. You're different with her." She waved a hand through the air. "What I think doesn't matter though. It's how you feel about her that counts."

"I love being with her."

"I already figured that much," she said dryly. "Can you picture a future with her?"

"I don't know. It's weird." Ryan raked his fingers through his hair. "One minute I can imagine having days like today when I get home and she's here waiting for me. Then I remember what she wants in life, and I wonder if we can make a future together."

"Medical school is demanding."

"Yeah. It's like her dreams and mine are completely incompatible."

"What do you mean?"

"I work summers. For now, she's off summers. I'm locked into a contract for the next four years. She would be looking at switching schools in two and starting her residency in six." Ryan leaned back on the couch. "And from what I've read, med students usually don't do their residency all in one place. It's hard to fathom how we can find time together when she's going through that."

"Have you talked to her about her plans?"

Overwhelmed, he nodded. "A little bit, but there's not much we can talk about until after she takes her MCAT and has an idea of where she will go to med school. Those decisions are at least a year away."

"You've never been one to make it easy on yourself."

"Isn't that the truth."

Susan fell silent for a moment before speaking again. "She's nothing like Brandi."

"I know." Ryan pushed himself forward and rested his elbows on his knees. "That's just the thing. Brandi was so focused on what she wanted in life, we never would have been happy together. With Kari, I'm afraid if I tell her how I feel, she'll let my dreams take over hers."

"You're in love with her."

"Yeah." His heart squeezed in his chest. "Is love supposed to be this difficult?"

"I don't exactly have the best track record in that area, but from what I've seen, anything worth having is worth working for. Sometimes that involves sacrifices."

"I guess it's not all fairy tales in the end, is it?"

"No, but that doesn't mean the effort isn't worth it."

His phone rang, and he looked down to see Kari's number.

Susan pushed herself up to a stand. "Take your call. I'll see you in the morning."

"Thanks, Mom."

* * *

Kari passed a box of books to Ryan and gave him an apologetic look. When she'd called him earlier, she had explained that she needed to stay home to help Maya finish unpacking before their friend arrived tomorrow. She hadn't expected him to volunteer to join the effort. "You know, you really don't have to do this."

"I don't mind."

"I'm sure there are other things you would rather be doing with your night off."

He carried the box across the room and set it beside a bookshelf. Then he turned to face her. "The only thing I had in mind was spending time with you. I'm doing that."

"But still." She knelt beside him and started shifting books from the box onto the shelf.

Ryan put his hand on her shoulder and waited for her to look up at him. She saw something in his eyes she wasn't accustomed to, an intensity that wasn't characteristic for him. He took a moment before he said, "Ben and Maya moved into their house the same day I did. I've been completely unpacked for two weeks. It doesn't take a genius to figure out that my house is all done because you've been helping me instead of your brother."

"I didn't do that much," Kari said. "Besides, most of your furniture came with the house. Maya and Ben didn't get their last furniture delivery until yesterday."

"Why did it take so long?"

"They didn't want the store in Phoenix to ship anything until after they closed on the house, and Ben asked them to delay it another week so he would be in town when it got here."

"That makes sense, but it doesn't change the fact that my house already feels like home because you spent the time to make it that way."

Kari smiled. As compliments went, it was a good one. "I had fun helping. You really picked a great house."

"Seems to me that we picked it together."

"Hey, Ryan. Where are you?" Ben said from the hallway.

"In here," Ryan called.

Ben poked his head into the living room. "Can I get you to help me set up the bed in the guest room? It's a two-person job."

"Sure." Ryan stood and followed Ben upstairs.

Kari watched him go and tried not to resent that Lauren's impending arrival had put a damper on her ability to spend more time with Ryan tonight. She shook that thought away. Ryan was right. Had she been helping Ben and Maya instead of staying at his house with Susan, Maya would have finished unpacking long before now.

Turning back to her task, she considered what the doctor had said today at Susan's appointment. If Ryan's mother didn't need someone with her all the time, that meant she would be free to go to Ryan's game tomorrow night. She finished shelving the books and went in search of Maya to receive her next task.

Kari entered the kitchen to find Maya rinsing serving dishes. "The books are put away," Kari said. "What else do you need done?"

"You're taller than me. Can you put these in the top of that cabinet?"

"Sure." Kari grabbed a dish towel and started drying the clean dishes, then proceeded to put them away. "Were you planning to go to Ben's game tomorrow?"

"Yeah. I thought since you've been staying with Ryan's mom, I could let Lauren use our extra ticket."

Kari's heart dropped. "Oh."

Maya turned to face her. "What?"

"I was thinking about going to the game. Miss Susan's doctor said she didn't need to have someone with her all the time."

"I'm sure we can figure something out. Maybe Ryan has a ticket you can have."

"I don't know . . ."

"Did I hear my name?" Ryan asked, walking across the family room toward them.

"Yeah," Maya answered. "I was just saying you might have an extra ticket for tomorrow night's game for Kari. I told our friend that's coming to visit that she could use one of ours."

"I can make sure we have one for you," Ryan told Kari. "Did you want to drive over to the game with me or hang out with your friend tomorrow?"

"I'd love to go in with you," Kari said with complete honesty, "but I should probably spend some time with Lauren while she's here."

"In that case, why don't you drive in with Maya, and I can bring you home," Ryan suggested. "That way we can spend some time together."

"What do you think, Maya?" Kari asked. "Will that work?"

"Sounds great. Ryan, would you mind giving Ben a ride tomorrow so we don't have to take two cars?"

"No problem," he said. "What else do you need help with?"

"Are the beds set up in the guest rooms?" Maya asked.

"All the furniture is in place, and Ben is putting sheets on the beds," Ryan told her. "I already took the boxes out to the curb with the trash."

"I think I'm ready to call it a night. Thanks so much for your help."

"You're welcome." As soon as Kari finished putting the last dish away, he added, "Kari, can I get you to walk me out?"

"Sure." She turned to Maya. "I'll be right back."

* * *

Ryan took Kari's hand and led her onto her brother's front porch. All day he had been looking for a moment to be alone with her, and he had finally realized it wasn't going to happen unless he forced the issue.

She pulled the door closed behind her. "Are you sure it won't be a problem to get me a ticket for the game tomorrow? I can always try to buy one myself."

"It's not a problem, Kari," he said, once again struck by how different she was from the other women he had dated. "I'm happy to get a ticket for you. I've missed having you at my games."

Her expression warmed. "I've missed being there."

"Besides, if you buy a ticket, you wouldn't be able to get one in the friends' box. I'm sure you'll want to be able to sit with Maya and your friend."

"That would be the ideal, but mostly I want to be able to see you play."

He moved closer and lowered his lips to hers, his stomach jumping into his throat as it had the first time he had kissed her. A cricket chirped in the background, and the heat of the night enveloped them. Sliding his hands to her back, he drew her closer and deepened the kiss.

When he drew back, Kari looked up at him and said, "I missed you."

"I missed you." He wanted to give her more words, words he ached to share, words he prayed would be returned. Instead, he asked, "Have you decided where you're going to school this fall?"

"I put in my application for George Mason yesterday."

"You're staying in Virginia?"

"That's my plan," she said. A touch of insecurity crept into her voice. "Is that okay with you?"

"It's more than okay with me." Though he wanted to ask what would happen after she finished college, he swallowed the question. Instead, he lowered his lips to hers once more and let himself enjoy the moment.

Chapter 29

KARI HEARD THE DOORBELL RING and tried to drum up some enthusiasm about Lauren's visit. She had spent the past several hours helping Maya finish cleaning the house to get ready for Lauren's arrival, which hadn't left them much time to spend with the guys.

She reminded herself that Lauren had been a good friend her freshman year. When Kari walked down the stairs, she discovered Maya had beaten her to the door. Lauren rushed in and gave Maya a hug.

"Oh, it's so good to see you!" She turned to Kari. "And, Kari, how are you?"

Before Kari could answer, she was trapped in a hard embrace. How the shorter girl could have such strength in her slender arms was beyond her. Recognizing Lauren's "how are you" question as just a greeting, Kari said, "Lauren, you look fabulous. New York must be agreeing with you."

"Thanks." She brushed her light-brown hair over her shoulder. "My internship has been so much fun, and, of course, there's nothing like the night-life in the city."

Maya pulled the door closed. "Let me show you to your room, and then we can all catch up over lunch."

"Sounds good." Before she followed Maya toward the stairs, Lauren added, "Oh, I almost forgot. Kari, I brought you a present. It's outside."

"You did?"

Lauren waved toward the door. "Go out and you'll see."

Suddenly wary, Kari looked over at Maya, who gave her an I-have-no-idea look. As the other two continued up the stairs, Kari opened the door and walked outside. She closed the door to keep the heat out and only managed to take three steps before she saw Lauren's gift was the one person she didn't want to see.

Slightly taller than her, his dark hair perfectly styled, Austin rushed forward even as she turned to go back inside. "Kari, wait."

She reached for the door, but he anticipated the action and positioned himself between her and the house. With no choice but to face him, Kari spoke with frost in her voice despite the ninety-degree weather. "I can't think of any reason for you to be here."

"I'm sorry to show up like this, but you have to let me explain."

"Explain what? That you were cheating on your fiancée with me?"

"It wasn't like that. Deb and I agreed to see other people while she was gone. We wanted to make sure we really did love each other enough to get married."

"And yet you never mentioned to me that you were in love with someone else."

"That's just it. When I started going out with you, I realized I wasn't in love with her, not really." His brown eyes bore down into hers. "You were the one I wanted to be with."

She folded her arms across her chest and let herself remember the embarrassment and hurt that had cut through her when she'd learned the truth. "I'm afraid it's a little late for that now."

"Kari, please give me another chance. I've been miserable without you."

"Let me get this straight. You deceived me, your father pulled my internship from me, and now, because you're miserable, I should just fall in line and take you back?" She shook her head. "I don't think so."

"I can understand you being mad, but my dad and I didn't have anything to do with your internship falling through. That just happened."

"You know, Austin, it doesn't matter." Kari threw her arms up and let them fall to her side. "I've moved on. I hope you can do the same."

He edged forward. "What if I don't want to move on? What if I want another chance to make this up to you?"

"There is nothing to make up to me," Kari said. "Not anymore."

"I don't understand."

"The truth is I'm involved with someone else. Looking back, I realize I didn't really know you when we were dating, and I know now that we never had a future together."

He stared at her as though trying to determine if she was telling him the truth. "I guess all I can do, then, is wish you the best."

Kari motioned toward the door. "Would you mind letting me into the house now?"

He moved to the side but not enough to let her pass. "There is one more thing I needed to ask you."

She crossed her arms again. "What's that?"

"Since you've obviously moved on, would you call Vanderbilt and drop the grievance? It's caused my father's ethics to be called into question, and I don't want him to suffer because of our misunderstanding."

"I see." Now she did see. He didn't really have any interest in her. He was here for a purpose, and she was the means to an end. Because all she wanted was for this conversation to end, she said, "I'll think about it."

Austin moved aside, and she reached for the door. Before she could open it, his fingers curled around her arm. An edge came into his voice when he said, "Don't think too long."

Before she could respond, he let go and turned to cross the lawn. She watched him for a moment before heading inside, his words playing through her mind. Was it her imagination, or had his last words been a threat?

* * *

Ryan couldn't stop looking into the stands. Where was she? He had caught a glimpse of Maya twenty minutes ago, but Kari had yet to make an appearance in the stands, even though the first pitch was scheduled to be thrown any minute.

Gavin, who was playing shortstop, called his name before throwing a ball to him as the infield continued their warm up. Ryan caught it and sent it to first.

Apparently noticing his lack of concentration, Ben motioned to him, and Ryan jogged over, the two men meeting where Gavin was standing.

"Is everything okay?" Ben asked.

"Yeah, sorry. I just didn't see Kari in the stands."

"Kari?" Gavin asked, turning to Ben. "Your sister?"

"Yeah," Ben answered.

"She's in the press box," Gavin told them.

"What's she doing there?" Ben and Ryan asked in unison.

"Beats me, but I saw Trent from public affairs walking her up there."

"That's odd," Ben said, voicing Ryan's thoughts.

The announcer's voice came on over the loudspeaker to introduce the person who would throw out the ceremonial first pitch. To Ryan's surprise, it was the serviceman who had caught his home-run ball in New York.

"Positions, boys," Gavin said, a subtle reminder that the game was about to start.

Ryan walked the few steps to third base and watched the man he had met a week earlier make his way to the pitcher's mound, a pronounced limp branding his gait due to his artificial leg. A hush fell over the stadium. Then he threw the ball, and the crowd went wild.

The veteran held a hand up in acknowledgment of the overwhelming response and then turned and pointed at Ryan before leaving the field.

Touched by the gesture, Ryan watched him exit. His eyes widened when he saw him reach the press area, and Ryan noticed Kari standing among the television cameras.

The umpire called out "Play ball!" and Ryan tried to push his curiosity aside. Regardless of why she wasn't in her seat, the important thing was that she was here.

* * *

Kari sat in the press box behind Alex Donaldson, the broadcaster she had met her first day in DC. Jaden Sampson, the man who had thrown out the first pitch, took a seat beside Alex. When Jaden glanced at her, she suspected he felt as she did, as though they had stepped into an alternate reality. Again.

Every time she was around Ryan, she wondered if she was dreaming and would wake up to find none of this was real. Every time he kissed her, that feeling intensified.

Now here she was, at the owner's invitation, sitting in one of the press boxes with the man Ryan had spoken of only days before. She still wasn't quite sure why the public relations staff had asked her to escort him during his time at Nats Park, but she rather liked exploring more of the facility.

Jaden wore a headset and sat between the two commentators for the Nationals local television broadcasts. As part of his trip to DC, he had been invited to help announce the first two innings of the game.

In between batters, the announcers guided the conversation to the wounded veteran's story and how he had come to be noticed by the Nationals.

The visit stretched from two innings to three before everyone said good-bye. Following the instructions the director of public relations had given her, Kari escorted Jaden down the hall to the owner's box, matching her pace with his.

"Thanks for staying with me in there," he said.

"It was my pleasure," Kari said. "That was the first time I had ever watched the game from that view."

"Did I do okay?"

"You did great. You were yourself, and you gave people a glimpse into what it's really like for veterans when they come home after battle."

"That was why I agreed to come," he said, lowering his voice. "I'm really a Yankees fan."

Kari chuckled. "Don't worry. I won't tell."

"Thanks. By the way, I think it's really great how you were helping Ryan Strobel with his mom."

"How did you know about that?"

"He told me when we were talking after the game in New York."

"He did?"

"Yeah. That's why I asked if you could be the one to come with me to the interview today."

Kari's eyebrows drew together. "I don't understand."

"I didn't want to get stuck being shown around by someone who was trying to put words in my mouth. After hearing Ryan talk about you, I knew I wouldn't have to worry about that with you."

"Thanks, I think."

They reached the door to the owner's box. He forced a smile. "Do I look happy to be here?"

Kari cocked her head to one side. "Maybe if you tell yourself you're happy to be here, you'll start to believe it."

"Right."

"And try to make your smile look less like a grimace," she whispered.

"Okay." He blew out a breath. "Here it goes."

Kari chuckled and escorted him inside. Within minutes, he appeared at ease with the rest of the group. When she finally left him during the seventh-inning stretch to sit with Maya and Lauren, the truth about his allegiance to the Yankees had come out, and good-natured ribbing had ensued.

Ball girls were throwing rolled-up T-shirts into the stands when Kari jogged down the steps toward her seat. She tugged on her ball cap to cut the glare of the setting sun and reminded herself that she wasn't in her usual spot as she approached. The ticket Ryan had given her put her two rows down and several seats over from where Maya was sitting.

She hoped an empty seat would be available closer to her friends, but unfortunately, the stands were packed for the Friday night game.

Resigned to sitting by herself, she searched for what would surely be the only empty seat in the section. Locating the correct row, she counted seats to where her ticket indicated she was supposed to sit. Instead of finding it empty, she saw a familiar face framed by long red hair. Brandi was back.

A stadium attendant approached Kari. "I'm sorry, miss, but you'll need to take your seat. The inning is starting." When Kari didn't respond, she added, "May I see your ticket?"

Kari was still too stunned by Brandi's presence to protest when the woman took her ticket from her hand. While Kari tried to regain her composure, the woman clearly went through the same exercise Kari just had only to find the seat occupied.

"I don't understand," she said, studying Kari's ticket again. "That's clearly your seat. I can have her move."

"No, it's okay. I'll find somewhere else to sit." Kari headed back up the stairs onto the concourse, her heart pounding uncomfortably. Dozens of thoughts raced through her mind, not the least of which was the way Ryan had held her last night.

Reminding herself that Brandi hadn't been invited the last time she'd shown up, Kari tried to push her insecurities aside. After all, Ryan hadn't mentioned anything about his ex coming today, and if he was really the man she thought he was, the least she could do was give him the benefit of the doubt.

She found an open spot on the concourse where she could see the game. Leaning her arms on the rail, she watched the rest of the game unfold. Shortly after the Nationals scored the first run of the game, several fans migrated onto the concourse, apparently planning to make an early exit to get ahead of the crowds.

Though she was beginning to feel a little claustrophobic with the extra bodies pressing along the rail beside her, she didn't relinquish her spot, determined to watch the game through to its conclusion.

She caught a glimpse of Celeste and Rachelle, two of the other Nationals' wives heading up the stairs toward where she stood.

Knowing that Rachelle was friends with Brandi, Kari tugged her ball cap lower on her head to shield her face from them. They were practically behind her when she heard her name mentioned.

"I'm surprised Kari stopped coming to the games. I really liked her," Celeste said. "And it looked like Ryan was pretty interested."

"Personally, I'm glad Brandi is back," Rachelle countered. "Kari seemed nice enough, but she's too much like Maya. They never want to go do anything. It's like hanging out at home is the best thing life has to offer."

"I don't know. Sometimes it's nice to have some time at home without everyone trying to ask for autographs and get Shawn's attention."

"It's okay sometimes, but I much prefer going out. Now that Brandi and Ryan are back together, I'm sure he'll be around a lot more."

"When did they get back together? I didn't even know he and Kari broke up."

"It just happened today before the game. I guess she ran into him when she went into the front office to say hi to the secretaries and pick up the ticket I left for her."

"I guess she had good timing."

"That's what I said."

Kari blinked against the tears trying to form. Could Ryan's feelings have changed so quickly? Or was he like Austin in trying to date two women at once? Had she simply been someone to spend time with until he decided what he really wanted?

The conversation continued behind Kari, morphing to talk about their travel during their husbands' upcoming road trip. As soon as Celeste and Rachelle moved beyond her, Kari swiped at her eyes and headed for the exit. She wasn't about to go home with Ryan after what she had just heard, and there was no way she wanted to go home with Ben, especially since she would have to face Lauren, the person responsible for letting Austin know how to find her.

Making her way to the main entrance, she headed down Half Street toward the subway station. She was a big girl, she reminded herself, despite her discomfort as she walked through the not-so-great neighborhood surrounding the ballpark. She would find her own way home, and maybe by the time she got there, she would know what to do about picking up the pieces of her broken heart.

Chapter 30

RYAN RUSHED TO THE PARKING lot, grateful he didn't have to hang around for the after-game press conference. In a truly defensive game, the stars of tonight had been their starting pitcher and Lanski, who had hit a solo home run in the eighth inning to win the game.

Eager to find out how Kari had ended up in the press area during the first pitch, he headed for his car, where he had arranged to meet her. He caught a glimpse of long hair falling over the back of one of his jerseys and was pleased to see Kari had opted to wear the one he gave her. He took several more steps before he caught a glint of red in the light and realized it wasn't Kari waiting for him but Brandi.

Instantly, his steps slowed. He looked around, hoping to see Kari nearby, but he didn't see her or anyone else, for that matter. So much for his great idea of beating the crowds out of the clubhouse tonight.

He was debating whether to turn around and go in search of Kari or anyone who could act as a buffer between him and Brandi when her eyes landed on him and she started forward.

"Ryan, I was wondering how long I would have to wait for you."

He stopped walking, but that didn't prevent her from closing the distance between them and putting her arms around his neck. Ryan pulled back, disentangling himself from her. "What are you doing here?"

"I heard you and that Kari girl broke up and I thought I would come see you."

"You heard wrong."

Her perfectly shaped lips pursed in surprise. "Oh. I thought since she stopped coming to your games the past few weeks, she wasn't in the picture anymore."

"Even if that were true, that doesn't change where we stand. We aren't getting back together. I thought I made myself clear on that the last time you showed up."

"We were together for more than two years. I don't know why you would want to throw that away." She put her hand on his arm. "I can't help it. I'm still in love with you."

Not so long ago, Ryan might have been swayed by her words, especially when delivered with such sincerity. Now that he had Kari in his life, he knew what real love felt like. He heard footsteps approaching and lifted his gaze to see Liam and Rachelle heading for their car. Shawn and Celeste followed behind them.

"Hey, Brandi. So good to see the two of you back together again," Rachelle called out.

Ryan opened his mouth to dispute the assumption, but Brandi spoke first. "Thanks, Rachelle. I'll see you at tomorrow's game."

"See you then." Rachelle led her husband toward their car. As Shawn and Celeste walked past, Ryan saw the confusion on Shawn's face as he let himself get dragged along.

Ryan looked down at Brandi, stunned. "Why did you do that?"

"Ryan, we're meant to be together. Isn't it time we make up and put the past behind us?"

"I'm starting to think we can just record this conversation and press replay." He jerked his arm free and stepped back once more. "I don't want to see you again. Period."

He stormed to his car and unlocked the door. He could only hope Kari wouldn't take long to get here. He wanted to get away from Brandi as soon as he possibly could.

* * *

Kari stared out the window of the subway train, not seeing anything beyond the tears that kept welling up in her eyes. She wasn't exactly sure how she was going to get back to Ben's house, but she had used the subway map on the side of the train to figure out her general direction. The first text from Ryan came shortly after she passed from the District of Columbia into Virginia. The second sounded when she reached McLean. She ignored both.

When her phone chimed a third time, she pulled it from her pocket to silence it only to see Maya's name on the screen, asking where she was. A similar message popped up from Ben a moment later. Realizing it wasn't fair to make them worry, she texted Maya.

Left the game early. On my way home now.

The response was instant. *Why?*

I'll explain later. She silenced her phone and tucked it into her pocket. Though she had left the game a few minutes early, the train was still crowded with people, most of them wearing Nationals T-shirts and jerseys. She tried not to notice the letters on the backs. Too many of the jerseys bore the name of the man she was currently trying to forget about.

First Austin, now Ryan. Why did she keep falling for guys who were emotionally involved with someone else? She should have realized Ryan still had feelings for Brandi with the way he had needed her to act as a barrier between them the first night they'd met.

She thought of her plans to transfer to a school in Virginia and wondered if she should reconsider. Why had Ryan bought the house across the street from her brother? She had thought avoiding Austin at Vanderbilt was going to be bad. Avoiding Ryan would be nearly impossible. Or would it?

Kari planned to get her own place before she started classes in the fall, and she didn't have to visit her brother at his house to see him. Besides, Ryan would be gone half the time during baseball season, and with Brandi around, he wasn't likely to spend many evenings at home. She straightened in her seat. She couldn't keep trying to avoid her feelings every time a man hurt her. Maybe if she faced the situation, she could figure out why she kept ending up in the same spot.

The driver announced her stop, and she stood. Several other passengers led the way onto the platform, and she followed the crowd to the main level. Realizing she was at least five or ten miles from Ben's house, she looked around for a sign to tell her where she could find a taxi, but there wasn't one.

She dug her phone out to look up a number for a cab. No service. "Great," she muttered to herself.

Not wanting to appear lost or vulnerable, especially at eleven o'clock at night, she let herself get swept along with the crowd, all the while praying she would miraculously find a cab waiting for her when she got outside.

When she exited, Ryan stood between his car and a sign that said *Kiss and Ride*.

Kari straightened her shoulders. As much as she wanted to avoid a confrontation with him, she realized she needed answers. Why would he have given so much effort to be with her last night only to dump her the next day without even talking to her first? And how dare he make himself so important to her and then just walk away.

Anger and hurt bubbled up inside her as she moved forward. "What are you doing here?"

"Looking for you." Ryan waved at the train pulling away from the station. "I'm glad I guessed which station you would get off at. What in the world were you doing taking the subway? I told you I would bring you home. And you know Ben would have driven you if you didn't want to wait for me."

"After I heard Celeste and Rachelle talking tonight, I figured you wouldn't want to drive me home."

"What do Celeste and Rachelle have to do with anything?"

"I heard them talking about you and Brandi. I know you got back together today."

"What?" His eyes widened, and she saw a flash of apology appear on his face. The look was enough to send her stomach dropping to the ground. She spotted two taxicabs a short distance away and turned toward them.

"Kari, wait." Ryan grabbed her arm to keep her from walking away. "It's not what you think."

"Oh, really? What am I supposed to think?" Kari demanded. "I went to sit in the seat listed on the ticket you gave me and found Brandi sitting there instead. Then everyone's talking about how they're glad you're back together with her, that I'm too boring, and we never go out with them. Obviously, you feel the same way."

"That's not true at all." Ryan lowered his voice. "Brandi ambushed me at my car. When she hugged me, that was all her. I didn't want anything to do with her."

Two subway patrons walked by, their progress stalling when they noticed Ryan. "No way! You're Ryan Strobel!"

Ryan lifted his free hand in a greeting, and Kari suspected he wasn't thrilled to be recognized. "Hey."

"What are you doing here? We were just watching you play."

"Just heading home," Ryan said. He pulled Kari a few steps toward his car and away from his fans. Again he lowered his voice, leaning closer to whisper in her ear. "You're the one I care about. Please let me take you home." When she remained silent, he added, "I want to at least make sure you get home safely."

Though she wanted to refuse out of spite, she realized he wasn't going to leave her alone until he was sure she made it home, and agreeing was her fastest course of action. She huffed out a breath. "Fine."

Ryan led her to his car and opened the door for her. She got in with every intention of remaining silent for the duration of her trip home. Memories tumbled over one another as Ryan climbed in beside her and pulled out onto the street.

The silent treatment only lasted three blocks.

"If you aren't back with Brandi, why was she here?"

"She thought you and I broke up." Ryan navigated his way through an intersection, but instead of continuing down the road, he pulled into the parking lot of a shopping center and parked. He turned off the engine and twisted to face her. "Someone apparently told her that you hadn't been to any of my games for a few weeks, so she assumed we weren't together anymore."

"So she came here again trying to get back together with you?" Some of the knots in her stomach loosened. "You had nothing to do with it?"

"Exactly. I don't know why Celeste and Rachelle believed her story, and I have no idea how she ended up taking your seat in the friends' box."

Her anger defused, Kari forced her eyes to meet his. "I'm sorry, Ryan. When I saw her in my seat, I tried to give you the benefit of the doubt. I planned to talk to you about it after the game, but then I heard Rachelle and Celeste, and I figured you really didn't want to have me around anymore."

"I'm never going to feel that way about you," Ryan insisted. "And I want you to know that Brandi is part of my past. That's it. I'm never getting back together with her." He paused and seemed to gather his courage. "I couldn't ever be with her or with anyone else. I'm in love with you."

Her jaw went lax, and she struggled to respond. "What?"

"I realize we haven't known each other long, and you probably think it's too fast for me to say that to you, but it's true." He put his hand on hers, his eyes darkening with intensity. "I've never felt for anyone what I feel for you."

Myriad emotions rushed through her, indescribable feelings of warmth, shock, belonging, mixed with a tiny seed of doubt. When she didn't respond, Ryan leaned forward and kissed her gently. "I do love you."

"I don't know what to say."

"Say you'll promise not to ever believe anything Brandi says about me again."

She managed to nod. "I promise."

"Good." He started the car once more. "Let's get you home. I'm sure your brother is worried about you."

Kari pulled her phone from her pocket, still reeling from Ryan's words. "I'll text him and let him know you're bringing me home."

Ten minutes later, he pulled in front of Ben's house and walked her to the door. He ran his hands down her arms, his fingers linking with hers. "I know your friend is here, but I'd really like it if you could drive in with me tomorrow." He lowered his lips to hers and kissed her with such tenderness she thought her bones might dissolve into a puddle. "I want to make sure everyone knows we're together, and I don't want anyone to ever come between us again."

She managed to nod her head. "I'll see you in the morning."

Chapter 31

Ryan made it until morning before the nuances of his conversation with Kari started eating at him. He didn't blame her for acting the way she did, but she hadn't been able to give him the security he had so hoped to receive from her. She hadn't told him she loved him too.

Last night had been an emotional roller coaster for both of them. Kari had ping ponged between being his girlfriend and feeling rejected. His emotions had gone through the ringer when Brandi had cornered him and then again when he couldn't find Kari.

His concern that she hadn't met him at his car had erupted into full-blown panic when she hadn't returned his texts and he discovered she wasn't with Ben or Maya either. He couldn't remember another time when he had been so scared, except when he'd learned of his mother's accident. Had his emotions not been so close to the surface, he doubted he would have admitted to them.

He pulled open his refrigerator door and stared at the contents—chicken salad, leftover meatloaf, and a few slices of Steak Diane. He chose the steak and put it in the microwave to heat. His gaze swept over the rest of the tidy kitchen.

A clear glass bowl on the counter held two glossy red apples, three bananas, and a cluster of grapes. He ran a finger along the bowl, realizing it wasn't something he had purchased. The bread box beside it was also new. Other than leaving Kari some cash for groceries while she was taking care of his mom, he hadn't given her any money to buy things for his house.

The home plate housewarming gift she had given him was displayed on a decorative easel in the other corner of his kitchen counter. He let himself read the saying again: *The best things in life happen at home.* He wondered if Kari realized that little by little she had made his house into his home.

He replayed their conversation from last night, reminding himself that he had known Kari for only a couple months. Admittedly, he'd already spent days sorting through his feelings for her, and his declaration had clearly caught her by surprise. Now he ached to know where she stood on their relationship. Did they have a future together? Was it possible that she would someday love him too?

"Good morning."

Ryan looked up to see his mother slowly making her way into the kitchen, her cane now the only outward sign of her accident.

"Hi, Mom. How are you feeling?"

"Hungry." The microwave dinged. "Any chance there's some of that meatloaf left?"

"Yeah. Do you want me to heat it up for you?"

"I can do it." Using her cane, she set about fixing her food while Ryan retrieved his own from the microwave and sat at the table.

"We're quite a pair, aren't we?" Ryan asked. "I'm having steak for breakfast. You're having meatloaf."

"There's nothing wrong with making sure good food doesn't go to waste," she said, joining him a moment later with her plate.

"True."

Susan took a bite of her meatloaf. "Kari's a pretty good cook."

"Yeah, she is." Ryan lifted his glass to take a sip of orange juice.

"Have you decided to marry her yet?"

Ryan choked, more of the orange juice going down his windpipe than into his stomach. His nose burned and his eyes teared up as he struggled to catch his breath.

"Careful there." Susan reached over and slapped him twice on the back. "I figured you'd already been thinking about marriage with what you told me the other night."

Ryan cleared his throat and blinked several times while his body struggled to remember how to breathe air. He took another sip of his juice, this time managing to swallow it as intended. Looking over at his mom, he attempted to put her comment in perspective. The truth was he had looked for rings more than once over the past week. He probably would have bought one if he had found one that suited Kari, but none of them had seemed quite right.

Deciding he could use a dose of reality right now, he confided in his mother. "Last night I told her how I feel."

"And? What did she say?"

"Not much. She was pretty shocked when I told her I love her."

"Don't fool yourself," Susan said. "She might not have gotten used to the idea yet, but she's every bit as in love with you as you are with her."

"How can you tell?" he asked, desperate to believe her words.

"Honey, the sun rises and sets on you as far as that girl is concerned."

Doubt colored his voice. "I thought Brandi felt that way about me too, and it didn't take long to find out how wrong I was."

"Brandi wanted the lifestyle. Kari wants to build a life." She reached into her pocket and pulled out a wadded piece of tissue paper. "I know you might want to get her something fancier, but if you want, you can give her this."

Ryan took the offering and unwrapped the tissue. Inside it lay an intricate silver engagement ring, the square-cut diamond set among four smaller stones, two on each side. "This is beautiful. Where did you get it?"

"It was my great-grandmother's. It's been passed down through the oldest daughters for generations. Since I won't ever have a daughter in the traditional sense, I thought you might want to give it to the woman you intend to marry."

Touched to the core, he turned the ring over in his hand and studied it. It was exactly what he'd been looking for, and Kari would love the sentimentality behind it. "Are you sure?"

"I'm sure."

* * *

Women's voices carried down the hall as Kari headed toward the kitchen. She supposed it said something that she had adjusted to having her breakfast at ten in the morning. Ryan's meals were at weird times because of his crazy schedule, and over the past few weeks, she had adjusted her eating habits to match his.

She smelled the Indian flatbread Maya often made in the mornings, and her mouth watered. The minute Kari entered the kitchen, Maya waved at the built-in warming tray. "I saved you some naan. It's in there."

"Thanks." Kari grabbed a paper towel in lieu of a plate and retrieved a piece. She glanced over at Lauren, who was sitting at the counter. "Did you get some?"

"Yeah. I was just telling Maya she should think about hiring a cook so she'd have more free time."

Kari laughed. "Maya wouldn't want someone else messing up her kitchen." She took a bite and rolled her eyes with pleasure. "This is so good."

"Glad you like it." Maya moved to the sink to start on the dishes.

Kari took the spot next to Lauren and broke off another piece of bread.

"What happened to you yesterday?" Lauren asked. "It's like the minute we got to the game, you disappeared."

"I was helping with a PR thing the team was doing," Kari said. "I didn't know about it until I got there."

Maya turned to face her as she dried a frying pan. "I assume you and Ryan got everything sorted out last night."

"Yeah, we did," Kari said, warmed by the memory of how things had ended between them. "Which reminds me, he wanted me to drive with him to the game today. I hope that's okay with you."

"No problem," Maya said. "I was thinking about going early too so I can show Lauren around and introduce her to some of the guys."

"Who's Ryan?" Lauren asked.

"Kari's boyfriend," Maya answered.

"Boyfriend?" Disbelief and embarrassment illuminated Lauren's face. "You're already dating someone else?"

"Yeah," Kari admitted. "We've been together for a couple months."

"Kari, I am so sorry." She was clearly distressed. "I never would have told Austin how to find you if I had known."

"Wait, what about Austin?" Maya asked.

"He was the 'present' Lauren brought me."

"Austin was here?" Maya set the pan down and looked at her with disbelief. "And you didn't tell me?"

"Things were kind of crazy yesterday," Kari said.

"Tell me more about the boyfriend. Who is he? What does he do? How did you meet?" Lauren said, cutting off Maya so she couldn't press for more information.

"He's one of my brother's friends," she said, feeling oddly protective of her relationship with Ryan.

"Will I get to meet him?" she asked.

"I'm not sure." Kari's cell phone chimed. She looked at it to see a message from her mom. Not revealing the source of the text, she held up her phone. "I'd better get ready to go. I'll see you at the game."

"Okay," Maya said, not letting Lauren question her any further. "We'll talk to you later."

Kari headed upstairs to shower and change. When she got dressed, she deliberately chose one of Ben's jerseys to wear instead of Ryan's. No reason to give Lauren any more clues as to whom she was dating. The last thing she wanted was for her college friends to start flooding her with questions about dating a professional baseball player. She'd already experienced far more attention than she was comfortable with when her friends realized Ben was her brother.

After collecting her purse and ball cap, she headed to Ryan's house. To her surprise, Susan opened the door.

"Hi, Miss Susan. How are you doing?" Kari asked as she walked inside.

"Doing well." She winked. "Give me another week and I might just try to take in a ballgame myself."

"That would be great. I'm sure it's been too long since you've been able to see Ryan play live."

"My thoughts exactly." She led the way to the living room. "Ryan should be out in a minute. He said he needed to make a couple phone calls before he leaves."

"Okay." Kari motioned to Susan's knee. "You know, I was thinking we should ask the doctor at your next appointment how soon you'll be allowed to drive. He probably wouldn't want you to drive all the way from Woodbridge up here, but I could get Maya to come with us and pick up your car if you want so you would have it here."

"I actually talked to the nurse about that very thing a couple days ago."

"And?"

"Do you think Maya is busy next Thursday?"

"Since the guys are heading to Atlanta that day, my guess is her schedule is wide open."

"Excellent."

Ryan walked in, keys in hand. "Oh, good, you're already here. Are you ready to go?"

"I am." Kari stood and spoke to Susan. "See you later."

"Have fun tonight."

"We will. Thanks." Kari followed Ryan into the garage. He had barely closed the door before she felt his hand settle on her shoulder to keep her from continuing forward. An instant later, she was facing him, and his lips were on hers.

His fingers tangled in her hair, and the ball cap she had been holding fell to the ground. Her heartbeat picked up speed, and goose bumps of pleasure danced along her skin. She let herself get lost in the kiss, her world spinning in that moment until everything settled and clicked into place.

"Sorry, but it's been too long since I've done that," he said when he pulled back.

Fighting a grin, Kari leaned down to pick up her hat and glanced at her watch. "Ten hours was too long, huh?"

"Much too long." He kissed her again. "I really do love you."

The warm sweetness of the words washed over her, along with the undeniable truth. "I love you too."

His eyes widened briefly, and his hand squeezed hers. "You aren't just saying that, are you?"

"No." Sincerity filled her voice. "I said it because it's true."

* * *

Ryan sat across the sleek mahogany desk from Trent Farley, the head of the Nationals' public relations department. "Trent, I don't know what to do. I thought the friends' box was restricted to people who had tickets to that section, but yesterday Brandi was in the seat that was supposed to be Kari's. How do I keep her from making a scene if she shows up again?"

"What makes you think she'll be back today?" Trent asked.

Ryan pulled out his phone and pulled up Twitter. "Because this is her post from twenty minutes ago. And I quote, 'Had a blast with Ryan Strobel last night. Heading to the ballpark to see what my boyfriend has in store for tonight.'"

"You said you made it clear that you don't want to see her anymore?" Trent asked.

"Several times." Ryan held his hands out in a helpless gesture. "I think she's using her friendship with some of the other guys' wives to get tickets and to access the restricted areas."

"I can put a stop to that."

A sliver of hope surfaced. "How?"

"I'll put her name on the security list so she can't get through."

"Even if she can't get into the clubhouse, there's no way to keep her from her seat if one of the other guys is giving her a ticket."

"Ryan, whether you want to admit it or not, she's wavering on that thin line between trying to make things work with you and stalking. Since the first is not possible, she's crossed over into the second."

"Brandi's not a stalker."

"If she wasn't, you wouldn't be sitting here right now." Trent motioned to his phone. "Let me ask you this—how often does she try to call or text you?"

"I don't know. We got back together for a couple weeks last December. When I broke things off again, she wouldn't leave me alone, so I blocked her number."

"Has she shown up at your apartment uninvited?"

"A couple times, but the doorman knows not to let her in," Ryan said, starting to see the pattern. "She doesn't know where my new house is."

Trent leaned back in his seat. "What about road trips? Have you seen her at games or at the hotels?"

"Every time we're in Boston. That's not too far from where she's from."

"The team controls the tickets for the friends' box." Trent waved in the general direction of the door. "I'll make sure we have alternative seating for Brandi and a friend in another section. If she shows up in the friends' box, she'll be given replacement tickets."

"You realize that's pretty much guaranteeing she'll make a scene."

"Don't worry. I'll make sure security is discreet. My plan is to invite her to sit in the owner's box."

"The owner's box. Why?"

"She'll feel like she's receiving special treatment," Trent told him. "We'll let her watch the game from there, and then we'll make it clear she isn't welcome in the restricted areas in the future. Our bigger issue will come after these security measures are in place."

"What do you mean?"

"She's obviously very active on social media. You have to assume she's going to lash out online before the night is over."

"What do you suggest I do?"

"I suggest you give me the tools to steal her ammunition before she gets a chance to use it."

"And exactly what kind of tools are we talking about?"

"I know you and Ben are good friends. How much do you know about his engagement?"

"I know the real story," he said, not comfortable sharing his friend's private information.

"Good." He picked up a pen and jotted something down on a notepad. "Ben got married to protect his reputation. I think you should consider a similar play."

"You want me to marry Kari to get rid of Brandi? Isn't that kind of extreme?" Ryan asked. It was one thing to ponder putting a ring on her finger but quite another to have his plans dictated by someone else.

"I was thinking more of making your relationship with Kari public. It doesn't have to include a ring on her finger," Trent said. "You said she's already here at the park. We can take a few pictures of you together, and I have some from yesterday when she was escorting Jaden Sampson around."

"I'll have to talk to Kari about this," Ryan said, not completely comfortable with Trent's plan. "I have to say, I'm not thrilled with turning what I have with her into a media circus."

"I can do subtle," Trent promised. "Trust me."

"Okay, but before you do anything, let's make sure Kari's willing to trust you too."

"Before you talk to her, I have to ask, what is the status of your relationship with her?" When Ryan hesitated, Trent added, "I only ask because I'll use a different approach if she's just a summer romance rather than if she's someone you expect to have around long term."

"I already have the ring," Ryan said. "But it's not on her finger yet."

"Congratulations on finding the right girl," Trent said with satisfaction. "This will make my job much easier."

"You do realize this is classified information, right?"

"My lips are sealed."

Chapter 32

KARI EMERGED FROM THE LADIES' room after changing into a new baseball jersey, one that matched Ryan's uniform. She looked up at Ryan and asked, "Are you sure you want me wearing this today? I put Ben's jersey on specifically so I could stay below the radar."

"I don't think staying below the radar is in the cards today." He guided her through a maze of hallways toward the batting cages. As they walked, he explained how his public relations director wanted to use social media to publicly announce their relationship.

"Ryan, are you sure about this?" Kari asked. "I don't really care if people know we're dating, but you normally don't like to put anything about your private life out there for the public."

"I know, but Trent is right. It's better to take control of the situation before Brandi tries to make either of us look bad in the press." Ryan took her hand in his. "She is going to flip out when she realizes she's being blocked from the team areas."

"I'm surprised the team is going to such extreme measures. She's still friends with lots of the wives," Kari said.

"Yes, but management doesn't want her harassing me, and I don't want her bothering you."

"I can avoid her if I need to."

"Yeah, but you shouldn't have to," Ryan said. "I don't want you to worry about running into her when you come to my games, and I certainly don't want her to keep using the other players' wives to gain access she has no right to have. From what I understand, she won't have any power if we let Trent lay the groundwork for us."

"What kind of groundwork are we talking about?"

"I'm not entirely sure, but he said to have you hang out during batting practice today."

"And what am I supposed to do while I'm hanging out?"

"I don't know. Just be you, I guess."

"Okay." Skepticism filled her voice. She waved with her free hand toward the now-empty batting cage. "I think it's your turn."

Ryan lifted her hand and kissed the back of it in a sweet gesture. "I'll be back in a minute."

She glanced around at the other players and noticed a photographer with a huge lens on his camera, his focus on Ryan. Ben stepped beside her, a bat in his hand.

"What are you doing over here? The club doesn't usually let anyone down here who isn't on the team or holding a press pass."

"It's a long story, and I'm not sure I understand it yet," Kari said. "Something about keeping Ryan's ex from spinning too much negative press."

"I'm clearly out of the loop on this one." Ben slung his arm over her shoulder and motioned with his bat toward Ryan. "You never told me what happened with you two last night."

She looked pointedly at the numerous people milling about. "That's not a conversation I want to have around here."

"Gotcha." They stood there together for a few minutes until Ben moved forward to take a turn. "Stay out of trouble."

"I always stay out of trouble."

Ben laughed. "Right."

* * *

"Okay, I give up. What's going on with you?" Shawn Nills plopped down in the seat beside Ryan as they prepared for their game. "I've been seeing you everywhere with Ben's sister, and then last night you were with Brandi. I have to say, I don't want to be around if Ben decides to break you in half."

Ryan saw the concern on his teammate's face and understood it. Players at odds with one another could undermine the entire atmosphere in the clubhouse. With the way the team had been winning lately, no one wanted anything to upset the balance. Deciding he could have a little fun with Shawn, he said, "I believe when I talked to Ben about dating his sister, the warning was something about how he was going to break me into little pieces if I hurt her." Ryan considered for a minute. "I think if he breaks me in half instead, my recovery time would be a lot shorter."

"This isn't good." Slowly, Shawn shook his head from side to side.

"Don't worry. I'm not going to get caught on Ben's bad side."

"Seriously?" Shawn shot him a look of disbelief. "Everyone saw you with Brandi yesterday, and I know she's here again today. There's no way you're going to be able to go out with her again without Ben knowing."

"Then I guess it's a good thing I'm still going out with Kari."

"You're cheating on Ben's sister?" The horror on Shawn's face was classic. "Are you insane?" he whispered.

"No, smart," Ryan said. "Kari is one of a kind. I've decided to keep her."

"I'm confused."

Deciding to set the record straight, Ryan turned to look at him. "I haven't dated Brandi since last December. She keeps saying we're going out, hoping to make it happen."

"But last night—"

"Last night I got cornered, and you happened to walk by when I was trying to tell Brandi—again—that I'm not interested," Ryan told him. "Apparently Celeste and some of the other wives have kept in touch with her, and she's been misleading them about what's really going on."

Understanding dawned, and Shawn's relief was apparent. "I'll make sure Celeste knows the truth. She was actually pretty disappointed when she thought you and Kari broke up."

"Really?"

"Yeah, she said she enjoyed hanging out with her and Maya at the games in Arizona."

"That's good to hear."

Gavin approached them and looked around the clubhouse before saying quietly, "Hey, Ryan, I just saw Brandi."

"Yeah, I thought she might be here today," Ryan said, keeping his expression neutral.

"I thought you were going out with Ben's sister." Beside him, Shawn tried to smother his laughter with a cough. Gavin leaned forward and continued. "I hate to break it to you, but you're messing with fire on this one. Ben and his sister are tight."

Shawn stood and managed to keep a straight face. "Ben's going to kill him after the game. Do you want to watch?"

"This isn't funny," Gavin said.

"I think it's pretty funny," Ryan said, looking at Shawn. "What do you think?"

"Yeah, I'm enjoying myself." Shawn raised a hand in greeting when Ben approached. "Hey, Ben."

"You two are crazy." Gavin stepped back, shot a look at Ben, shook his head, and said again, "Crazy."

As Gavin moved away, Ben's eyebrows drew together in confusion. "What's with him?"

"He thinks I'm cheating on Kari."

Ben didn't miss a beat. "That wouldn't be good."

"Yeah, that's what they said." Ryan motioned to Shawn and Gavin.

"It's good to know they value your life."

"Nah," Shawn said as he stood. "We just value his batting average."

"At least now I know why they keep me around." Ryan finished buttoning his jersey. "Let's go get this game started."

* * *

"You're dating Ryan Strobel?" Lauren's voice vibrated with disbelief. "Why didn't you tell me that you were dating *that* Ryan?"

Kari looked over at her friend, not sure what to say.

"How did you know Kari was dating Ryan?" Maya said, saving her from coming up with a response.

"It's right here on Instagram." She held up her phone. On it, a photo of Kari with Jaden, the veteran she had met yesterday, was displayed along with the caption *Ryan Strobel's girlfriend, Kari Evans, shows a special guest around Nats Park.* "Is this why you weren't sitting with us yesterday?"

"Yeah," Kari admitted. It was one thing to say she didn't care about her relationship being on social media, but she hadn't expected to face the results so quickly.

"And you're dating Ryan Strobel." Lauren pointed at the field. "The really hot guy right down there."

"I think we've already established that," Kari said dryly. "It's not that big a deal."

"Are you kidding me?" She leaned back in her seat and propped one foot on the seat in front of her. "I feel like an idiot for thinking you would even want to see Austin again, much less date him."

Kari caught a glimpse of movement and saw one of the stadium attendants barring Brandi's entry to their section. She braced for a scene and was amazed when Brandi fell in step with the man as though she were happy about her circumstances.

"What are you looking at?" Maya asked, turning to follow her gaze.

Kari automatically censored her response to avoid giving Lauren any more gossip to spread around. "I just saw the friend who was in my seat yesterday."

"I'm glad the team was able to get you a seat with us today. We missed having you here yesterday."

"I missed it too," Kari admitted, glancing at the security guard and Brandi disappearing onto the upper concourse.

"Here's another one," Lauren said, bringing her attention back to her screen. "That's a cute picture."

Kari's stomach fluttered with unexpected emotions when she saw the photo. The image captured the moment when Ryan had kissed her hand, her gaze focused on him in adoration. "I guess there's no question that we're dating in this one."

Maya leaned forward. "It is a cute picture of you guys."

Kari's phone vibrated, and she looked down at it to see a text message from one of her other college friends. *You and Ryan Strobel? That's awesome. When do I get to meet him?*

"Seriously?" Kari held the phone out to show Maya.

"Let me see that." Maya took Kari's phone from her. She turned it off and gave Kari a satisfied look. "There you go. Problem solved. Now you can enjoy the game."

"I guess that's one way to do it."

Maya dropped Kari's phone into her purse.

"You don't have to hold my phone for me," Kari said, reaching out so Maya would return it.

"If you have it, you'll be too tempted to turn it back on and see what's happening," Maya insisted. "Trust me. This is the only way."

* * *

Ryan didn't know if it was having Kari back in the stands where he could see her or knowing that Trent was keeping Brandi at bay, but he had a good night. Two doubles, a single, and a walk had given him a nearly perfect night on offense and had landed him in the spotlight at the after-game press conference.

He was surprised to see Kari standing inside the clubhouse with Marty and wondered if her presence was courtesy of Trent's kindness or if it was a deliberate move to protect her from any interaction with Brandi.

Regardless, when her name came up during the question-and-answer portion of the press conference, he was caught off guard.

"We saw mention of your relationship with Kari Evans on social media for the first time tonight. How long have you been dating?"

"We've been together a few months."

"Is she any relation to your teammate Ben Evans?"

"They're brother and sister," Ryan confirmed.

The manager stepped in and helped steer the line of questions back to the game. After the press conference ended, Kari approached him.

"Looks like you're stuck with me whether you like it or not," she said.

"I like it," Ryan told her. "Let's get out of here."

They headed for the exit, and Ryan noticed one of the security guards fall in step behind them. "Marty, where are you going?"

"Trent asked me to walk you out to your car. It's just a precaution."

Not sure what to think of the extra security measure, Ryan continued forward. He scanned the area as they approached his car. Thankfully, tonight's journey through the parking lot was without incident.

He waited until they were on their way home before he asked, "I'm afraid to know the answer, but I have to ask: How bad was Brandi's reaction to our relationship going public?"

"Do you want me to check?" Kari reached for her purse.

Ryan glanced over at her, stunned. "You haven't already looked?"

"No." When he didn't respond immediately, she added, "One of my friends texted me when they saw something about me going out with you. Maya suggested turning off my phone so I wouldn't be bothered."

"You're telling me your name has been deliberately leaked all over the Internet, and you weren't watching the reactions at all?"

She looked confused. "I was at your game to watch you, Ryan, not stare at my phone."

A grin broke out on his face. "I really love you."

"That's good to hear," Kari said. "Because whether I was watching it or not, it would be pretty embarrassing to have your team link us together only to have you decide you didn't want to see me anymore."

"I don't know how that could ever happen."

"I may have to hold you to that."

"I don't mind at all."

Chapter 33

Kari watched Lauren get into her car with a last wave good-bye. "Is it bad that I'm glad to see her go?"

Maya giggled. "I thought you were going to string her up by her toenails if she brought up Ryan again."

"Her perfectly painted toenails," Kari added. She offered another wave as Lauren pulled away from the curb. "I never realized how much you must have dealt with when you and Ben got together. What a pain."

"The media only affects you if you let it," Maya told her. "Other than one bad week, we haven't had any real issues. And now that your relationship with Ryan is out in the open, Brandi won't be able to keep lying about things to everyone."

"True."

"Celeste called this morning and told me Brandi is leaving town today. It looks like Trent's plan worked."

"I hope so," Kari said, relieved. "Ryan doesn't need the stress."

"I agree." Maya led the way into the kitchen. "Ben and I are going to head over to the hardware store to look at blinds. Do you want to come?"

"Hmmm. Walking through a hardware store with my brother. I think I'll go with no on that one."

Maya chuckled. "I'll see you later."

"Have fun," Kari said. "And text me if you need rescuing. If you let him anywhere near the power tools, you'll be there all day."

"I know. I found that out the hard way when we were looking for paint."

Kari glanced down at her watch and wondered if Ryan was up and moving yet. He had come over the night before, after his Sunday afternoon game. Hamburgers on the grill, potato salad, and corn on the cob. The late July barbecue had felt so blessedly normal after all the chaos of the past few weeks.

Ryan and Ben had even managed to put Lauren at ease, and by the end of the night, she seemed to finally understand that they were more than the uniform they wore.

Kari wandered into the living room, where her study materials were lying on the coffee table. She knew she should study but couldn't muster the energy for it. Besides, it wasn't often Ryan had a day off. She wanted to spend it with him.

She looked around for her phone so she could text him. After a thorough search of her room, pockets, and purse, she remembered Maya had put it in her purse the night before.

With a shake of her head, she slipped on her sandals and walked outside. She was at the edge of her brother's lawn when a car pulled up beside her. Her eyes narrowed when the driver climbed out and she saw it was Austin.

"What are you doing here?"

"The grievance committee hasn't heard from you yet. I thought I could make things easier and bring the paperwork to you."

"Paperwork?"

"Yeah, you know, the document saying you're dropping your grievance."

Her back straightened. "I never said I was dropping the grievance. I said I would think about it."

"Kari, what's the point of continuing with it? The summer's almost over, and things obviously worked out okay for you." His tone made Kari wonder if he should pursue a law degree rather than medical school. "Why put my dad through this? He didn't do anything wrong."

"If he didn't do anything wrong, then the grievance process will show that," Kari replied. She stepped around the car and started past him.

He moved to block her path. "The accusation alone can affect his career."

A door opened and closed. Kari saw Austin's gaze shift briefly before returning to hers.

"You really aren't going to drop this, are you?" he asked.

"I'm sorry, Austin, but I don't think I can. The truth needs to come out, and I'm as interested as anyone to know what it is."

"I really have missed you," he said, changing tactics.

"Don't go there."

"I can't help it." Before she could evade, he took her by the arms and leaned down to kiss her.

Kari turned her head, and the intended kiss landed on her cheek.

"What are you doing?" she asked.

The question had barely crossed her lips when she heard Ryan's voice behind her, fury vibrating in his words. "Who's he?"

"I'm her fiancé," Austin said, shifting to put his arm firmly around Kari's shoulders. "Who are you?"

"Austin, stop lying." Kari tried to break free of Austin's grip, but he only tightened his hold. "Ryan, it's not what you think. He's nothing to me."

Ryan's eyes hardened. "What I think"—he looked at Kari briefly before focusing solely on Austin—"is that he'd better get his hands off you before I decide to use him as a punching bag for my workout today."

"Look, I don't want any trouble." Reluctantly, Austin dropped his hand, but he didn't drop the pretense. "Kari and I talked about taking a break for the summer, but that doesn't change the fact that she promised to marry me."

The muscle in Ryan's jaw tensed, and now his gaze landed on Kari. "Is this true?"

"No, it's not true. We dated for a few months, and then we broke up because *he* was engaged to someone else."

"Come on, Kari," Austin said smoothly. "Just because I didn't want to get married this summer is no reason to start making up stories. Haven't you led this guy on enough? You're going to be back in school with me in a couple weeks and will have forgotten all about him."

"I'm not going back to Vanderbilt," Kari retorted. "And I'm not going back to you."

She noticed Ryan's hand clench into a fist, and she stepped between the two men. "Ryan, he's not worth it."

"Oh, I don't know," Ryan said, clearly considering. "I think I'd get a lot of satisfaction from breaking his nose."

"And risk injuring your hand?" Kari shook her head. "I don't think so."

Clearly not taking the threat seriously, Austin changed tactics once more. "You know, I saw all sorts of feel-good stories on you two on the Internet this weekend. It would be a shame if they were followed up with the news that the Nationals' third baseman is dating an engaged woman."

"We aren't engaged."

"It's your word against mine," Austin said. "As we were just discussing, the appearance of misconduct can be extremely damaging to someone's reputation."

Anger caused her own fist to curl, and before she could consider the consequences, Kari's fist struck out and connected with Austin's eye.

Stunned, he stumbled back two steps.

Pain jolted through Kari's hand, but she refused to give Austin the satisfaction of knowing she was hurt too.

Ryan moved in and grabbed Austin by the front of his T-shirt to hold him in place. "I think it's time you leave. And I suggest you never come back," Ryan said evenly. "And if I see anything negative about Kari or me anywhere, you will find yourself dealing with my lawyers until you're forty. Do I make myself clear?"

Austin's eyes lit with fear, and he managed a weak nod.

"Good." Ryan released him, but he didn't move back. Instead, he held his ground until Austin retreated to his car and hastily started the engine.

Ryan moved back to give Austin a clear exit and then turned to Kari. "You went out with that loser?"

She tilted her head to one side. "Do I need to mention your ex-fiancée?"

"Point taken." He lifted her hand, her knuckles red and beginning to swell. "Come on. Let's get some ice on this hand."

Kari followed him into his house and sat on one of the kitchen stools while he put ice into a plastic bag. After wrapping it in a thin dish towel, he pressed it gently to her bruising knuckles.

She looked up at him, realizing how similar this situation had been to the one at the ball field when she had believed Brandi's story. "Thanks for not buying into his lies."

"I'll admit, I had a moment when I saw him kiss you." His shoulders lifted. "Then I remembered how everyone made assumptions about me and Brandi. You never would have been so upset about that if you were dating around behind my back."

"I would never date around behind anyone's back," Kari said.

"I know." He leaned across the counter and kissed her. "Just so you know, I would have fought that guy for you."

"Yeah, but there's always a certain satisfaction in knowing that he has to live with the fact that it was a girl who gave him a black eye."

"I can see your point." He lifted the ice pack from her hand, and she winced. "I think I know where I'm taking you today."

"You don't have to take me anywhere. I thought we could hang out here and go swimming or watch a movie."

"Change of plans. We'll pick up your purse on our way."

"On our way where?"

"The ER. Austin may end up with a black eye, but I think you broke your hand."

"Great."

* * *

Ryan led the way into the waiting room of the urgent care closest to his house and wondered if perhaps the ER at the hospital would have been quicker. An entire men's volleyball team dominated one corner, identifiable both by their uniforms and the volleyball one of them carried. An older couple sat beside the reception desk, and a mother with two young children wheeled her youngest back and forth in a stroller while trying to occupy her three-year-old with a coloring book.

Kari approached the reception desk, where a woman in her thirties sat, her demeanor calm despite the crowded lobby. "How long is the wait?"

"About thirty minutes."

Kari looked back, questioning.

"That's not bad," Ryan said and asked the receptionist, "Do you have an X-ray machine here?"

"We do," she said. "Who is the patient?"

"I am." Kari held up her hand. "Possible broken metacarpal."

The receptionist picked up a clipboard and handed it to Kari. "I'll need you to fill this out."

Ryan took it from her and led Kari to an empty seat beside the volleyball team. "I assume you'll need me to write for you."

"Yeah, thanks." She looked at her hand again. "What was I thinking using my right hand?"

"Don't ask me. You're the one who was all worried about me getting injured." Ryan started filling out the information on the form, asking questions as he went. When everything was complete and Kari signed the form with her good hand, he carried it back to the desk.

When he returned to sit beside Kari, she was chatting with the volleyball team. "Who's the patient?" he asked.

A tall lanky man around twenty lifted a hand. "That would be me."

"Let me guess. Twisted ankle."

He shook his head. "Separated shoulder."

"How did you do that?" Kari asked.

"He and a pole had a disagreement. He lost," one of his teammates answered for him.

"Ouch."

"What are you here for?" one of them asked.

Kari lifted her hand. "Punched the ex."

Several sets of eyes shifted to Ryan. He held up his hand and shook his head. "It wasn't me. I'm the good guy here."

The volleyball player's name was called, and Kari continued to chat with the rest of the group. Ryan found himself drawn into the conversation as they joked about the perils of unusual injuries.

Twenty-seven minutes after their arrival, Kari's name was called. "Do you want me to wait for you here?"

"You can come back with me if you want." Kari stood and followed the nurse. They reached the exam room, but after a brief conversation with the nurse, the woman led Kari away for her X-ray.

When she returned, Kari sat in the chair beside Ryan. "I'm really sorry you're stuck with me here today."

"It's been an adventure," he said. "Besides, if I hadn't come, those volleyball players would totally have been hitting on you."

"Oh, I doubt that. They just needed someone to distract them from worrying about their friend."

"You did a good job of it," Ryan said. "How's the hand feeling?"

She looked down at it. "I liked it better before it started turning purple."

"You certainly got that guy's attention though." Ryan shook his head. "How did you meet him?"

"We had some classes together, and we were both studying pre-med. After we broke up, I realized we didn't have as much in common as I thought."

"Lucky for me."

"I'm the lucky one."

The door opened, and the nurse entered holding the X-ray in a manila sleeve. She pulled it free of the protective covering, clipped it onto the display screen, and flipped on the light. "The doctor will be right in."

"Thank you." As soon as the nurse left, Kari stood and crossed to the X-ray. She studied it a moment and turned back to look at Ryan. Her nose wrinkled. "Well, you were right. It's broken."

He stared at the image, unable to identify the problem. A moment later, the doctor walked in and introduced himself.

"Let's see what we have here." He motioned for Kari to sit on the exam table. She did so, careful to use only her good hand to boost herself up. The doctor studied the X-ray for a moment before moving over to probe the injury.

"I'm afraid you have a fracture of one of the metacarpal bones."

"Yeah, I know," Kari said. When the doctor gave her a puzzled look, she said, "I looked at the X-ray before you came in."

"The good news is that we should be able to put it in a splint instead of casting it."

"For how long?"

"You'll need to follow up with your regular doctor, but for an injury like this, you're looking at about eight weeks."

For a minute, Ryan thought Kari was going to try to negotiate her sentence down, but instead she said, "Thank you, Doctor."

"I'll be right back to splint that for you."

"Do you realize you diagnosed yourself faster than the doctor did?" Ryan said as soon as the doctor left.

"Yeah, but I knew where to look. He had to analyze the entire image."

"It was still pretty impressive."

"What would have been impressive is if I could have given Austin a black eye without breaking my hand."

"Next time," Ryan said.

"There isn't going to be a next time. After seeing you, I doubt he'll be coming back."

"I can live with that."

Chapter 34

KARI SAW THE WAY MAYA clasped her hands together, a sure sign of nerves. "Don't worry. It's going to be good news. I can feel it." Maya pressed her lips together, and Kari was surprised to see the depth of emotions evident on her friend's face. She put her hand on Maya's arm. "The doctor said your surgery went well. You did the extra chemo to prevent any new tumors from forming. Why are you so worried?"

"Because every time I've had scans, it's been bad news."

"You're getting good news this time," Kari assured her. "I've decided."

Maya's amusement chased away some of the worry. "Oh, you've decided, have you?"

"Yep." Kari scratched at the edge of her splint.

"I still can't believe you broke your hand," Maya said, clearly attempting to distract herself.

"I don't think Ryan is going to let me live it down."

"What do you mean?"

Kari gave her a wry smile. "I kept Ryan from punching Austin to make sure he didn't injure himself, and then I did exactly what I told him not to do."

Maya chuckled. "Oh, I'm sure he's having fun razzing you about that."

"He is," Kari said. "It wouldn't be so bad if I hadn't just told him I didn't want him to hurt his hands."

The door opened, and once again, Maya gripped her hands together.

"Hello, Maya. How are you doing?" the doctor said.

"You tell me."

"Your scans look great."

Tears of relief filled Maya's eyes. "Really?"

"Really," he assured her. "I can still see a shadow at the base of your skull where the tumor was located, but the PET scan didn't light up at all."

"Does this mean I can start playing tennis again?" Maya asked.

"Absolutely."

"She's been pretty eager to take advantage of the tennis court in her backyard," Kari said and then asked, "Any chance we can see the actual scans?"

"Sure." He pulled the images up on his monitor, discussing each one with Kari. Finally he said, "You must be studying medicine."

"Planning on it," Kari said. "Thanks for showing us these."

"You're welcome." He turned to Maya. "I'll see you back in three months for the next scans."

"Thank you."

Kari and Maya walked out of the office and made it only a few steps before they saw Maya's friend Henry.

"Henry! How are you?" Maya asked. "It's been too long since I've seen you."

"I agree. You shouldn't have moved so far away."

"It's thirty minutes," Maya said. "And if you came to the games, I would see you all the time."

"You know I can't handle the heat. Come September I'll be there all the time."

"I'm going to hold you to that."

"What are you girls up to today?" Henry asked.

"I was meeting with Dr. Schuster."

"Good news, I hope."

"Very good news," Maya confirmed. "In fact, I think we should go out and celebrate. Can you take a lunch break?"

"I might be persuaded." Henry walked with them as they headed toward the main entrance. He motioned to Kari's hand. "What did you do to yourself?"

"She was protecting the Nationals' third baseman," Maya answered for her.

"This I've got to hear."

Kari looked over at Maya. "You know, I think I like your explanation a lot better than mine."

"I thought you might." Maya headed for the door. "Come on. I know this great little Brazilian restaurant you're going to love."

"Lead the way," Kari said.

* * *

"Are you sure you don't want to bring your wheelchair?" Ryan asked his mother as they prepared to leave for his game. "Even if I drop you off close to the entrance, you'll still have to do a lot of walking."

"I'll be fine. In case you have forgotten, I have every intention of being able to pass the stairs test next week so I can move back home."

"I know, but the last thing we want is for you to push it too hard."

"Ryan, even if I agreed to the wheelchair, it would be too hard to use. I wouldn't be able to get myself to my seat, and Kari certainly can't push me with her broken hand."

"I guess you're right."

"Moms are always right," Susan said. "You should know that by now."

"Sorry. I forget sometimes."

"I'm always available to remind you." She headed for the door, and Ryan had to admit she was moving well and no longer had difficulty getting down the step into the garage.

"Kari's riding with us, isn't she?"

"Yes. If she isn't here when we're ready to leave, we'll swing by and get her on our way out." He opened the garage door and noticed Kari crossing the street. "There she is now."

Ryan opened the front door for his mom at the same time she reached for the handle of the back door. "Mom, why don't you sit up front?"

"I can take the back." She climbed in and positioned her cane in the seat beside her.

Kari reached them. "Miss Susan, you can sit in the front."

"I'm fine." Susan closed the back door.

Ryan gave Kari a kiss in greeting. "I guess you're sitting in the front."

"Okay, then." She clutched her purse with her left hand to keep from getting tangled in the strap and took her seat.

"How's the hand?" Susan asked as Ryan took his place behind the wheel.

"It's not as sore as it was the first couple days. I haven't had to take any pain meds today."

"What are you on? I assume the doctor gave you a prescription."

"He offered, but I had him leave it with my chart because I knew I wouldn't fill it anyway. I'm not big on the heavy-duty stuff unless it's really necessary."

"I hear you. It's scary how many people get hooked on them."

Ryan listened to them chat about the challenges in the medical field, appreciating the way his mother now treated Kari. When the women finally took a breath, he asked Kari, "Have you figured out what you're doing for fall semester yet? Classes start in a few weeks."

"I meet with the counselor tomorrow morning," Kari told him. "It will be nice to get that settled so I can finally shift my focus to finding a place to live."

Ryan glanced over at her, his eyes focusing on her hand. "Are you sure you want to get your own place right away? With your hand, it might be nice to wait until you have the splint off."

"I hate to impose on Maya and Ben for that long," Kari said. "They haven't even been married a year. I'm sure it would be nice for them to have some privacy for a change."

"Yeah, but we're traveling half the time anyway," Ryan reminded her. "In fact, we're on the road week after next to New York and Philly. I was hoping you would come with us."

"I don't know . . ." Kari said.

"And don't think I'm letting you pay for your hotel room and airline tickets," he said, recognizing her hesitation likely had to do with the cost of her room.

"Ryan, I already told you I don't feel comfortable having you do that."

"Why not?" Susan asked from the back seat. "He wouldn't offer if he couldn't afford it."

"That doesn't mean I should expect him to spend money on me that way," Kari countered, turning to look back at Susan.

"I think it's great that you don't expect it," Susan said.

"See," Kari said as though she'd won a small victory.

"That's why Ryan is so insistent," Susan continued as though Kari hadn't spoken. "He wants you there. You're doing him the favor by being at his games to cheer him on."

"Exactly," Ryan said.

"I guess if you put it that way . . ."

"I put it that way the last time you came with the team, and it still ended up being Ben who paid for your room," he said.

Now she smiled and looked back at Susan again. "I have to admit, it is kind of nice having guys fighting over me, even if one of them is my brother."

"Last time I tried to fight over you, you ended up with a broken hand," Ryan reminded her.

"True." Her brow wrinkled in concentration. "You're right. No more fighting."

"Agreed," Ryan said firmly.

Kari looked at him mischievously before turning back to his mother. "And since we've decided not to fight anymore, I think it's time you two settle your argument."

"What argument?" Susan asked.

"The debate about why you won't let Ryan buy you the house he keeps trying to give you."

"Oh, that's not an argument. I'm not moving. End of argument."

Kari looked over at Ryan and gave him an apologetic shrug. "I tried."

"It was a good effort," Ryan said.

"Not bad for her first try," Susan said.

"How do you know I'll try again?" Kari asked.

"Because you two work as a team, and Ryan hasn't admitted defeat yet," Susan said. "I'm going to have to keep on my toes with both of you."

"And you'll love every minute of it." Ryan glanced at Kari. "She hates to lose even more than I do."

"Thanks for the warning."

Chapter 35

KARI SAT IN THE REGISTRATION office at George Mason University, hoping the woman across the desk could help her. Though she had been admitted as a visiting student for fall semester, every class she had tried to add was full.

She scratched at the skin where her splint chafed against her arm. The past few days had been an adventure, trying to learn how to do things left-handed.

"It looks like most of your classes will transfer, but I'm afraid we don't have openings in the pre-med classes you need next." The counselor tapped on her keyboard. "We do have some general ed classes you can take in the meantime."

"I was really hoping to use my last few GE classes to keep my academic load balanced," Kari said. "Isn't there anything available in my major?"

"Not that you haven't already taken," she said apologetically. "Of course, you can always use this down time to study for your MCAT. Ideally, you will want to take that this spring so you can start your med school applications next summer."

"I've been studying the past few weeks," Kari said. "I've found that it's hard to prepare when you aren't actively taking classes."

"I'll put your name on the wait lists for the classes you need, but unfortunately, our admitted full-time students will take priority if any openings occur."

"I understand." Kari stood. "Thank you for your time."

She left the office and made her way out to her car. Though part of her knew it would be nice to stay on track for graduation, the idea of paying out-of-state tuition for general ed classes irritated her on principle. She could just as easily take them online from her community college in Cincinnati, and then she wouldn't have to worry about commuting.

She started toward Ben's house, another task looming over her. Baseball season was more than half over. At some point, she really needed to find an apartment and a job. Her hand, unfortunately, didn't make her the most attractive potential employee.

An hour later, she related her challenges to Ryan as they drove to his game.

"You know, if you want to take classes at a community college, you might try NOVA. They have a bunch of campuses, and it's supposed to be a really good school."

"That's an idea," Kari said, considering. "I just hate the idea of getting behind."

"They might have some medical classes you can use. Jenny got her nursing degree there."

"I'll ask her about it," Kari said. "Speaking of Jenny, I thought your mom was going to come to the game with us tonight."

"She was going to, but Jenny decided to come up. They're going out to dinner and a movie together."

"That's sweet of Jenny to make the drive up here."

"Yeah. I think part of the reason for her visit is because my mom has told her so much about my house that Jenny decided she needed to see it for herself."

"Your home is pretty awesome."

"Thanks largely to you."

"I haven't done much."

"You've done more than you realize," he countered. "I would still be living out of boxes if it weren't for you."

"I'm sure your mom would have whipped you into shape had I not been around," Kari said. "It's going to be weird when the doctor clears her to go back home."

"I know. Less than two weeks."

"That's going to be strange for you to have your mom out of the house, and I'll be moving into an apartment a week or two later."

"I thought you hadn't found a place."

"I haven't, but I need to find something soon. I can't keep putting it off forever."

"Personally, I think you should wait until after the season ends. It doesn't make sense for you to pay rent when you probably won't be in town half the time anyway."

"I hate to break it to you, Ryan, but once classes start, I'm not going to be able to travel with the team."

"You can if you take online classes. Even if you decide to take some locally, you might be able to make the weekend games."

"Maybe."

Ryan motioned to the clock on his dashboard. "It's still pretty early. Why don't you call the community college and see if you can meet with a counselor tomorrow?" he suggested. "You've said yourself that you'll feel a lot better when you can make plans."

"That's a good idea," Kari said. "I'll call when you're at practice."

"And I know it's selfish of me, but I would really love it if you could come to some of my games, especially if we make it to the postseason."

"You'll make it to postseason. You guys are too good not to make it in."

"I hope so, but we haven't clinched our spot yet."

"Trust me," Kari said. "You'll make it.

* * *

Ryan dropped onto one of the chairs overlooking his swimming pool and surveyed his new kingdom. His game had ended early tonight, a three-to-one victory that had taken only two hours and three minutes. His team had been playing well the past few weeks, and all of them were beginning to believe that a postseason bid was theirs to lose. No one was willing to see that happen.

Their two-week home stand was a much-needed break for all of them. Getting off work at a reasonable hour was a bonus he hadn't expected at this point in the season. Now, with a breeze cooling the August night, he watched the lights from the house shimmer off the water, and he let himself ponder his future.

Kari and his mom had been chatting about school when he had left them in the kitchen to go change. When he had come back to the living area, they hadn't been anywhere in sight, but their voices had carried from his mom's room.

The friendship the two women had developed over the past several weeks was something he never dared hope for, and yet the easiness of it increased his resolve to keep Kari in his life. Not once during his two years dating Brandi had she spoken to his mother unless they were forced to be in the same room. Ryan suspected that even if he hadn't started dating Kari, she would have offered to help with his mom.

Her selfless nature and genuine kindness were among the many traits that reminded him why he wanted to keep her in his life. He still wasn't sure what to think about how his ambitions in life would mesh with hers, but surely if they loved each other enough, they would find a way to make things work.

He heard the sliding-glass door open behind him and turned to see Kari coming toward him, a tall glass in her hand.

"Here, I thought you might want something to drink." She set it down on the patio table before turning back to close the door behind her.

"Thanks, but what about you?"

"I can only carry one at a time." She held up her bandaged hand, a touch of humor lighting her eyes. "Besides, I already had a sip of yours."

"Then I guess I don't need to offer to share."

"Nah, I'm good." She took the seat beside him.

"Did my mom go to bed?"

"She's heading that way."

"What were you two talking about for so long?"

"We were talking about jobs. She was giving me ideas of some places I might be able to work while I'm finishing my undergrad. I really want to do something in the medical field since my internship fell through this summer."

The realization of how much life was about to change struck him. So far, the entire time he and Kari had been dating, their schedule had revolved around the demands of his career. Things were about to make an abrupt change, and he dreaded not being with her for such a significant part of his day.

"Did you ever talk to Maya about staying with her until the season ends?"

"I did." Kari leaned back and stretched her feet out in front of her. "You'll be happy to know she agrees with you. She said she was hoping I would hold off on getting a place until Ben finishes out this season. Besides, if I end up at the community college instead of George Mason, that will change where I want to live."

"I think you should live near here."

Her eyebrows lifted. "Oh, you do, do you?"

"I do." Ryan sat up and shifted to face her. He wanted her with him always and wondered how soon he could edge her into a more permanent relationship. He leaned forward and kissed her, his hand lifting to caress her cheek.

Leaves rustled in the yard, a car alarm went off only to be silenced a moment later. Everything else faded away as his lips moved slowly and easily over hers, his whole world focused on her.

When he drew back, her eyes lifted to meet his, and her lips curved into an easy smile. "You do make a pretty convincing argument."

"Glad you think so. After all, once you get an apartment, you'll be in school at most five days a week, but we'll want to see each other seven days a week."

She leaned forward and kissed him again. "Yes, you make a very good argument."

Chapter 36

A SENSE OF DÉJÀ VU played over Kari as she waited silently, watching the academic adviser at the community college look over her transcripts. When the adviser finally glanced up, she said, "We've already received your official transcripts from Vanderbilt, so we shouldn't have any problem getting you registered for classes."

"Are there still classes open that would transfer toward a pre-med degree? My plan is to start at George Mason in the spring."

"We can help you with the general ed classes. Unfortunately, a lot of the medical classes are limited by program. I don't suppose you are interested in nursing instead of pre-med?"

Kari shook her head. "Not really."

"Let me show you what we have available. Even though some of these may not directly transfer into requirements in your pre-med program, you may find them useful when you get further into your program. And, of course, it never hurts to beef up your résumé before you apply for med school."

Kari looked at the list of medical courses offered. Besides several nursing programs, she saw offerings in radiology, sonography, and dental hygiene. "Would I be able to take one of these?" Kari asked, pointing at the radiology courses.

"Technically, you're supposed to be admitted to the program, but if there's room, we might be able to get you a waiver since you've already completed the prerequisites and your grades would most certainly gain you admittance into our program."

"That would be great." Kari waited while the counselor tapped a few keys on her computer.

"We have two classes we can get you in. They're in the second year of the radiology program, but we had two students wash out."

"That's great. Thanks." Kari waited while the counselor input the classes. Several minutes later, she handed Kari a class schedule, a bill for her tuition, and a student handbook.

"In the back of the handbook, you'll find the requirements for our various programs. One thing you might want to consider is completing your associate's degree before transferring to Mason," she said. "The tuition alone would be several thousand dollars less, and we have an automatic acceptance agreement with them provided you maintain a high enough GPA. Looking at your transcripts, I'm sure that won't be a problem for you."

"I'll think about it. Thanks." Kari stood. "It was nice meeting you."

"You too. I hope you enjoy your last few weeks of freedom before classes start."

"I'll certainly try."

* * *

Ryan's hands shook as he dialed the phone. He couldn't put this off any longer. He wanted Kari to be his future, and before he tried to put a ring on her finger, he needed to talk to her father. The team would leave for New York tonight, and he already had reservations for an elegant restaurant overlooking the city for Wednesday after the game. He didn't know if he was quite ready to ask Kari to marry him, but he wanted to have everything in place in case the timing felt right.

"Hello?" Kari's father's voice came over the phone.

"Mr. Evans? This is Ryan Strobel. I play for the Nationals with Ben."

"Is he okay?"

"He's fine."

"And Kari?"

"Everyone's great," Ryan assured him. "I'm sorry. I didn't mean to worry you. It's actually Kari I'm calling about."

"Does this have anything to with the fact that you've been dating her for the past several months?"

"Yes, sir." He mustered his courage. "The truth is I'm very much in love with your daughter, and I want to know if you can support me in asking for her hand in marriage."

Silence hummed over the line for a moment. "Can I assume that you've already discussed this with her?"

"No, sir. Not yet. I felt it was appropriate that I speak with you first."

"Well, I appreciate that." He fell silent again, and Ryan felt like his heart might explode. "Ben has spoken very highly of you, Ryan, so please don't think my hesitation is a reflection on you."

"But you have reservations," Ryan managed to say. "I know we haven't been dating long . . ."

"It isn't that," Steve said. "My concern has more to do with Kari's goals for her future."

"You're talking about medical school," Ryan said, beginning to under-stand.

"Yes. It's been something she's talked about a lot this past year. If you really love my daughter, her future goals and plans need to be part of your discussion about marriage."

"I've already thought a lot about that. There are several good medical schools in this area, and she's already planning to finish her undergrad here."

"The logistics are something the two of you will need to discuss," he said, and Ryan wasn't sure exactly what to think when he added, "If the two of you do decide to get married, you will have to recognize the challenges that will come from her goals and the obstacles your career could put in front of them. If you get traded at an inopportune time, the two of you will have to be uni-fied on how to handle it."

"You make a lot of good points," Ryan said, deflated.

"With that said, if you love each other and want to get married, I'm certainly not going to stand in your way," Steve said. "In fact, I hope things do work out. Every time I've talked to Kari on the phone since she moved to Virginia, she has seemed very happy."

"Thank you, sir. I appreciate your time."

"And, Ryan?"

"Yes."

"Best of luck to you."

"Thank you." Ryan hung up the phone, his gut churning more now than before he had called Kari's dad. Steve Evans was right. If Ryan really loved Kari, he couldn't get in her way. He had expected the result of the call would leave him wondering when to pop the question. Instead, he was faced with a more pressing question: how could he make sure he wouldn't derail Kari's dreams if he tried to make his own come true?

He opened the drawer of his nightstand and retrieved the ring his mother had given him. He wanted nothing more than to see it on Kari's finger, and he was afraid that the promise it held could also be a noose around her neck. His heart breaking, he replaced the ring and closed the drawer once more. He couldn't let her go, but he couldn't move forward. What in the world was he supposed to do for the next ten years while Kari pursued her medical career?

Chapter 37

KARI LOOKED UP AT THE skyscrapers of New York City, the dizzying heights leaving her off-balance. Every time she thought she had her footing, the frantic pace of the pedestrians walking by reminded her she was most certainly not in DC anymore.

"This city never ceases to amaze me," Kari said, looking forward again so she could keep pace with Ryan without running into the throngs of people on the Manhattan sidewalk. "I don't know if I could ever get used to the pace here."

"I imagine if you had to, you would adapt," Ryan said. He steered her toward the revolving door of a hotel.

"This isn't our hotel, is it?"

"No, but there's a restaurant on the top floor I thought you would like. It's got a great view of the city."

"Sounds fun." They walked into the lobby, and Ryan led her to the elevator. Part of her wished Maya and Ben had decided to join them on their first night in New York, but another part of her appreciated some time alone with Ryan.

Several other patrons crowded onto the elevator with them, and Ryan remained silent on the long ascent to the top floor. When he led her to the restaurant, her eyebrows lifted. White linen tablecloths and flickering candlelight set the tone of the dimly lit room. The fading daylight illuminated the New York skyline through the bank of windows that lined the walls.

The maître d' took Ryan's name and efficiently led them to their table near the corner beside a window.

As soon as they were alone, Kari said, "Ryan, this place is amazing."

"I'm glad you like it." He smiled, but it didn't quite reach his eyes.

"Is everything okay?" Kari asked, sensing something about him was different but unable to ascertain exactly what it was.

"Were you able to meet with the school counselor yesterday? You never told me how it went," he asked rather than answer her question.

"I did."

"And?" Ryan prompted.

"It was a mixture of good and bad news," Kari said. "I was able to get into a couple classes in radiology that seem really interesting. Apparently that isn't easy to do since I'm not admitted to their program."

"What was the bad news?"

"While these classes are interesting, there weren't any classes available that are required for my major."

"What will that do to you as far as graduation?"

"I'm guessing I'll have to go to school next summer to make up for the classes I should have taken this semester." Her shoulders lifted. "It's kind of annoying because that's when I should be putting together all of my applications for med school."

"That is tough." He seemed to ponder her answer for a moment. "When will your classes start this fall?"

"August 23."

"That soon?"

"Yeah. I ended up with four classes, but I'm hoping the homework load won't be too bad so I can still go to your home games. At least the night ones."

"I'll miss having you at the others."

"I know, but it's not any different from when I was staying with your mom."

"I guess."

A little unsettled by his somber mood, she changed the subject. "By the way, did you hear Shawn and Celeste's news?"

"No, what?"

"Celeste is pregnant," she said, a bubble of excitement surfacing.

"Really?"

"Yeah. She's due at the end of spring training." Kari considered the way she had heard the news and the oddity of how Celeste had expressed the timing. "I guess that's around March, right?"

"Yeah." Ryan fell silent again. Kari let herself get lost in the view of the city until he brought her back to the present with an unexpected question. "Have you thought about having kids?"

"I don't know." She thought for a moment. "I mean, I always assumed someday I would get married and have kids, but I never really planned anything beyond that. It's one of those things that has always been too far in the future to really think about."

"I have to imagine it would be tough to have a family with a medical career."

"It can be, but it depends on your specialty. When I was growing up, the pediatrician I went to worked part-time, and so did all of her partners. They found a way to balance their family lives with their careers. I guess I always assumed I would find a similar kind of compromise."

"That makes sense." Again the conversation stalled, but this time Kari narrowed her eyes.

"Is something bothering you?"

"No, I'm just tired."

"We can cut our evening short," Kari offered.

"I don't think you really want to do that," Ryan said, his mood lightening. "Their chocolate mousse is supposed to be incredible."

"You did it now," Kari said. "You're stuck with me here through dessert."

"I'm sure I'll manage to suffer through it."

"Glad to hear it."

* * *

A bruised shoulder, a strained calf muscle, and a tight quad were among the many minor injuries Ryan found himself facing as the Nationals slid into a five-game losing streak. The lack of success on the field and his battered body were minor inconveniences compared to the ache in his heart.

Every day, he tried to remind himself how lucky he was to have found Kari and to have her as part of his life. And every day he could hear her father's words echoing through his mind, a constant reminder that what he wanted wouldn't mesh with Kari's plans for at least a decade. Ten years. It felt like an eternity.

The ring his mother had given him, the ring he someday hoped to give Kari, lay in his bedside table. Every time he opened the drawer and saw it, another pang resonated through his core. He needed her in his life, and the thought of having to steal snatches of time together for so many years overwhelmed him.

Kari had started her classes two weeks earlier, and already her homework load had taken a toll on their time together. True to her word, she made it to most of his games, but she had taken to driving herself so she could leave early enough to get to bed at a reasonable hour. He missed sharing his commute with her. Her class schedule had also robbed them of the mornings they had once shared. He didn't want to think about how much worse things would be when she no longer lived across the street.

He supposed he should be grateful that she would be nearby for the next two years, but then what? If she was accepted into medical school locally, he was pretty sure they could find a way to make it work, but the more he researched the possibilities, the more he realized how difficult it was for medical students to get into programs in the first place, much less narrow their possibilities so significantly. And what would happen if they had to choose between being together and her going to medical school? Could he survive being separated from her for the whole baseball season?

Four years of residency was yet another crushing thought. The simple truth was he could see Kari light up every time she talked about her radiology classes, and the more he saw her passion for her chosen field, the more he could feel her slipping further and further away. He didn't want to put out that spark in her, but he didn't know how to keep her in his life without extinguishing her dreams.

An alarm sounded on his phone, a reminder that it was time to leave for the ball field. And a reminder that once again he would be driving there alone. He stood and winced when the muscle in his calf protested the moment he put weight on it. Aches and pains were part of life, he reminded himself. He hoped he could find a way to endure both the short-term injuries and the uncertainty of his future.

Chapter 38

KARI DIDN'T KNOW WHAT WAS going on with Ryan, but something had changed over the past few weeks. And it wasn't just the drop in his batting average.

She could sense the weariness in him and Ben as they moved from August to September. As much as she wanted to help them weather the exhaustion common at this part of the season, she found herself struggling with her own schedule of going to Ryan's games and keeping up with her classes. Not having the use of her right hand was yet another obstacle. Typing one-handed was decidedly hindering her efforts when she needed to use the computer.

Though she didn't particularly mind the balancing act or the fact that most of her homework was completed at Nationals Park, the growing strain between her and Ryan was dragging her down. She wished she knew what to do about it.

A five-game losing streak followed by a single win and two more losses had taken its toll on the whole team and their fans. Six more wins were all the Nationals needed to clinch a playoff spot, and everyone was starting to wonder if those wins were ever going to happen.

Susan had moved back to her apartment three weeks ago, thrilled at having her freedom back and still refusing to let her son upgrade her living conditions.

After spending the past few weeks looking at apartments, Kari was starting to understand Susan's resistance. It wasn't just the prospect of moving her belongings into a new space. It was also trying to find a neighborhood that felt like home. Kari had yet to discover that particular amenity in any of the complexes she had looked at so far.

Why was it that the process of looking for houses for Ben and Maya had felt so much simpler than searching for a one-bedroom apartment for herself?

Maya had helped her research several in the area, both in Great Falls, near her house, and in Springfield, near the community college. Unfortunately, the prices were significantly higher than what she had expected. She had found a studio apartment with promise only to discover the complex had no vacancies.

Armed with a new list of prospective apartments, Kari headed out to her car. She was reaching for the door handle when Ryan's front door opened and he stepped outside.

Changing directions, she skirted around her car and crossed the street to meet him in his front yard. She glanced at her watch. "It's only nine in the morning. What are you doing up so early?"

"I missed you." He slid his arms around her waist and leaned down to kiss her good morning.

"What made you think I would be awake so early?"

"Lucky guess." He released her, and his eyes narrowed. "Where are you off to? I was hoping we could have breakfast together."

"I'm going to Herndon to look at some apartments."

"Herndon? That's twenty minutes away in the wrong direction from your school."

"I know, but I found some there that I might actually be able to afford."

"Kari, I can help you out with rent so you can stay close by."

Immediately, she shook her head. "Paying for my rent is not your responsibility."

"Kari, we talked about this. It's going to be hard on you to deal with school and come over here to see me if you live so far away."

She took a step back and folded her arms. She couldn't say why his words hit her, especially since they had been spoken before, but her spine stiffened, and her mood darkened. "Did it ever occur to you that once baseball season ends, you would be perfectly capable of coming to my apartment to see me?"

The expression on his face told her the truth before he managed to recover. "Well, of course I would come to see you too, but I just assumed we would want to spend most of our time here."

"Because it's your home and it's convenient for you."

Now Ryan took a step back. "It's convenient for you too. Your brother and best friend live across the street."

"And I imagine when I move, they'll be more than happy to come see me as much as I come to see them. The question is, will you?"

"What do you mean?"

"It occurs to me that all this time we've been together, everything has centered around you."

"That's not true."

"Isn't it?"

"Of course not. I'm the one who insisted on paying for your flights and hotel rooms so we could spend time together. I got tickets to the games for you any time you wanted them."

"I'm grateful you have been so generous," Kari began, her stomach clutching as clarity seeped through her. "But listen to yourself for a minute. You paid for hotel rooms. You paid for airline tickets. You got me game tickets. Ryan, everything you did was so that I would be around for your convenience. How much of that was for me, and how much of it was for you?"

"It was all for you."

"Are you sure?" Shaken by her new perspective, she said, "I have to get going. My first appointment is in half an hour."

Appearing both confused and frustrated, Ryan raked his fingers through his hair. "Why don't you wait a minute and I can go with you."

"You have to leave for your game at noon. I don't know if I'll be back by then." Needing some distance, she took another step back. "I'll see you later."

She didn't wait for his response; she crossed back to her car and unlocked the door. When she pulled forward and drove around the circle of the cul-de-sac, she glanced over to see him still standing where she'd left him. His eyes followed her, but neither of them waved.

* * *

His side ached from last night's slide into home, and his glove seemed to have formed a hole in it since last night. Every third grounder during practice seemed to slip right through it. He didn't want to think about batting practice any more than he wanted to replay his earlier conversation with Kari. That didn't stop both episodes from looping over and over in his mind.

The lack of success with his bat was easy enough to remedy. See ball, hit ball. Repeat. He hadn't been terribly consistent with that today, but he knew the problem was something he could work through in the near future.

His conversation with Kari, however—he kept trying to manipulate it over and over again. If only he had explained himself a little differently, she would have understood. Surely she knew his motivations for buying her tickets and hotel rooms had been as much for her as for him. Sure, she had resisted at first, but she wouldn't have ultimately agreed if she hadn't wanted to go to his games. Everyone else he'd ever dated had hoped for him to make such offers. Brandi had certainly spent many afternoons shopping in New York and playing tourist in Philadelphia.

His thoughts stalled, and clarity bloomed. Kari hadn't. She hadn't shopped. She hadn't gone sightseeing. She hadn't done any of those things unless they were together.

How many afternoons had she sought out the shade of the concourse on a ninety-degree day while she'd studied for her MCAT? How many times had she skipped dinner so she could eat with him after the game? And how many times had he asked her what she wanted to do?

Jack approached where Ryan stood on the side of the field.

"Hey, Jack," Ryan said, trying to push aside the emotional cloud hanging over him.

"Has the doc taken a look at those ribs since last night?"

"No, but the X-ray came back clean."

"I want him to check you out again. I'm thinking about sitting you tonight."

"What?"

"Ryan, it's not a punishment. I just think you can use a day of rest."

"But we're playing the Mets. We win this series and we can clinch the division."

"I'm well aware of that," he said. "But you've been struggling for a few weeks. I think rest will do you good." He held up a hand before Ryan could protest further. "I'm not saying you can't go in later in the game, but the start is going to Monroe."

Ryan opened his mouth to argue, but thought better of it. His coach was right. He wasn't in top form. Maybe a night sitting out would give him the motivation he needed to remember why he loved this game. And maybe he could discover the secret of knowing how to be the man Kari would be able to love for a lifetime.

The thought crossed his mind that he should text Kari that he might not play today. His eyes were drawn to the stands and the empty seat he knew belonged to her.

The realization that they had never fought before crossed his mind, and he assured himself that she would come around soon enough. If he gave her some space and time, she would reach out to him. After all, their challenges were in the long term. Surely this misunderstanding would resolve itself by morning.

Chapter 39

KARI DIDN'T GO TO THE game on Saturday or to the games on the two days after that. She didn't call Ryan or text him. She didn't follow the team on Twitter or Facebook. And with each minute of silence that passed, she was dying a slow, painful death.

She refused to call first. Hadn't she made herself clear three days ago that it was time he started putting some effort into their relationship? She wasn't asking for much, just the acknowledgment that her goals and dreams deserved as much consideration as his.

His name might appear in the news every day, even if it was in the form of a box score, but that didn't make his dreams any more valid than hers. Sure, she might have made it seem like she was willing to let the demands in his life take priority, but he could hardly blame her for that. It wasn't like either of them expected for his mother to have major health issues or for her to take so long in making her educational plans for this semester.

Admittedly, she hadn't been very aggressive in her job search, largely so she would have the flexibility to watch his games, but that decision had also hinged on her educational plans. She couldn't very well commit to a job without knowing when she was available to work.

She looked at the MCAT review books on her bookshelf and sighed. What was she thinking? For more than two months, she had studied and prepared for the mother of all tests, and she still didn't feel like she would ever be ready. It was as though she saw the starting gate but couldn't quite bring herself to step up to the line.

Ten years. Just the thought of surviving the next two years made her cringe. Transferring from the community college to George Mason, finishing her undergrad, taking the MCAT, applying for medical school. And some-where in there she had to find time to work to make sure she could cover her living expenses. The college fund her parents had created for her would cover most of her tuition, and she was determined to avoid going into debt before she reached her postgrad.

A knock sounded on her open door, and she looked up at Maya. "Am I interrupting?"

"No, come on in." Kari shifted back onto her bed and crossed her legs. She glanced at the window to see the sun had nearly set. "I'm all finished with my homework. I was just working ahead for the next day."

"How is everything going?"

"Pretty good. I'm so glad they gave me the waiver for the radiology classes. I never expected to enjoy them so much."

"That's great." Maya sat on the edge of her bed. "How is everything else going?"

"Okay," Kari said without enthusiasm.

Maya's eyebrows lifted.

"What?"

"I'm worried about you. For months, you've spent nearly every spare minute with Ryan, and now, all of a sudden, you two are never together." Maya's voice held understanding. "Did the two of you break up?"

"Not exactly."

"I don't want to pry, but I see you looking miserable, and Ryan isn't himself." Her gaze narrowed. "This isn't a cheesecake kind of day, is it?"

"I guess I'm trying to figure out what to do with the rest of my life, and I have no idea how Ryan fits into it," Kari admitted.

"Do you love him?"

The simplicity of the question cut to the core of the matter. "Yeah, I do. Unfortunately, he expects me to fall in line with what works in his life. I want to help people. I want to make a difference."

"Then you need to make sure he understands that," Maya said.

"You're right."

"And for the sake of all the Nationals' fans out there, would you have this conversation with him sooner than later? Ryan doesn't play nearly as well when you two are at odds as he does when his life is in harmony."

"He didn't have a good game yesterday?"

"He hasn't had a good week," Maya said. "The guys are off today. Maybe you should see what he's doing tonight."

"I don't know, Maya." Kari wavered. "If I'm always the one to try to make things work, what kind of relationship will Ryan and I really have?"

"If you don't talk to each other, you won't have a relationship at all," Maya said bluntly. "And I know you. You're a problem solver. You hate having things hanging over your head like this."

Kari considered the truth of Maya's words. "I'll think about it."

"Ben and I are heading out to dinner. Do you want us to bring something back for you?"

"No, I'm fine. Thanks."

"See you later."

Kari watched her go, her stomach twisting in knots. She hated not knowing what was going on with Ryan, but she also worried he would never learn to appreciate her if she didn't take a stand and make sure he really cared about her as an individual. That included caring about what she wanted for her future beyond sitting in the stands and cheering him on.

Not quite ready to call Ryan, she crossed to her bookshelf and retrieved one of her study books. Her student catalog came off the shelf with it and fell to the ground. Lifting it from the floor, she started to put it back but paused when she thought of the counselor's comment about getting her associates degree from the community college prior to transferring to George Mason. Not in the mood to study for her MCAT, she replaced her study guide and carried the student handbook to her bed. She flipped through the pages, instinctively starting with the medical programs. She read through the descriptions of each, focusing on the radiology and sonography programs. Considering her options in a new light, she retrieved a pencil and used her left hand to check off the classes she had already completed.

Now seeing multiple paths before her, she looked at her cell phone. Maybe Maya was right. Maybe it was time to have a serious talk with Ryan.

* * *

Ryan looked at his phone for the fifteenth time in less than five minutes. Why hadn't she called him? Or texted? At this point, he would settle for smoke signals. He certainly wouldn't miss them, considering he had paced by his front window dozens of times today hoping to catch a glimpse of Kari.

He should have known she would force him to make the first move. Hadn't she been the only girl in years who had waited for him to ask her out? And hadn't he always appreciated how she didn't make him feel like he was a prize to be won, instead always showing she cared for him as a person rather than as a public figure? He now knew he hadn't appreciated her nearly enough.

Her words had been more true than he liked to admit. Though he had felt justified in expecting her to conform her schedule to meet his, in reality he'd never considered things would change, not even when he finished the season and the demands on her time became more extreme. He may have paid for various travel expenses and made sure she could come to the games, but she had always been appreciative of the gestures and had consistently been clear that she didn't expect such treatment.

The bottom line was that she wasn't interested in him for his money, and he needed to stop acting like such things should matter between them.

His phone rang, and he held it up. His heart sank when he saw it was his mom and not Kari. He debated ignoring the call but realized he wouldn't be able to handle both of the women in his life being mad at him at the same time. "Hey, Mom."

"You sound exhausted. Is everything okay?"

How is it, he asked himself, *that moms can always tell when something is wrong?*

"It's been a rough couple days," Ryan said.

"I saw your game last night. You didn't look like yourself. Are you feeling okay?"

"The usual stiffness that comes at this point of the season." He knew he could leave it at that and his mom wouldn't press, but he needed to talk to someone. "Kari and I had an argument, and it's been hard not having her to talk to."

"Have you tried talking to her?" Susan asked.

"No, not yet."

"That's a mistake right there," she said. "If you want to build a future with Kari, both of you need to learn how to communicate with one another. The silent treatment might seem like a good idea, but it only keeps people from moving forward."

"I talked to her dad about asking her to marry me."

"How did that go?"

"He seems like a really nice guy, but he basically told me the same thing Kari and I ended up arguing about. She has her own dreams for her future, and if I stay in her life, I'll probably get in the way."

"Her dad said that?"

"Not exactly. He just said I needed to keep her goals in mind when planning for the future."

"He's right."

The arrow in his heart dug a little deeper. "Which circles back to the root of the problem. My career and her goals don't mesh. Her dad obviously doesn't think this can last long term, and it sounds like you agree with him."

"That's not what I said, and I don't think it's what he said either," she told him. "The two of you need to sit down together and be open about what it is you want for your future and then decide how you're going to make your dreams happen."

"And if my dreams get in the way of her dreams?"

"That's always a risk, Ryan. The important thing is to talk to her and make sure you make your decisions together, taking both of your dreams into account."

Ryan wandered into the kitchen, and his eyes landed on the words displayed on his counter: *The best things happen at home.*

"Mom, I've got to go, but I'll talk to you later."

"Good luck, Ryan. I'm pulling for both of you."

"Thanks." He hung up the phone and dialed Kari's number. She answered on the second ring. Just the sound of her voice sent his heart racing. "Hey, is there any way we can talk?"

"Actually, I was hoping to talk to you."

He picked up the trivet shaped like home plate and asked, "Would you mind coming over here? I can come to you, but I thought we would have more privacy at my place."

"That's fine. I'll be there in a few minutes."

"Thanks, Kari."

"I'll see you soon."

As soon as she hung up, he set the decoration down and headed for his room. He didn't know if Kari was ready to hear what he had to say, but it was time he put all of his cards on the table.

Chapter 40

KARI KNOCKED ON THE DOOR, not sure if this was a new beginning or the beginning of the end. Ryan hadn't sounded like himself when he had called, but, then, she hardly knew what to expect from him since they had never fought before. She really hated fighting. It was such a downer.

A sense of anticipation sent her nerves humming. She had already decided on one huge change in her life today. It scared her that her first thought after making such a monumental shift in her future was to share it with Ryan. His call had come at the perfect time. She only hoped his friendship, and their relationship, would continue and that he would support the changes she intended to make in her life.

The door opened, revealing a weary-looking Ryan, several days' worth of growth on his face. His hair was tousled as though his comb had gone on strike and his fingers had taken over the job.

"Thanks for coming over." He stepped back to let her in. The absence of a kiss in his greeting sent another ripple of trepidation through her.

They hadn't spoken for three days. What did she expect? She reminded herself of this fact and hoped it was the only reason Ryan was giving her such a wide berth as he showed her inside.

They passed by the kitchen, and it took only a glance to notice what was missing—home plate. Her stomach sank. Was he already trying to get rid of anything that reminded him of her?

A piece chipped away from her heart, and she forced herself to straighten her shoulders. Ready to cut through the tension between them once and for all, she remained standing and waited for him to face her when they reached the living room.

"Are we breaking up?" she asked.

"No." A horrified expression appeared on his face. He reached for her good hand and squeezed. "No," he repeated.

Kari let out the breath she hadn't realized she'd been holding.

"Please, sit down." Ryan motioned to the couch and waited for her to sit before he took the seat beside her.

She let her gaze wander long enough to notice a few other minor changes since she'd been here last. The decorative bowl she had put on the coffee table had been moved to the end table, and a square box lay in its place.

Her stomach still a ball of nerves, she forced herself to look him in the eye. "We're not breaking up?"

"No. I hope we never break up," Ryan said earnestly. His hand squeezed hers, and he waved his other nervously. "I've been thinking about what you said."

"And?"

"And you were right about a lot of things." He let out a sigh. "I've been so used to you being here, to us being here together, that when I think of us hanging out, I always think of us being here." She opened her mouth to respond, but he continued before she could. "It's not because I'm not willing to meet you halfway. I always think of us here because this is home." His free hand came to rest on hers so her good hand was caught between both of his. "We've been making a home together, and I've struggled with knowing how long it might be before your life will settle down enough to make it permanent."

His last word resonated through her. "I'm not sure I'm following you."

He seemed to muster his courage. "I talked to your dad awhile ago."

The implication of such a conversation nearly left her speechless. She managed to swallow the lump that had formed in her throat. "You did?"

"Yeah." Now he appeared to be at a loss for words. "We talked a bit about what you want for your future."

She opened her mouth to tell him everything had changed, but he rushed on. "Ten years of school is a long time, and I've really been struggling with what your goals mean to our future."

"Ryan, there's something you should know—"

"I'm sorry I made you feel like your goals weren't important to me and that I let my schedule take over our time together. I want to spend time with you, and if that means driving across town to visit you after you move, I'll do it. I'll do anything I can to help you reach your dreams." He drew a deep breath. "I know it might seem like it would never work for the long term, but I know if we want it to, we can push through the challenges."

"What exactly are you saying?" she forced herself to ask as her heart-beat quickened.

Ryan released her hands and reached for the box on the table. "We've been making a home together without even realizing it. I want you to share that home with me, to be part of my forever."

He lifted the lid off the box. Inside lay the ceramic home plate, a piece of twine tied around it. Looped onto the bow hung a diamond ring. "Kari Evans, will you marry me?"

Both hands lifted to cover her mouth. Her throat closed, her heart swelled, and tears welled up in her eyes. She blinked hard to see him still staring at her expectantly, a look of near-panic on his face. Her head bobbed up and down, and she reached for him. "Yes." She nodded again. "Yes, I'll marry you."

His lips found hers, the stress and frustration of the past few days falling away to be replaced with hope and an indescribable feeling of belonging and unity.

He pulled back, fumbling to untie the engagement ring so he could slip it on her hand. "This was my great-grandmother's, but if you don't like it, we can get you something else. I thought you would prefer something with some history to it over flash."

Her eyes welled up again at the thought that he would understand her well enough to know that the sentimentality of a family heirloom would mean so much more to her than how much money he spent.

Her eyes lowered to the ring. "It's beautiful." She looked up at him. "It's perfect."

"So are you." He kissed her again, his expression serious when he pulled away. "I know you have a lot going on with school in the next year, trying to apply for med school and everything. I know it may seem fast, but what do you think about getting married in the spring? I thought I might be able to get the team to give me some time for your spring break. If you want a big wedding, we could go for All-Star break so we would have more time." She started to respond, but again he rushed on. "I'm happy to hire a wedding planner so you still have time to keep up with your studies."

"I think I'd feel more comfortable planning my own wedding," Kari said. "I always envisioned something on the smaller side. Would you mind that?"

"It sounds perfect." He hesitated a moment before he added, "If you want to plan it yourself, maybe we should wait until next fall or even the following winter. You're going to be so stressed with everything else you'll have going on with your life."

"I started to tell you this earlier." Kari held up her right hand, lifting it so her splint was in his line of vision. "Do you remember how I saw the break in my hand when we were at urgent care? You made a comment about how quickly I was able to find the problem?"

"Yeah, I remember."

"I was going through the program offerings at NOVA, and it finally dawned on me that what I've always wanted is to work in the medical field and to make a difference."

"Right." He looked at her, confused. "That's why you're studying medicine."

"It's why I started out studying medicine," Kari corrected. "And it's why I'm switching to radiology."

"What?"

"Every time I try studying for the MCAT, the section on diagnostic tools and their uses is so easy for me, but everything else, I really struggled with. I mean, I know about the basic anatomy and such from my pre-med classes, but what I love is seeing scans and X-rays. Using those tools to help doctors make the right diagnosis, knowing I can be there to hold someone's hand, so to speak, when they're going through a tough time, that can be my way of making a difference."

His gaze stayed on her, and he finally managed to ask, "Are you sure that's what you want?"

"It is." She smiled. "And the best part is that with the classes I took at Vanderbilt, I should be able to complete the entire program by next December."

"Really?"

"Really. I have to apply officially, but the counselor seemed to think I could get in when I first met with her. I also thought I might be able to get you to pull some strings for me."

"What kind of strings?"

"I have to do clinicals and an internship before I finish my degree. I thought maybe someone I knew would be able to help me get on with the Nationals' medical staff."

His eyes lit with understanding. "You realize you'd have to come to all the games?"

"For those six weeks anyway."

He grinned. "I think I could make a call."

She returned his smile. "As for the wedding, how would you feel about Valentine's Day weekend?"

"I would love that, but I doubt we would be able to find a venue so quickly."

She let her gaze sweep the room. "You really do have a great house."

"Yeah." Confusion and wariness colored the single word.

Now Kari motioned to the box on the table. "I read somewhere that the best things happen at home."

"You mean get married here?"

"Exactly."

He took her hand and lifted it to his lips, kissing the knuckle just above her engagement ring. "You're absolutely right. The best things do happen at home."

* * *

One game. Only one more game to clinch the division. Ryan glanced at the scoreboard as he stepped into the on-deck circle. Bottom of the ninth inning, down by one run, one out.

Ben took his spot in the batter's box, and Ryan saw his determination. The fans were on their feet, the cheering deafening. They would have one more chance to lock in the division tomorrow night, but Ryan wanted it today. Kari would be in class during tomorrow's game, and he wanted to share this moment with her.

Several fans shouted encouragement and demands. They wanted a home run.

Ryan gave his bat a few practice swings while Ben worked the pitch count in his favor. Ryan watched the pitcher wind up and timed his next swing as though he were standing in the batter's box himself.

He saw the mistake, saw the placement. He swung his bat at the same time Ben did.

A loud crack sounded, and the ball lifted into the air, Ben's bat shattering and pieces flying toward the pitcher and down the third-base line.

Ryan cheered with the crowd when he saw the ball fly into the air and fall into the sweet spot in front of the centerfielder and behind the second baseman.

Ben made it safely to first base but couldn't go beyond.

Ryan took a few steps toward home plate, glancing over his shoulder to where Kari sat. He couldn't hear her, but he saw her mouth the words, "Have fun."

He lifted his chin in acknowledgment and reminded himself to live in the moment. A big game, the ability to make a difference, the woman he loved looking on.

Anything but a double play would keep the line moving. He had a brief fear that he would end the game in exactly that way. Then he shook that thought away. *Focus on what you want to happen*, he reminded himself. *See the future and make it happen.*

He looked down at home plate, his lips curving slightly at the symbolism it would always hold for him. Then he positioned his feet and raised his bat.

Three pitches later, wood connected with ball. The home run the fans had demanded rocketed over the fence of the Nationals' bullpen.

Ryan jogged around the bases amid the roar of the crowd. He glanced up into the stands again as he came down the third-base line. Kari was barely visible, but he knew she shared his thoughts when his foot crossed home plate. The best things were most definitely happening for them at home.

About the Author

TRACI HUNTER ABRAMSON WAS BORN in Arizona, where she lived until moving to Venezuela for a study-abroad program. After graduating from Brigham Young University, she worked for the Central Intelligence Agency for several years, eventually resigning in order to raise her family. She credits the CIA with giving her a wealth of ideas as well as the skills needed to survive her children's teenage years. She has written more than twenty novels, including multiple Whitney Award finalists and Whitney Award winners, *Code Word*, *Deep Cover*, and *Failsafe*. She currently lives in Virginia with her family, where she enjoys sports, travel, writing, and coaching high school swimming.